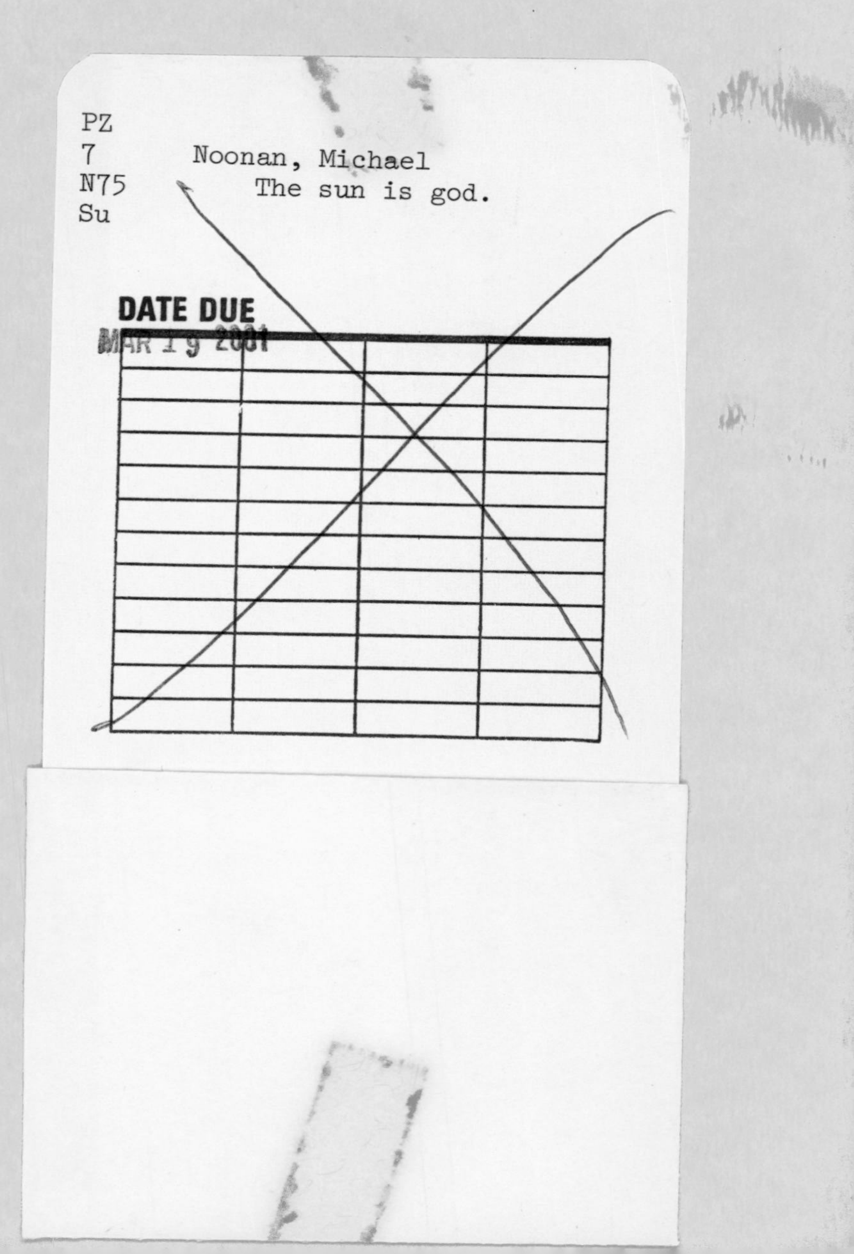
PZ
7
N75
Su
Noonan, Michael
The sun is god.
DATE DUE
MAR 1 9 2001

THE SUN IS GOD

Also by Michael Noonan

THE PATCHWORK HERO
THE DECEMBER BOYS
THE PINK BEACH

Michael Noonan

THE SUN IS GOD

DELACORTE PRESS / NEW YORK

Originally published in Great Britain by Barrie & Jenkins

Manufactured in the United States of America
First printing
ISBN: 0-440-08496-2

'A Man's life of any worth is a continual allegory, and very few eyes can see the Mystery of his life ...' Keats

This novel is the outcome of a search for a story to account for the secret double life and seafaring masquerades of the greatest of all English painters.

Prologue

There was nothing instantly remarkable about the three occupants of the light skiff which moved slowly and gently across the smooth flood-tide waters a hundred yards from the Margate shore on the estuary of the Thames: a husband and wife with their fourteen-year-old son—holiday-makers from London, enjoying the sea air towards the close of a blazing June day.

A close observer would have noticed that the boy had a sketchbook in his lap and was engrossed in making a pencil drawing of the anchored ship towards which his father was rowing. But the stocky middle-aged man who occupied the centre seat, his eyes drowsy and half-shut against the sun, his shirt-sleeves rolled up and his arms working rhythmically as he ploughed the blades of the oars through the water, would not have commanded a second glance—nor would his wife, in the stern seat. She was about forty-four, the same age as her husband; a frail woman with frizzy straw-coloured hair and pale blue eyes which gazed into a distance that had nothing to do with the scene around her.

The surface of the sea had become a mirror for the sunset, and under the glowing canopy of scarlet, lilac and lemon a great silence had fallen over the water—a silence so deep that it seemed to amplify the few noises that disturbed it. The dipping of the oars splintered the soundless tide, and the wings of seagulls and petrels creaked drily as they flew overhead.

Will Turner brought the skiff under the ship's soaring bowsprit and figurehead: a freshly-painted bare-breasted Boadicea. This ship, a 98-gunner with furled sails—a floating fortress of stout timbers and stubby iron fangs, converted by the setting sun from a machine of war into a gilded ark—was destined to take part in one of history's greatest sea battles. But now it lay at rest from patrols and skirmishes, the air around it reeking of oil and tar stirred from its rigging and seams by the heat of the day. Several seamen leaned on the foredeck railing high above the three in the skiff; one of them puffed at a clay pipe from which writhed cloudy pink smoke suffused with the sunset.

Will swung the skiff side-on to the big ship and then pulled both oars aboard, letting the boat drift as the sea tapped against its planks. From here, his boy Billy would be able to draw the man-of-war in greater detail. Will sat astride his seat so that he could watch the lad at work, careful to make his interest seem casual since Billy did not appreciate an audience when he was sketching. On this occasion, however, the boy was so wrapped up in what he was doing that he did not notice his father's scrutiny.

Will was delighted with the drawing of the ship. It would look well in the window of his barbershop back in Covent Garden: and it would fetch at least two shillings. He turned his head to communicate his pleasure to his wife, but there was no response.

Mary Turner was as oblivious to what her son was creating as she was to her husband's pride in it. There was an unnatural stillness about her that set her apart from them—from everyone. Only a week earlier Will and Billy had brought her here to recover from one of her 'attacks'; and the change of surroundings seemed to have had some effect. Always a wispy, febrile creature, she now seemed placid—no longer the raging madwoman of Maiden Lane. But there was something in her attitude at this moment that should have alerted her husband and son.

Billy went on with his drawing and Will watched him; but a subtle change stole over Mary as she gazed at the sunset. Its mounting splendours—the play of light and switches of colour—woke the sleeping demon, until she was possessed by a craving for violence. Insanity illuminated her pale eyes as she reached down to grasp a small anchor lying by her feet.

With a strength born of her madness she began to rise and lift the anchor, almost as weightless and insubstantial as the smoke rising from the seaman's clay pipe above her. Slowly she raised the anchor higher and higher until she held it with the barbed flange poised over Will's head.

In the moment of pause Billy looked up to see the black apparition of his mother with the raised anchor against the sunset. Horror clamped his throat as he tried to cry out to his father, but the look on the boy's face was enough to make Will twist round and throw himself to one side just as the anchor shaved past him and embedded itself in the seat where he had been sitting.

As Mary fell forward with the force of her action, dangerously rocking the skiff, Will quickly enclosed her in his arms, calling on all his resources to overcome her frenzied resistance. She struggled violently, screeching and snorting as she fought to break free, her inarticulate ravings mingling with the yells from the seamen on the high foredeck. They leaned over the railings, their numbers growing, and heads appeared at empty gun-ports—all of the men gleefully taking sides in what they presumed to be a domestic brawl.

'Give it to 'er, matey!' cried one.

And another bellowed, 'Fight 'im, missus! Fight 'im!'

Drenching waves hit Billy as he clung to the gunwale, his face bloodless with shock. Of all the attacks he had witnessed, this one seemed the most savage—the more appalling because it had taken place outside the confines of Maiden Lane, where such events were hidden from the gaze of strangers. He could make no move to help his father.

But suddenly there was no need. As swiftly as it had come, the surge of insanity ebbed from Mary; she lay inert in Will's arms, sobbing her bewilderment at the dark force that had overwhelmed her.

The oars had gone overboard in the struggle, and one of them now drifted alongside, striking the side of the skiff. Billy reached for it and used it to draw in the other oar, which floated nearby, recovering it and fitting both into the rowlocks.

'Row, son,' Will urged him, Mary now a trembling bundle in his clasp. 'Row for the shore.'

With most of the weight at its stern, the skiff rode at a steep forward angle and it was as much as Billy could do to keep it going. From his high rowing position, and in the aftermath of his agitation, he had difficulty in controlling the oars

—splashing them untidily and sometimes missing the water altogether, scooping only thin air.

The mocking laughter of the seamen rang out across the water and echoed in his ears as he desperately pulled for the shore. But worse than that was the picture imprinted on his memory—a shape, a silhouette of his mother against the sunset, the anchor held aloft. It filled his mind now. It would never leave him.

PART ONE

Chapter 1

Billy Turner opened his eyes and saw a shimmering pattern of pink and gold on the ceiling above him—patches of it trembling and overlapping, as if set in motion by the calls of the dawn birds in the trees outside the house. He watched for almost a minute as he came fully awake, his fascination growing at the combinations of the pink and gold.

He disentangled himself carefully from the bedclothes and left Sarah sleeping as he crept barefoot to the window and drew the curtains aside. As the sudden strong light hit his eyes, he whispered, 'Look at that sky! Miraculous!'

Evelina was awake in her cot beside the bed. Six months old, rosy and beautiful, she watched her sturdy young father throw off his nightshirt and start to drag on his clothes. As he did so, he pulled faces at her and she responded with happy gurglings; but when his head disappeared into his shirt she let out a cry of cheated dismay that woke her mother.

Sarah rolled over, muttering and rubbing the sleep from her eyes. She propped herself on an elbow and swept her rich red hair back with her free hand so that she had a clearer view of Billy. He sat on the edge of the bed, feverishly tugging on his boots, then fumbling in his haste with his gaiters.

'William!' she said, making it sound a crime. 'You woke me up.'

He glanced around at her and saw the exasperation in her amber-green eyes and the flush on her creamy skin.

'Sorry,' he mumbled, standing up, reaching for his coat and heaving himself into it. 'Got to catch that sunrise.'

He bent over the cot to give Evelina a farewell tap under the chin, but in his haste he made it sharper than intended and the baby started to howl.

'Now look what you've done!' Sarah cried.

Billy hesitated a moment, caught between two hostile parties, and then decided to pacify them by uniting them. He lifted the baby out of the cot and deposited her in Sarah's lap.

Before she could speak he was out of the bedroom and clattering down the stairs—waking the four other children on the way. Amid the growing sounds of wakefulness above he thumped about as he sorted out his equipment and then, slamming the front door after him, he slipped out, his boots ringing in the empty square as he ran to find a hackney cab to take him to the landing stage at Charing Cross.

Sarah was left to fume as she quietened Evelina and tried to cope with the four older girls calling for her from their bedroom below. It was quite beyond her why any man, painter or otherwise, should leap out of bed at daybreak to catch a sunrise; or, for that matter, rush from the house at night at the glare or smell of a neighbourhood fire to gaze at a blazing building; or be away for days or even weeks at a time hunting down storms at sea or ships on rocks or whales cast up on the shore.

It was Sarah Danby's misfortune that she couldn't get along with a man unless she could dominate him. John Danby, before his illness, had been just the mate for her—never quite believing in the good fortune that had given him such a young and vital wife, always willing to do what would please her and bind her to him. In Billy Turner she had picked on a man of exceptional individuality, one whose temperament she simply would never understand. She resented his work being given precedence over all else, especially paying some attention to her; and when he fobbed off her attempts to accompany him to exhibitions and other functions, that resentment deepened. It was clear to her now that he deliberately avoided being associated with her in public—not, as he tried to suggest, for the sake of her good name, but for fear that he might make himself more vulnerable when the pressure to marry was put on him.

At first she had assumed that he would marry her when a suitable interval had elapsed after John Danby's death; if not before the birth of Evelina, certainly not long afterwards. But Billy skilfully dodged the issue when she began to hint at it and then turned a very deaf ear when she tried to discuss it outright. If he was prepared to live with her, why wouldn't he marry her? And why did their relationship have to be secret? She couldn't find any reasonable answer; and Billy probably wouldn't have been able to give one either. The truth was that it was an escape—an escape from the cramped room at Maiden Lane and his mother's madness—an escape from the fear that he too was tainted with insanity.

As she raged in the house at Fitzroy Square, taking out her exasperation on the woken children, Sarah regretted ever having become entangled with Billy Turner. Yet she herself had arranged for a friend of his, a young fellow artist called Tom Girtin, to bring him to a musical evening at their house. She had encouraged him in an illicit relationship while her husband's health grew worse and worse, fully realising that Billy regarded the fact that she was married as a protection against any permanent involvement. She forgot for the present that after John Danby's death, when she was faced with destitution, Billy had decided not only to shoulder the responsibility for his own as yet unborn child but also to provide a roof over all their heads—though, in his curious way of reasoning, he had decided that she would be more a housekeeper than a mistress.

But the initial electrifying impact that she had made on him was waning, and although he might once have been excited by the brazen sexuality he had detected underneath her outward refinement and elegance—something he had encountered and enjoyed among the girls who worked in the taverns and lodging houses where he stayed on his early sketching tours—it was steadily losing its attraction for him.

Billy, meanwhile, had reached the river in time to wake a sleeping waterman, hire a boat and drift out in the middle of the sunrise—not merely to capture something of it with his paint-box and brushes, but to search out its secrets of colour and effect. He was at peace here on the river. He had been born within a few minutes' walk of its banks in Maiden Lane and it was both friend and inspiration to him, the scene of his first discoveries about the wonder of water, the magic of light and how to obtain his effects. It was here, when he had been drifting alone—as he did now—that a heavy admiral's barge thrust by weighty oars headed towards him. The junior officer at the bow yelled at him to row out of the way. Billy was so absorbed in his work that at first he heard nothing; then, when he realised what was happening, he resented being shouted at. He had as much right to the river as anyone else—including admirals! The barge swept past dangerously close, the oars splashing water on to the colour sketches drying in the boat. Billy was incensed—until he saw what the water had done to his sketches. The colour had run. He picked up one of the sketches and rubbed it with the cuff of his coat, then held it up in triumph.

This was one of the techniques he used on the morning after leaving Sarah in bed with the howling infant. The tide turned, and as his boat was carried down towards Blackfriars Bridge he made colour studies of the sun rising through flimsy veils of mist. The traffic on the river began to build up: fishermen's coracles, watermen's wherries, bumboats with bread, cheese, greens and liquor for ships at anchor. Billy remained oblivious to these vessels, and the owners and occupants were too concerned with their own affairs to give more than a casual glance at the boat drifting with the young man seated amidship. But a neat private barge hove to at a quiet order passed to its lone oarsman from someone under the curtained scarlet awning. A jewel flashed on a thin hand as it reached down to the water to pick up one of Billy's cast-off sketches. Hand and sketch vanished behind the curtains as the barge drifted closer; and then the curtains were parted a little so that the owner of the hand could peer out through the narrow gap.

The stranger stared in amazement as Billy dipped an entire sheet of paper into the river, withdrew it, shook a shower of water from it and set about applying colour to it with his fingers, rubbing with the side of his hand and scratching with his fingernails.

'What in God's name do you think you're doing?'

Billy jumped and turned to see a face between the parted curtains—narrow, high-bred and indignant.

He was too startled to answer, despite his own indignation,

before the owner of the private barge went on to state: 'That's no way to paint.'

Finding his voice at last, Billy replied heatedly, his Cockney accent coming out strongly: 'I'll paint any damn way I like!'

'Dip your paper in river water? Use your bare fingers? You call that painting?' the man derided, disclosing the cushioned interior of the barge as he widened the gap in the curtains and tossed the sketch he had rescued back on to the water. 'You must be mad.'

With this, the scandalised connoisseur disappeared behind the scarlet curtains, and his oarsman started rowing again, heading up the river towards Westminster. The man could not have said anything more certain to destroy Billy's creative mood and flow.

He was confronted with that image of his mother rearing with the upheld anchor against the sun and reminded of the thing that threatened to possess and destroy him too. The fear was always with him. And it was his realisation that he would need to conserve so much of himself emotionally in order to devote his mind and energies to his vocation that made him shy away from other commitments—such as marriage.

He gathered the sketches lying around to dry in the boat, and put out the oars, drifting at first with the tide, then rowing downstream under Blackfriars Bridge, shooting the rapids between the platforms that protected the piers of London Bridge, spending the rest of the day roaming among the forests of masts of moored ships, seeking anonymity and finding another escape, until he returned to Fitzroy Square to be greeted by Sarah with a sarcastic: 'That was a long sunrise!'

Chapter 2

It was a joke among Will Turner's regular customers to start him talking about his son. At his barbershop, entered just off Maiden Lane from an alley called Hand Court, Will would readily oblige with accounts of Billy's latest successes, the mark his entries were making at exhibitions at the Royal Academy and elsewhere, the important people and publishers who were buying and commissioning work from him, and the prices his boy was being paid for them. The drawings displayed in his windows in Maiden Lane and Hand Court and around the walls of the shop itself might once have been purchased for shillings, but now the prices were in guineas and increasing all the time.

Will's boasting was taken in good spirit for the most part; it was no more than the honest pride of a father seeing his son going up in a hard world; and it was some compensation to the otherwise unassuming little barber for the torment of his life with Mary.

He understood why Billy had made the move from his cramped quarters above the barbershop to a room in Harley Street; besides, their friend, Dr Thomas Monro, had recommended it. But Will knew nothing of Sarah Danby, nor of Billy's move to a house in Fitzroy Square. He was conscious of his boy's secretiveness, and believed that it was caused by his need to conceal his mother's condition.

On one subject Billy was far from secretive: that of his election as an Associate of the Royal Academy. As he approached the minimum age—twenty-four—his anxiety increased to the point of obsession. One morning he called at Maiden Lane.

'I might just as well forget about m'chances,' he said, pacing around the empty barbershop.

Gently and tactfully Will said, 'Son—I was talking wi' Dr Monro only the other day. He said it were only a matter o' time.'

'With my background and them snobs at the Academy, I'll never get it! Never!'

Will knew what the reference to his background meant—his humble origins and his mother; but he ignored this as he took up Billy on the other point. 'Snobs they well may be, some of 'em. But they won't stop 'ee. I'll show you why.' He went to a drawing on the wall—a delicately detailed cathedral interior—and wagged his forefinger at it. Dr Monro had done much the same thing with an oil painting at his house in Adelphi Terrace when Billy's prospects of becoming an Associate had been discussed. 'This is what'll get 'ee in,' he went on in the accent of his native Devon, repeating what Dr Monro had said. 'With work the like o' this, they can't keep 'ee out.'

Billy would not be placated and kept prowling around the shop, muttering to himself. It was a constant wonder to Will how he had come to father such a son; the only thing he saw of himself in his boy was his sturdiness—his smallness and strength. Now there was something in Billy's conduct that struck Will as being curiously familiar—and he realised that his son was acting as Mary had done before her early attacks. From this time on he was conscious of other signs in Billy—switches of mood, flashes of impatience and temper, exhaustion, lack of appetite—and with a dread that he kept to himself he wondered whether Mary's condition might be repeating itself in her son.

Despite Billy's doubts, his artistic impact was such that he was elected an Associate to the Royal Academy six months after his twenty-fourth birthday.

It was a cold November night when Billy received the news and he rushed to Maiden Lane, finding his father alone in the barbershop, tidying up after a tiring day.

'I'm in!' Billy cried, thumping himself on the chest. 'In after all!'

And then he saw the look of concern mixed with the tears of pride that shone in Will's eyes; his father was worried that a raised voice might disturb his mother.

In a lower voice he asked, 'How's she been?'

'Much the same as ever,' Will said, then brightening added, 'but earlier on she were asking for 'ee.'

'I'll go upstairs and see her,' Billy said, knowing that telling her what had happened might be impossible.

He found her in the sitting-room, a tinier figure now, staring out into the darkness of Hand Court.

She didn't hear him enter, so he spoke softly, careful not to startle her.

'It's me, mother,' he said. 'I'm back.'

She turned slowly and looked at him for a moment before registering any recognition. He could see that she was still sealed off in the black, joyless prison of her private despair. Presently, she said, 'Joseph?'

Although this was his first name, Billy had never been known by it; now he couldn't be sure whether she meant him —sometimes she confused him with her brother, Joseph Mallord William Marshall, after whom he had been named.

Then she asked, 'Where's Mary Ann?' and he knew that she was lost in the past.

Mary Ann, who had been three years younger than Billy, had died when he was eleven. His father had told him that the shock of the little girl's death had started his mother's illness, but he was no longer sure. He believed that the seeds of her madness must have always been there, germinating, waiting to flower, as they had done at sunset at Margate and many times since.

In her present state all he could do was to try to humour her, so he said, 'I'll see if I can find her.'

He left the room, conscious that he was taking the easy way out; but how else was he to handle her when she was in this state?

Back in the barbershop he found Will waiting with a decanter of port and two glasses.

'How was she?' he asked, preparing to pour two drinks in order to toast his boy's success.

Billy said nothing, just shaking his head; and before Will

was able to tip a drop of the port into the first glass, Billy brushed past him and went out into the night.

Will understood how it upset Billy to find his mother in an increasingly detached state, yet he wondered where his boy was heading. Surely not back to a room in Harley Street to plunge into his work when he had such an occasion to celebrate. He had the feeling that Billy was involved in some situation about which he couldn't bring himself to speak.

To occupy himself, and to find some way to celebrate his boy's success on his own, he took up a pencil and went to some of the early drawings on the wall and printed the letters A.R.A. after Billy's signature. And such was the man's ability to rise above his troubles that, having done this, he was able to chuckle to himself and say aloud, 'And I'll be bound it won't be long before 'ee are a full R.A., either.'

He was about to drink a port on his own when there was a knock on the door, and Will opened it to admit Dr Monro.

'I've been out visiting a patient,' the doctor explained. 'It was there that I heard the result from an Academician who voted at today's General Meeting. I thought I'd drop by on my way back to Adelphi Terrace—just to make sure you'd heard.'

'Thank 'ee, doctor, I have; indeed, I have,' said the little barber, bobbing up and down on his toes with pride. 'Billy himself rushed in to tell me.'

'I'm delighted,' said Dr Monro. 'Not that I ever had any doubt, in spite of William's views to the contrary, that it was only a matter of time before the Academy "snobs" had to recognise him.'

The two men laughed and then when Will suggested a port the doctor readily accepted.

As they raised their glasses Dr Monro said, 'William's quite the best architectural and landscape draughtsman in the country—and he's barely started yet.'

This was music to Will's ears, coming from a man whose house seemed to him to be crammed with the works of masters—Claude, Poussin, Rembrandt, Canaletto and Gainsborough. He had seen them for himself when he went with his striped apron and tools of trade to the house overlooking the Thames to trim the doctor's hair and attend to his wigs.

He had also seen several of Billy's paintings hanging alongside these great works.

And so the two men drank their toast, the doctor, a tall, beaky, urbane man in his middle forties, towering over Will.

Dr Monro had inherited wealth. He was an enthusiastic amateur artist but had long ago accepted the fact that he would never be more than that. He found his outlet by acquiring fine paintings and encouraging young painters. He was one of Billy's earliest patrons, and one of Will's most eminent clients. He was a prominent physician and, by coincidence, a pioneer in the treatment of mental illness. This made him especially interested in the Turner family since he had heard rumours and first-hand accounts of Mary's outbreaks of violence.

He accepted a second glass of port from Will to warm him against the black cold outside, and as he was about to leave he asked bluntly about Mary's health.

Taken by surprise, Will mumbled, 'Oh—the wife ... well, she's doing nicely, thank 'ee. Very nicely.'

But his defensiveness belied his words, and the distress that suddenly clouded the little man's friendly face was obvious.

'If ever you need me, you know where I'm to be found,' said the doctor, preparing to leave. 'I've made that clear to you—and to William.'

Will could do no more than bow his thanks. His fear of what might become of Mary—of where she might be taken were he to reveal the full truth about her outbursts—was so great that he couldn't bring himself to discuss her condition with any outsider, not even with the one man who might be able to help.

Pausing at the door Dr Monro asked one final question. 'William's quite happy with his room in Harley Street, I trust?'

'Oh yes, doctor—quite,' Will said, relieved to be asked something he felt he could answer frankly. 'He's at work round the clock there. But no matter—he calls in every day he's in town to see us—me and his mother.'

Dr Monro nodded and smiled as he went outside, but once alone his expression changed. He had received confirmation of what he suspected: many people, including the young artists who came to his house, knew about young Turner's association with Sarah Danby, but obviously his own father was still ignorant of it.

Billy called at Maiden Lane the following day to tell his father that he had joined the Academy Club and was on his way to his first dinner there.

Will had spent part of the day telling customers and neighbours the latest news about his son. Now his eyes blurred as he gripped his boy's arm with both hands in an effort to convey his pride and affection and escorted Billy to the barbershop doorway to see him on his way. But then he stopped suddenly, exclaiming, 'Hold on, son! You won't do for the Academy Club looking like this.'

Billy writhed, as he had done often as a boy when his father had decided that he needed attention, and found himself steered back into the shop and across to a work bench. Will tugged the end of the red ribbon at the nape of Billy's neck, releasing his son's thick brown hair over his collar and shoulders. The ribbon was grubby, so he tossed it away and took up a pair of steel scissors, then snipped a length of clean red ribbon from a roll set on the wall.

'Hold still!' Will said, as Billy continued to fidget. He sleeked the hair into a tail and wound the ribbon around it, tying it in a neat bow.

Having made this start, Will found more and more to attend to. He pushed Billy into the chair by the bench and trimmed the hair around his ears, his sideboards and the fringe above his eyes. Then he decided, despite protests, that his boy was in need of a good clean shave, so he removed his cravat and set to work.

Billy tried to endure his father's ministrations with some good grace, but he was embarrassed when a customer entered the shop and sat down to enjoy watching the father at work on a reluctant son.

He was conscious of the customer's grins; more than that, he had the feeling that the man had his eyes on him in a curious, calculating way, as if dwelling on something, and he was relieved to be able to get out of the chair and on his feet again.

All wasn't over yet. Will insisted that Billy should wear a clean cravat, then surrender his coat so that some stains could be sponged out, before standing back to make a final appraisal of his workmanship. After a grunt and a nod, he said, 'That's more like it.'

And so Billy was allowed to depart, leaving the waiting customer to take his place in the chair.

The man, a scrawny lamplighter who prided himself on being well-informed about many things, was only too ready to encourage Will to talk about his son. He, too, had something to say, but he managed to contain himself with malevolent satisfaction until Will had finished telling him about Billy's election to the Royal Academy and what a help it would be in his career to have the letters after his name. Then, savouring every moment of it, the lamplighter started to lead up to his item of news about the rising young artist.

'I understand your lad's got hisself a room in Harley Street, too,' he began.

'He has,' Will granted, open and unsuspecting. 'More space, better light.'

'Pleasant neighbourhood that. I was on the lamps up that way once. Handy to Fitzroy Square, too.'

'Fitzroy Square?' Will repeated, puzzled.

'I got an ol' workin' mate on the lamps around that area now. Marylebone. He was tellin' me he often sees your William—although it was his opinion the lad spends less time in that room o' his than with the widow Danby in Fitzroy Square. Easy walkin' distance.'

Will moved round to the rear of the chair to work on the back of his customer's head, concealing his reaction.

'Wife o' that songwriter who died last year,' the lamplighter droned on. 'Danby. Seen her m'self a number of times. Well-built, upstandin' red-head. Used to be an actress. Strikin' looker. It's hard to believe, but I'm told she had four girls by Danby in less than half a dozen years. *And* she's just had another. Seems she thrives on havin' 'em.'

The lamplighter paused to spice his malice with a dark humourless chuckle. Will had to fight to keep his hand steady as he snipped with his scissors, still out of sight.

'Of course, she was only eighteen when he married her—

and he was gettin' on for twice her age. Death to a man. A woman like that needs a strong, husky young lad. Like your William ... As a matter of fact—not that you can blame the lad—there's a very strong rumour up around Marylebone that the widow's newest baby girl was fathered by your boy ...'

Will managed not to show any emotion. It was only afterwards, when he was alone, that he could digest this malicious gossip. Or try to digest it. The secretiveness of Billy's nature had never been more apparent to him. And while Will could just—although only just—stomach having to learn in such a roundabout and cruel way that he was probably a grandfather, his main concern was for his boy. How had he landed himself with this woman? Was it due to the streak of instability he had detected in Billy and put down to something inherited from his mother? And how might it affect his boy's work and career—something to which Will in his way had dedicated himself as deeply as Billy?

Chapter 3

As the relationship between Billy and Sarah disintegrated into constant exasperation and resentment on her part, and more and longer absences on his, a little physical attraction lingered—but that was all.

By their second Christmas together Sarah was pregnant again—to Billy's fury and her own secret satisfaction. She no longer hoped for marriage, but she needed to be assured of his protection. Two children would be more shackling than one child. She thought she knew enough of his nature to be certain that he would never abandon his children—or even hers.

Billy got on very well with all the children, and for their sake he and Sarah called a truce that Christmas. But it was shaky from the start and ended abruptly the day after Christmas when Billy rugged up in his warmest clothes and prepared to leave the house.

'You can't be rushing away again!' Sarah exclaimed.

'I'm not,' he said, trying not to flare back at her.

'But you're going out.'

'I'm going to Maiden Lane.'

'And leaving *us*?'

'I promised Dad,' he said, and slipped out before she could prolong the argument.

He was relieved to be out of the house, even though he was not happy at leaving the children to face Sarah's temper on their own. The weather was bitter, but he enjoyed the walk through the streets of crusted snow and ice.

After the prickly atmosphere at the house in Fitzroy Square it was good to be home. His father had roasted a duck in the basement kitchen and steamed a pudding that a customer had given him as a present. In the parlour it was almost like far-off boyhood days when Mary Ann was alive, but for his mother's complete detachment.

Mary had shown no particular pleasure at seeing her son, but at least she was calm and quiet. That gave Will hope. It was a good sign when she ate a little of the duck and seemed to enjoy it. He went down to the kitchen, hoping she would want some of the pudding which he brought up decorated with a sprig of holly snipped from the nearby churchyard.

'What a delicious looking pudding!' Billy exclaimed, picking up a bottle of brandy and pouring some over it. He smiled at his mother but there was no response.

Her lack of reaction didn't perturb Will. It was enough that the three of them were together, he thought, as he lit a taper in the fire. He had been afraid that the unmentioned ties which Billy had at Fitzroy Square might, at this time of the year, prevent him from coming. He carried the burning taper back to the table and held it to the brandy-soaked pudding.

Blue and yellow flames flared. Mary screamed.

Will and Billy froze.

For a moment it was a tableau: Mary sat rigid; then she snatched up the carving knife from the table and raised it menacingly at the two men. But as she stood facing them, something of their crushing disappointment and utter despair must have communicated itself to her. She sobbed and let the knife slip from her hand. It clattered on to the table.

Will and Billy, as if released from a trance, started towards her from opposite sides of the table. She backed out of the door that led to the barbershop, but Will caught its edge before it could slam shut. He and Billy reached her as she tried to wrench open the door into Hand Court. In more recent attacks and outbursts she had rushed from the house, on at least two occasions heading for the river, where she had tried to throw herself into the water from the end of a jetty. Will and Billy had the same intention—to stop her from leaving the house and get her up to her bedroom. When she pulled away from them and made across the shop towards the darkened staircase they let her go. But from a walk she swiftly moved into a run, stumbling up the stairs and past the sitting-room on the first floor, not stopping at her bedroom on the second landing but continuing at the same hectic pace right up into the attic. By the time they reached her she had the window open and was half way through it. As they pulled her back into the room she clawed at the ledge and struggled to get back out of the window. Her cries and pleas left neither her husband nor her son in any doubt that it had been her intention to put an end to their misery.

To make it worse, the violence that had been by-passed in the parlour was now unleashed. The demon that possessed Mary seemed to give her unprecedented strength as she fought against the two men to break away; but they found added strength in their fear for her, and eventually managed to get her to her bedroom.

There exhaustion suddenly seemed to sweep over her; and although she continued to struggle, Will was able to hold her down by himself.

It was then that Billy made the decision: the one he knew his father would never be able to make, no matter what the circumstances.

'I'm fetching Dr Monro,' he said.

As he hurried from the shop the open attic window banged overhead in the wind, and in the darkness he was aware that a few neighbours were standing at their closed windows with lanterns, peering out. It no longer mattered.

He ran all the way across the Strand and along Adelphi Terrace to pound the knocker on Dr Monro's door, oblivious to the icy spumes that the wind carried in from the waves on the river. A manservant let him in and called Dr Monro from the dinner table, and the doctor began putting on his hat and coat even as Billy was panting out his story. Together, Billy and the doctor hurried back to Maiden Lane.

Mary had found hidden pockets of strength but now Billy helped Will as Dr Monro opened a small bottle and tried to empty its contents into Mary's mouth. She writhed and jerked her head, spitting most of the liquid out but swallowing a little of it.

'That may have some effect,' the doctor said. 'I fear, though, that she's liable to make another attempt at suicide.' He took over from Billy, saying to him, 'Get me some rope.'

'Rope?' Billy echoed in a shocked whisper.

'I'm sorry,' Monro said firmly, 'but that is the way it has to be—rope.'

Billy rushed to his room and came back with a weathered coil of rope he had used on sketching tours to haul himself up to eyries from which he got his views of the land and the sea.

Dr Monro cut the rope into lengths and bound Mary's hands together, then her feet; he tied her to the bed as Will and Billy held her. It was unbearable for them to have to watch, but impossible not to. Through it all, Mary made grating, unnatural sounds—sounds unrelated to human speech, as if her voice had been taken over by some vicious predatory creature.

When it was done, Dr Monro led Will and Billy out to the landing where, towering over both of them, he laid a comforting hand on the shoulder of each of them.

'Tonight I'll make arrangements for her to have the best possible treatment right from the start; and we'll take her to the hospital in the morning. With my influence I can arrange that for her.'

'What hospital be that?' Will asked although he knew with a dull certainty what the answer would be.

'Bethlehem,' Dr Monro said, articulating the name distinctly because he knew what was in Will's mind.

'You call it Bethlehem,' Billy said. 'Most people call it Bedlam.'

'That is a corruption of its real name—and a most unfortunate one.' He repeated the name again. 'Bethlehem.'

But to Will and Billy it was still Bedlam.

It was a long night; and the morning, when it came, was one of dazzling whiteness and bitter cold. A two-horse carriage eventually drew up in Maiden Lane, and Dr Monro hurried from it into Hand Court. Alert neighbours immediately linked it with the cries they had heard coming from the Turners' attic window the previous night. A dozen of them hung about as Mary Turner was carried out, the rope on her hands and feet concealed by the blankets in which she was swaddled. All that could be seen of her was a tiny face in an aperture formed in the enclosing blankets. She was limp, inert and in a remote, mindless stupor.

The carriage braked and rumbled into the Strand, along Fleet Street, past St Paul's, along Cheapside and up through Moorgate. Will and Billy sat with Mary lying across their laps. Patches of snow caught the sun and reflected light into the carriage, invading the privacy of what to father and son was a funeral.

Tears welled out of Mary's eyes and zigzagged down her cheeks with the movement of the carriage. They could have been caused by the coldness but Will interpreted them differently. And she was so passive now that he clutched desperately at what was a last tiny strand of hope.

'Billy, she be better now, don't you think? Better now ...'

Billy had never had his father's optimism, and he looked to Dr Monro for help.

'It's best this way, Mr Turner,' the doctor said kindly. 'She'll be well looked after. I promise you that. And she'll get better much more quickly in the hospital.'

The carriage reached Moorfields and pulled up at the gates of the long, low, gloomy hospital. Looming over the carriage, from the tops of the two solid pillars to which the gates were hinged, were two reclining statues proclaiming in blackened stone the brutish attitude of the times towards those afflicted with illnesses of the mind—a macabre pair of effigies: moping madness on one side and raving madness, chained, on the other.

Shiny bold faces suddenly appeared at the carriage windows —local sightseers, jeering and laughing at the bundle Will and Billy held across their laps.

Dr Monro lifted his cane and shook its thick silver-topped head at them.

'You call this a hospital!' Billy shouted, making it an accusation against Dr Monro. 'It's a free show for the mob— that's what it is!'

Monro started to protest that he and his colleagues had no jurisdiction outside the hospital walls, but Mary took fright at Billy's outburst and began writhing and crying out.

The provocateurs whooped with delight, and rocked the

carriage. At this point the iron gates swung open and the gate-keeper waved the driver through. The carriage jerked forward and rolled into the hospital forecourt, with Mary still screaming hysterically.

As soon as the carriage had stopped, attendants rushed from a stone archway and pulled the door open to subject Mary to a swift, practised routine—dragging her out and then racing her in through the arch. Will and Billy stumbled out of the carriage after her, but by the time they had their feet on the ground she had been carried out of sight.

Her cries echoed back to Will and Billy, and other voices started up in the depths of the vast living tomb. Like a rising tide, the sound engulfed the two men; and with this in their ears and the stench of the place assailing their nostrils they stood helplessly for a moment, looking at the dark opening into which Mary had disappeared, saying their silent farewells.

The carriage dropped Will and Billy in the Strand. It was far enough; and Dr Monro understood why. They wanted to slip quietly back into the house at Maiden Lane, hoping the neighbours wouldn't see them returning without Mary.

Once inside, Will made a colossal attempt to convince himself that the terrible step just taken had been for the best. 'Like the doctor said, son—she'll get better quicker there.'

Billy muttered his agreement, but in his heart he didn't believe it. The thought of his mother in that place filled him with despair and dread; and as the day wore on, Will's dogged determination to make a show of cheerfulness became more than he could endure. As soon as he decently could, he excused himself and went out to walk the streets and the paths by the river, eventually ending up in his room in Harley Street. Here he remembered what Dr Monro had told him when he had confessed to the doctor that he believed his mother's affliction was in his blood too. 'It's in all of us,' Dr Monro had said. 'In a way it's a matter of mood—and we are all creatures of mood. We all have our elations, we all have our despairs. In some of us those emotions are stronger, more pronounced; and in a few they are uncontrollable, and so they are called insanity and madness. Those who lose control go under. They are the ones we have to look after. But most people can fight their inner feelings—and do. Especially those who can absorb themselves in their work—as you can. Through your work you get it all out of yourself. It's like the device that stops the new steam-engines from blowing up—a safety valve.'

This had made sense to Billy then—and ever since. He set to work on a storm scene, turning it into a huge threatening canvas as he tried to drown out all the horror in a scene of wrath and whirlwind, freezing the image of his mother with the anchor in the form of a grim tree in sharp black outline.

It was here that Sarah found him. What was he doing here alone? Why hadn't he come home to her and the children? Where had he been all night?

'Putting my mother in a madhouse!' Billy hurled at her, keeping his back to her and painting on.

This only infuriated her more. She cared nothing about his mother and had no word of sympathy for him. 'That's where you'll end up if you carry on like this. You rushed out of the house, you've been gone all night and day. It's not normal ...'

Billy turned from the canvas and looked at her with sudden calm. 'Sarah—I don't have to answer to anyone for what I do or where I go. And I shouldn't have to remind you that I took you on as a paid housekeeper.'

Sarah's cheeks turned scarlet. 'And I shouldn't have to remind *you* that I'm carrying your child. A paid housekeeper, am I? For that I'll never forgive you.'

Chapter 4

Within a year Mary was discharged from the Bethlehem hospital uncured. In her absence Will's business had picked up, and it was clear that it would be impossible for him to look after her himself and keep the barbershop going. On Dr Monro's advice, Billy decided to put his mother in a private asylum at Islington. He could afford it.

His work was in greater demand from publishers and engravers —and his fees had risen. He was able to meet all his financial responsibilities and still put some money by. With this security he felt free to experiment with more adventurous works, but in doing so he stirred up something that was to pursue him for the rest of his life.

Critics who had before praised him now turned sour. He was accused of affectation, capriciousness and insulting tradition. The attacks upset him badly, but didn't deter him. In a break in the war with France he crossed to Calais; and from notes taken when the packet was waiting in stormy waters for the tide to rise over the bar, he painted one of his largest and most arresting pictures to date. But to the critics the sea was soap and chalk, and the sky a heap of marble mountains.

He needed sympathy, but he got none from the woman he supported in Fitzroy Square.

After the arrival of his second daughter, Georgiana, the situation with Sarah became intolerable. Billy gave up his single room and rented larger premises in Harley Street. Here he set up a spacious painting-room in which he could take refuge from Sarah's unabating complaints and nagging.

His sketching tours provided another escape, although they had become an essential part of his professional life. Sometimes he walked, sometimes he hired a pony. From cliff-tops and escarpments he gathered rivers and mountains, castles and ruins into his sketchbooks. As he did so he found himself confronted by the mystery of the conflicting aspects in nature and man. Nature could be serene or violent, as he saw in sunrises and sunsets, gales and thunderstorms. So could man, as he saw in the churches and abbeys, built by man to express hopes and aspirations, and then destroyed by him in mindless eruptions of hate and violence. He had a growing intimation that just as beauty and terror existed in nature, they existed in a parallel way in man. Also, that beauty and terror might both originate in the same cosmic sources of darkness and light. But he was wary of allowing such overtones to creep too deeply into his work. Few of the potential customers who would leaf through his sketchbooks would have much concern for the destinies of men and nations.

His most convenient escape from Sarah, or from anyone or anything that happened to bedevil him, was closer to home —the Thames, the river that was part of his life. One day he dragged his boat up on to the mud a little downstream from the Tower of London on the opposite bank and went into a nearby tavern for a pot of ale to wash down the bread and cheese he had brought with him. At a corner table four men were having a noisy argument, the gist of which soon became clear to Billy. It appeared that a close companion of the four had been forced to leave their company and was unhappily on his way, by courtesy of King George III, to His Majesty's penal colony in New South Wales. The time taken by the voyage was in dispute; and Billy suddenly found himself involved, one of the men having taken him for a sailor.

How many years did it take to sail to Botany Bay?

'Takes years to get back,' Billy said wryly, unconsciously adopting rougher speech. 'As for gettin' there in the first place, I've not made the voyage m'self, but I'm told three months is fast sailin'. With storms an' calms it can be anythin' up to nine.'

To have been taken for a seaman, and to have carried off the part, gave Billy a curious sense of elation. On his sketching tours he had dropped into many taverns and alehouses where he had been recognised as an artist simply because he carried the tools and materials of his trade. That had been part of the business of establishing himself as an artist—to look like one. But having achieved his aim, the need no longer existed and he had begun to wear plain durable clothes, often bought at shops specialising in apparel for seamen. Even his hat was the style of beaver favoured by watermen. Without realising it, he had taken the first steps into a disguise that could also be an escape.

He finished the last of his bread and cheese, emptied his ale pot and took his leave of the men and the tavern-keeper to stroll back to his boat. The interlude had pleased him and put him in the mood to work, so he decided to make some notes of the Tower across the water, sitting on the gunwale of the boat with a sketchbook on his knee.

After studying a subject carefully, Billy's gift for visualisation was such that he could retain the image for quite some time without further reference to it as he went ahead and made his sketches and notes. On this occasion, one look was enough to occupy him for almost a minute.

When he glanced up again, he found that he was not alone.

Three of the four men who had been arguing in the tavern had silently approached over the mud and now surrounded him. The fourth—the one to whom Billy had given the Botany Bay information—hung back.

'Spying, eh?' said the closest of the three.

'Spying?' Billy repeated, confused.

'Drawin' secrets. Then sellin' 'em to the Frenchies, like as not.'

The accusation was outrageous—but, as Billy knew, the country was alive with rumours and spy-scares. In every village he had passed through on his last sketching tour he had seen recruiting posters and crude slogans saying 'God bless the King and damn the French.' Anyone behaving in any way out of the ordinary was liable to be treated as a suspect.

His sketchbook was snatched from his hands and examined amid mounting indignation as the men found proof of their suspicions. The river scenes they immediately identified as invasion notes to supply the enemy with suitable places for river landings. It was all that they needed. The sketchbook was ripped apart and the pieces were tossed over the mud. Then Billy was manhandled into his boat and launched into the stream without oars, the three men swearing and cursing him. At this point the fourth man—perhaps less inebriated than his friends—defied the others and shot the oars out into the water so that Billy was able to recover them. For his trouble, the wretched man was set upon by the other three as Billy rowed rapidly away from the brawl.

After this, he was careful not to draw attention to himself by carrying any equipment or materials openly. One simple article removed this danger. He bought a compact seaman's chest—a travelling-box as he came to call it—in which he carried the simple essentials for day to day living when on the move; and hidden away underneath these innocuous items were his drawing and painting materials.

And so he began to pass himself off as a seaman.

'Any chance of a berth for the night?' he asked the landlord of a riverside tavern on the first evening of deliberate disguise, flavouring his request with a nautical tang.

'Aye. There's a room upstairs cryin' out for someone to use it. Sixpence an' it's yours—an' a good meal in the mornin' into the bargain.'

'I'll have it,' Billy said. 'And I'll have a tot of rum to be goin' on with.'

'Been on a far voyage?' the landlord asked.

'Far enough to lose m'land legs,' Billy the seaman replied, delighted with his success so far. 'Naples.'

'Naples? T'other side of the world. How'd ye find things there?'

And so Billy extemporised, drawing on paintings he had seen of crowded roadsteads and dreamy anchorages, giving ancient ships modern rigs but somehow still describing what he had seen in the paintings of his idol Claude at Dr Monro's house and during his visit to the Louvre in Paris. As he grew increasingly eloquent, customers gathered round to listen; and he was filled with exhilaration. He was a seaman—not Billy Turner at all. And it was as though he had found a key that opened the door to a secret world: an escape route unconsciously sought and now discovered.

Meanwhile, on his visits to Maiden Lane his father saw

much of his mother in him. Will knew nothing of the masquerade, but he noticed the style of clothing that had become Billy's everyday attire; the toughening not only of his physique and physical features but also of his speech—the forthrightness, the abruptness, and at times the curious leavening of seafaring phrases and nautical terminology. But he still asked no questions, even though there was so much of his son's life that was a mystery to him.

Chapter 5

Mary Turner lingered on in the private asylum for three years. Billy and Will kept up their visits to her, but she rarely recognised them; towards the end, she didn't know them at all.

Dr Monro was with them when Mary was laid to rest in the asylum grounds, yet to father and son it seemed that her funeral had taken place when they left her at Bedlam. It was as if she had been dead since that day, and that this was a rite in which her remains had simply been exhumed for final burial. In its way, her death was a release for her, Will and Billy; but Billy believed that the dark thing which had stolen his mother's reason still lived on in him. And on that bleak day the cries of the inmates drifted across from the asylum buildings as Mary's coffin was lowered into the grave.

During those three years of Mary's confinement in the private asylum, Billy had been elected a full R.A., reaching this pinnacle within two months of his twenty-seventh birthday. And shortly after this, he had made the final break from Sarah.

He had realised by now that both his father and Dr Monro knew about the relationship, but there was never any mention of it to him. The quarrels with Sarah had meanwhile become so frightening to him that he felt the rages that boiled up in him were part of his heritage from his mother and he was afraid that at some stage he might not be able to control them. He stayed away more and more, his increasing absences only making Sarah more impossible than ever when he returned. She had now found a new cause for complaint about him. The appalling workmanlike attire he now habitually wore irritated her intensely; also his speech with its tang of the waterfront.

In the end, he shut his ears to it all, packed what he needed and went to Harley Street—and stayed there.

This gave him the chance to devote some time to a plan that had been forming in his mind after some of his brushes with critics, dealers and Academy officials. He took over the lease of the whole premises and carried out extensive alterations. On the first floor he built a gallery that extended out over the garden, giving him plenty of space to show his works just as he pleased, without Academy tyrants or other busybodies interfering. And to an extent it did away with the need of grasping dealers.

Will's business in Maiden Lane had declined with the passing of the fashion of wearing wigs, the tax imposed on wig powder being partly to blame. He had worked hard to keep the shop going in the hope that Mary might become well enough to leave the asylum and have a home to return to. Now there was no need to keep the shop, so Billy persuaded Will to close down and come to live with him in his enlarged premises in Harley Street.

It was a totally new life for Will at the gallery, but he fell into the way of it immediately, watching over his boy's interests, handling inspections of work for sale, settling the prices, buying materials and bargaining for them, too—and even running errands. In effect, he became his son's servant and general factotum: but the two, who had been brought even closer by Mary's death, remained deeply dependent on each other.

Sarah and the children stayed on at Fitzroy Square, on an allowance paid by Billy. Although adequate, Sarah considered it a pittance. Her grievance, she felt, justified an appearance at Harley Street to complain in person; but when she went there, ready to do battle, Billy was out and she had to be content with his father.

Rumour had prepared Will for Sarah Danby, but even so it was a shock to find himself face to face with the lady. Nothing had prepared him for the fact that there was a second child. He had only one way of accounting for how Billy had become involved with such an unsuitable woman—a lapse of control or judgement—somehow due to something inherited from his mother. He could only promise to have a word with Billy on her behalf. And Sarah, sensing that she might have found a manoeuvrable intermediary if not an ally, promised to come again soon and bring his grandchildren to see him.

Will had to tell Billy who had called; and from then on, Billy—still without giving his father any details about the affaire with Sarah—used him as a buffer against her. He always managed to be somewhere else whenever she called, and she never set eyes on him.

Sarah really daunted Will. But she always managed to win him over, on what became frequent visits, by bringing along Evelina and little Georgiana. No matter how much he might steel himself against being used or manipulated by Sarah, Will's heart would melt at the sight of the children. He had sweets for them when they came, and he bought rag dolls for them to play with—although they usually preferred the unadorned tight-jointed wooden skeleton-doll that Billy used as a limb guide in his figure work.

Among the numerous things with which Sarah was highly dissatisfied was the house in Fitzroy Square and, through Will, she nagged Billy into agreeing to a move to a new house in Marylebone. But when, not much later, she began to demand another move to something even grander—arguing that Billy could well afford it with his growing fame and the income that went with it—he decided that he had endured enough. She could move all right: but it would have to be to somewhere well away from Harley Street.

With this in mind, Billy went to see his lawyer, George Cobb, in his chambers in Clement's Inn, just off Fleet Street. Cobb, who had been introduced to Billy by Dr Monro as a suitable man to handle his affairs, was a competent, good-natured person who was amused by Billy's entanglements.

'I don't care where you find a place for her, Mr Cobb,' Billy told him, 'just so long as it's out of town. I can't have no more of her sailing round to Harley Street in full rig every time it takes her fancy.'

'I'll get Gascoigne on to it,' Cobb said, calling in the junior associate who was later to become a partner in the firm—a young man who already had a high opinion of himself and was showing the first signs of self-indulgence in overweight.

When Gascoigne had been told the situation, he asked Billy,

'How soon would you like this done, sir?'

'Forthwith! The *Victory*'s at Spithead and she's due to sail for Sheerness with Nelson's body. I'm hoping to be granted permission to go on board and do some drawings. I could be there for three or four days; I could be a couple of weeks. The matter must be settled before I get back.'

At Sheerness, on the morning that the late admiral's flagship was expected at the mouth of the Thames, Billy was out waiting well before dawn. Since it was almost the shortest day of the year, it was a late sunrise: but slowly the fog and mist thinned away to leave a great grey grounding out over the sea and the horizon: then a slow suffusion of pink through the grey, the gradual bloom of gold and orange. In the heart of this a ship materialised, its sails filled out although the sea was as yet unruffled by any sign of wind.

It was not, however, the ship for which he was waiting. This one, as it made signals and fired salutes, he recognised as the *Dreadnought*—one of the four 98-gunners at Trafalgar and a sister ship in type to the sunset ship that Billy had sketched when a boy at Margate with his mother and father.

The *Victory* arrived later, anchoring at noon. After the great hero's body had been transferred to a smaller vessel and taken to Greenwich, leave was granted for a number of distinguished people to go on board, Billy among them. For all of the privileged visitors it was an historic occasion but for Billy it was also work. He made notes and sketches and interviewed officers and men who had fought in the battle; and by the time he left he had three or four important pictures already taking shape in his mind.

In Billy's absence, Sarah was informed that arrangements were in hand for her and the children to be moved to a cottage in Epping. She wasted no time in storming round to Harley Street to have it out with Will.

'It's preposterous,' she fumed. 'Whoever heard of Epping? Why, it's—it's the wilderness! If he thinks he's going to get me to leave London ...'

This was the first that Will had heard about it, but he listened patiently to the tirade. When Sarah paused for breath, he managed to take some of the sting out of her attack by saying, 'I hear Epping's becoming quite fashionable, even if it is a little way out. And to be honest, I'll miss 'ee, won't I?'

Momentarily disconcerted, Sarah blinked at him. 'Miss me? Will you really?'

'Of course. Won't be treating my eyes to the sight of the little 'uns so much, will I now?'

Sarah could see that he really meant this; and although she continued to complain it was in a more subdued tone. 'I'm not a fool,' she said. 'I can see what William's doing. He's trying to get rid of me—of us—all of us—and this is just the first move. By the time he's finished we'll be destitute.' There were tears in her eyes, but they were tears of vexation.

Will, who had never had much in the way of height and now at sixty seemed even smaller, drew himself up. On his dignity now, he said, 'No, Mrs Danby—never. I know my Billy.'

'You may think you do, Mr Turner; but you certainly do not know him as I do.'

'He'll not abandon 'ee,' Will affirmed categorically. 'Not any of you. That I promise.'

Sarah sniffed, unconvinced. 'How can you be so positive?'

'I know.'

Sarah had to be content with that. But although she resigned herself to an eventual move to Epping, she managed to frustrate every ploy by Gascoigne and his young probationary clerk Morley to shift her. Her final excuse was that Christmas was upon them, and surely no civilised person could expect her to undergo the upheaval of a move at such a time.

When Billy returned from Sheerness he gave no thought to whether or not Sarah was still within easy nagging distance. He was suffering from one of his uncontrollable bouts of impatience—an anxiety that caused real physical pain—to get his vision of the *Dreadnought* and that delicate cold dawn on canvas, and he closeted himself in his painting-room.

Will was well aware of his son's state and was apprehensive about disturbing him, but he had made a promise to Sarah and was determined to honour it without delay. He took the unusual step of invading the painting-room shortly after Billy had settled in.

'Before you get too far into it, son, can you spare a minute?'

'Can't it wait?' Billy replied absently, working on.

Will hesitated, but only for a moment. He was genuinely concerned for the children. And also his boy's honour was at stake.

'No,' he said simply.

Billy stopped work and turned, arrested by the tone of his father's voice and then surprised by the determined look on his face.

'Forgive me for taking up your time when you wants to get on wi' things,' Will continued, 'but this be a particular matter. Kindly hear me out.'

Billy had never known his father to make a request such as this—any request, for that matter—and it disturbed him.

'What is it, Dad?'

'Sarah and the little'ns.'

Billy lifted the brush he was holding as though he would dash it to the floor in anger, but nothing was going to stop Will now.

'I asked 'ee to hear me out, son.'

With a visible effort, Billy managed to contain himself. He lowered the brush and waited for his father to go on.

'If this be the last thing I ever ask 'ee, Billy, I want 'ee to make me this one promise: that you'll see to it that Sarah and the children—not only Evelina and Georgiana but also the rest of 'em—that all of 'em never wants for the roof over their heads, the fireside at their feet and the wherewithal to keep body and soul together.'

It was a long speech for Will, and it made Billy feel suddenly ashamed. Perhaps he *had* been too hard on Sarah. He was so moved by his father's earnest plea for her and the children that the only immediate reply he could manage was a succession of nods. Then he said, 'Yes, Dad. Of course. I promise.'

'Thank 'ee, son,' Will said. 'That's all. Get back to your picture.' And he was gone before Billy could even begin to frame an explanation for his apparently callous attitude towards Sarah.

* * *

Will headed straight for Sarah's house, stopping on the way only to buy oranges for the girls. He was happy and proud to be able to tell Sarah that his boy had lived up to expectations and had promised faithfully that she and the children would always be looked after. In return for his intervention, though, he had a favour to ask. Would she kindly now fall in with the arrangements made by the lawyers and not create any further delay or difficulty?

Sarah turned the matter over quickly in her mind and then agreed. She felt that she had done well, thanks to Will. Very well. The man didn't realise it, but he had forged a weapon for her to use against his son and had delivered it into her hands.

Chapter 6

The following summer, the Harley Street gallery was again open to the public. Among the pictures on view were four that had been inspired by Billy's visit to Sheerness. A pair of them were finished: the 98-gun Trafalgar veteran sailing out of the dawn, and the *Victory* beating up the channel. The remaining two were much larger and unfinished, both of the battle itself.

These four paintings came in for special attention a week or so after the opening, when Will noticed that they were being scrutinised critically by a gentleman for whom his boy had no great affection. It seemed prudent to let Billy know.

Will found his son in the painting-room, crouched over the window-sill under a heavy black cloak with only his legs showing. To make the spectacle even more astonishing, from under the cloak Billy held a hat with the stove-pipe part protruding over the sill into the sunlight.

'Bless my heart!' Will exclaimed. 'What are you at now?'

From underneath the cloak came a muffled, 'Ah-ha!'

Will smiled and shook his head.

'Get down under here, Dad, and take a look.'

'At what, son?'

'You'll see. Come on.'

Will placidly did as he was told, stooping down and lifting the cloak. Sharing Billy's view into the hat, he saw how the light coming through the tiny hole pierced in the crown was broken up by Billy's new prism into seven colours on a small sheet of white paper.

'Beautiful, don't you think?' Billy said.

'Magical,' Will replied in a sort of boyish wonder. 'Like a piece o' rainbow.'

Leaving Billy to watch on his own, Will came to the point of his intrusion. 'I thought I better warn 'ee, son—there be someone outside I think y' ought to know about.'

'Who might that be?' Billy asked, his voice muffled again and not much interested.

'Sir George.'

There was a moment of absolute stillness under the cloak, as if some spectral shadow had invaded the pristine colours there, and then it was flung back and Billy stood facing Will.

'Beaumont?'

Will nodded. He had recognised Sir George from a visit the previous year. 'Wi' a pair of officers,' he added.

'Officers?'

'One navy, one marine.'

At first Billy was amazed that Beaumont should be here again in his private gallery. Since his previous visit the baronet had become increasingly abusive in private and public about the upstart Turner's work. His most recent attack had been aimed at Billy's two pictures in the inaugural exhibition of the newly-founded rival group to the Royal Academy, the British Institution. According to Sir George, they were like the work of an old man who had lost his powers of execution. Since Billy was still only thirty-one and quite certain that the pictures did justice to his vision, he considered the insult too absurd to worry about. Not that Beaumont's opinions were without influence. He himself was a landscape artist, but of limited range and meagre talent. Through his wealthy and privileged background, combined with a highly articulate and dominant personality—and even though, in fact, younger than Billy—he had established himself as one of the prime arbiters of artistic standards and taste, a defender of tradition, a natural enemy of experimentalists. Billy came to the conclusion that Sir George was here to pronounce ultimate judgement on what was on show.

It struck him as being damned brazen. But if Beaumont wanted it that way, Billy could be brazen too. Much as he loathed and despised the reigning convention whereby the instigators and victims of criticism were expected to maintain reasonably civilised social relationships, he went out into the gallery, carrying his hat upside down by the brim with the prism bouncing very gently in the bottom. Will trailed along after him—the faithful retainer, but a distinctly apprehensive one.

Beaumont stood out at once among the twenty or so men and women viewing the pictures. He liked to think of himself as patrician, the epitome of elegance, and was conscious of his classical profile and noble head—but that head, in Billy's opinion, contained the mind of a tarantula. The fact that Beaumont had been one of the first to champion John Constable did nothing to alter that opinion. With Sir George, in scarlet and blue and heavy with gold braid, were a marine captain and a naval lieutenant.

What was Beaumont doing with these two in tow? Billy asked himself. There was something odd about it. He managed to remain outwardly at his hospitable best as he sauntered across, bowing and passing the time of day with the other visitors.

Sir George had already dismissed the *Victory* painting as trivial and the dawn seascape of the 98-gunner as an indistinct daub. As for the first of the two unfinished battle pictures, he thought it would be best left in its uncompleted state—although he ventured to observe that had Lord Nelson survived to come here and see with his one remaining eye what the upstart Turner had done to his victorious naval engagement the shock might well have accomplished what the sniper's bullet had already achieved at Trafalgar. And the larger of the battle pictures—well, that was nothing but a highly irresponsible and reprehensible fabrication of a sacred event.

'Sir George!' Billy began. 'How nice to see you back. I should be honoured. Which I am, of course. And it's a rare pleasure to have two real serving officers seeing my naval work at first hand.'

Sir George's naturally superior expression underwent no noticeable change as he introduced: 'Captain Bentley of *Britannia*, and Lieutenant Osterham of *Swiftsure*.'

Billy seized upon this information with delight. 'Well, now —*Britannia*—"Old Ironsides"! And *Swiftsure*. If I know anything at all about my boats, both them ships-of-the-line were at Trafalgar.'

'Indeed,' Beaumont said. 'Both of these officers were also there. In the action.'

Billy grew even more excited. 'Then I'm more honoured than I realised. Gentlemen, you have my admiration and my envy. It was a great occasion for the peace of the world. And it would have saved me a great deal of trouble if I'd been there with you. Most of what I needed to know for these pictures I got from others who were in the battle. I was allowed on board *Victory* at Sheerness, y'know.'

'Ah,' said Beaumont, 'so it was there that you obtained your information for these two battle pictures?'

'There and elsewhere, Sir George. I move about, y'know—around the coast and ports. One way and another, I'd say I'd set eyes on a good three parts of the British Navy as it is now afloat.'

'It would appear, then, that you've been seriously misinformed.'

'In reference to what, Sir George?' Billy maintained his cordiality; but where he stood and listened a short distance away, Will detected a subtle change.

'I'm very much afraid I must take you to task about it,' Beaumont went on.

'Do so, by all means. We rough and ready jack-tars of the artistic world, as it were, look to the likes of yourself to keep us in line.' He winked at the two officers, but was not perturbed when they remained impassive.

Beaumont drew off his calf gloves and grasped them in one hand, giving himself a loose bunch of empty fingers to assist him as he launched into his attack, confining it to the larger of the two battle paintings. He believed sincerely that in the defence of art in general, and the limits of dramatic licence in particular, he was about to do to Turner what Nelson had done to the French and Spanish fleets at Trafalgar.

'Here we have the Admiral's famous signal to the fleet before the engagement—"England expects ..."' he said, with a light flick of the fingers of the gloves towards the signal shrouds. He turned to the younger of the two officers. 'At what precise time was that, Lieutenant?'

'11.40, Sir George.'

'*Before* the start of the action?'

'Most certainly. The main action didn't commence until noon.'

Beaumont twirled the fingers of his gloves in a sort of general gesture of disparagement, taking in the whole picture. 'Yet here,' he observed, 'the battle would appear to be at a peak. Great clouds of cannon smoke, a ship sinking, another on fire, masts falling, the sea strewn with men from abandoned ships.' He flipped the limp fingers towards the sinking ship and addressed himself to the other officer. 'I understood you to say, Captain, that you had identified this vessel ...'

'That's the French 74-gunner *Redoubtable*.'

'Any comment, Turner?'

'The Captain was there. He recognises the ship in question, so I got it right,' Billy answered evenly, although into his voice had crept an edge which Will noted with mounting unease.

Other visitors to the gallery began to gather around, attracted by Sir George's raised voice.

'But the ship is sinking,' Beaumont stated.

'She's meant to be.'

'Well, Captain?'

'*Redoubtable* was taken in tow, Sir George. She didn't sink until after the storm struck the next night.'

'I see,' said Beaumont; and believing that he had annihilated Billy on this point he went on to the next, turning this time to the naval officer. 'This burning ship, Lieutenant. You said you thought you knew which vessel it was meant to be.'

'The French *Achille*. It must be. No other ship burned the way she did.'

'Well, Turner?'

'I'll have to be honest with you, Sir George—I'm delighted.'

'Delighted?'

'Yes. This young gentleman has put my mind completely at rest. I don't recall it causing me any sleepless nights, but it's good to have it confirmed that I got this part right too and didn't make a bonfire out of the wrong ship.'

Beaumont glanced at him to make sure that he wasn't concealing a grin; but Billy appeared to be utterly straight-faced, so Beaumont proceeded to call his next item of evidence.

'Lieutenant, you said you could confirm the actual time that this ship caught fire.'

'Yes, Sir George. Almost at the precise time that we knew for certain that we had the battle won. Half-past four.'

'Is there any possibility that because of the confusion of battle you might be in error on this point?'

'I shouldn't think so, sir. All the survivors witnessed it.'

'I know *I* did,' the marines captain averred. 'She burned for an hour and a half, then blew up at sunset. We took it as a delayed victory salute.'

'Then what on earth is this we have in front of us?' Beaumont asked. He started to sum up the case for the prosecution with the aid of the fingers of his gloves, first flicking them towards the signal to the fleet. 'It is a matter of historical fact that these flags went up at 11.40, *before* the action commenced.' Another flick, this time to the sinking *Redoubtable*. 'The *next night*.' And then the burning *Achille*. 'Half-past four.' He faced Billy. 'Yet you clearly have it all happening at the *same* time, Turner.'

'That's a fair comment,' Billy granted coolly.

'But this painting is a travesty. What you've done here is most grievously at odds with eye-witness accounts of the event.'

'No, Sir George. I wouldn't go so far as to say that,' Billy replied, at last showing annoyance.

'I suggest you enlighten us, then. For instance, what particular time did you have in mind?'

'None that damned particular.'

Beaumont stiffened. And Will began to look desperate, fearing that Billy might be provoked into a rage that could not be controlled. The small audience of visitors, meanwhile, pretended not to be aware of what was going on but gathered expectantly.

Billy pointed to the other battle picture, showing Nelson lying mortally wounded on the deck of the *Victory* and the *Téméraire* among the ships in the background. 'I imagine you've a round or two to fire at this one as well.'

'I most certainly have. Apparently, the sequence of events there is also incredibly wrong.'

'I wasn't painting time-tables of the events. Let's have that clear and understood for a start. I know the facts. It took me weeks getting 'em, and then months sorting 'em out. What I was doing here was putting the whole event—the spirit of it, the real truth of it—into the one picture. But you don't see that, do you, Sir George?'

'Indeed I don't.'

Billy dipped his hand into his hat and took out the prism.

'Now, Sir George. If you were commissioned to paint a picture of the vital element we call light, how would you do it?' He held up the prism in the palm of his hand. 'Make it out all white and silver, like you see it in this prism as it looks now? Or split it up into the essential parts, as we understand 'em, of what light really is and paint colours of the spectrum?'

'Either I would paint light or I would paint the colours of the spectrum.'

'With a little imagination, whichever you paint, it's still the same thing.'

The young naval lieutenant was re-examining the larger of the two Trafalgar pictures with fresh eyes. He let out a whisper. 'Jove!'

Beaumont whirled around at him.

Billy laughed. 'Watch out, Sir George ... watch out ... Your naval escort's in dire danger of striking his colours and going over to the enemy.' He planted his hat on his head. 'Help yourselves to a good look around, gentlemen,' he invited them. 'If there's anything further you need, my father here is in charge and he'll do his best to oblige. I'm taking a little fresh air, so I'll say good-day.'

He raised his hat to Beaumont and the two officers and then kept it aloft as he bowed around to the others present, including Will, before replacing it. Then, tossing the prism up and down in his hand, he strolled out of the gallery.

'Mr Turner has a point, you know, Sir George,' the lieutenant said awkwardly, not wishing to offend Beaumont further but trying to justify his apparent about-face. The fact was that he had suddenly seen the picture for what it really was—the whole battle contained in one panoramic scene of action.

'I see nothing whatsoever of what Turner claims,' Beaumont said tersely.

'Nor I, Sir George,' said the captain.

'Besides,' Beaumont added, 'no man in his right mind would try cramming a whole battle into one picture. This is what comes of allowing mental defectives to meddle with our artistic standards.'

Beaumont and the two officers moved on, with no thought to the fact that Billy's father had been well within earshot. They left the gallery almost immediately.

Will was thankful that Billy had gone before this parting comment. He was all too aware of his boy's eccentricities and what they betrayed. Through his work Billy seemed able to keep control of himself as he progressed steadily from one artistic goal to another, but a remark like Beaumont's could have done untold harm. Billy was so sensitive on the subject that it took just a hint that he might be mad, or that this trait showed in his work—as had already been insinuated in print—to plunge him into a black, brooding depression. It was as well that he hadn't been there.

But Billy's day was not yet over. As he ambled down Harley Street towards Oxford Street, enjoying the quick glances of those whose eyes were caught by the piece of polished glass flashing in the air as he tossed it up and down like a ball of light, he suddenly decided that he would like to show the prism to the children—his two small girls and Sarah's four—so he hailed a hackney cab.

'Eppin'?' growled the cabman suspiciously from his perch. A long drive like that would put him out of local business for the rest of the day. And it would cost a penny or two.

Billy dug into a pocket and produced the necessary credentials in the form of a handful of silver and copper coins.

The cabman swiftly nodded him on board.

Ragged and boggy stretches on the roads slowed the cab down, and it took the best part of two hours before they reached Sarah's house. Billy had been paying the rent for over six months now, but it was the first time he had seen it—a pleasant double-storeyed thatched cottage in good repair, with a well-tended garden for which, he reflected, he also paid a gardener.

Telling the cabman to wait, he alighted and went to the door. His arrival had already been noted. There were eager young faces at the window. He took the prism out of his pocket and began to toss it up and down, looking forward to using his hat and coat to treat the girls to the magic of this piece of glass.

The first ripple of concern struck him when the faces suddenly withdrew in alarm from the window. And then, when the door was opened by an elderly local woman employed by Sarah as a servant, he was puzzled to see all the girls hanging back nervously behind her. He waved to them, but they began to back away. And when he tossed the prism up and down again, one of the little girls cried: 'He's going to throw it at us!'

'Throw it at you?' the woman said, turning to stare in astonishment at the retreating children and receiving a chorus of answers as they fled in fright down the hallway and out of sight.

'His mother used to throw things!'

'And she chased people!'

'With razors!'

'And red-hot pokers!'

And then the woman servant herself joined the retreat, leaving the hallway empty—until Sarah appeared and stared along at the man standing at the open doorway. She didn't invite Billy in, and she did nothing to quieten the girls; nor did she chide them for what had been said. Will's promise had given her this weapon to use against his son without fear of reprisals.

Billy squeezed the prism tightly in his hand as though he would crush it, its edges cutting into his palm and fingers. He was shocked far beyond being able to say anything. Turning, he stumbled back into the hackney cab; the jolting all the way back to London only added to the dark confusion of his thoughts.

Chapter 7

While Sir George Beaumont continued to wage his holy war against Turner and his paintings, Sarah Danby intensified her campaign to hound and harass the man who had spurned her. She tried to corner him at Harley Street, to find out what he was doing, where he had been; and, of course, to complain that her allowance wasn't enough and that the more money he made the more niggardly he became.

She was right about him earning more money. Because of it Billy placed an increasing amount of business in the hands of his lawyers, particularly now that he was investing some of his earnings not only in stocks and shares but also in property—including a house by the Thames, at Hammersmith. At each meeting in the Clement's Inn chambers the name of Mrs Danby was prominent on the agenda. Time and again he would be confronted with details of expenditure which Sarah had incurred, allegedly on behalf of the fast-growing girls.

On one of these lists a new name suddenly appeared.

'Hannah? Hannah?' Billy demanded in a sudden rage. 'Who the devil's *Hannah* Danby?'

'The late John Danby's niece, apparently,' George Cobb said, accustomed by now to his client's eruptions. 'His brother's daughter. A girl of twenty-two, I'm told, from the country.'

'What's this sum of five shillings doing set against her name?'

'Her weekly wage.'

'Wage? What wage?'

'Mrs Danby's taken her on to help in the house—as a maid, I presume.'

Billy was furious. 'I thought I said she wasn't to have a maid no more.'

'Mrs Danby insists that she can't look after the girls unless she has some help.'

'But there's less of 'em!'

'Less?' Cobb repeated.

'Yes, less. It means not so many.' And then heavily, as Cobb still looked blank, 'Mrs Danby's eldest—Marcella—married, ain't she?'

'Oh, I see what you mean. Yes, indeed, she is.'

'And wasn't I given to understand that Caroline was being courted by some young man with much the same intention?'

'You were, Mr Turner.'

'Besides—I don't seem to recall being consulted about a maid.'

'You weren't.'

'Was it you, then, that gave permission, Mr Cobb?'

'It wasn't, Mr Turner.'

'So it was Gascoigne.'

'No,' Cobb asserted. 'The young woman was engaged entirely without consultation with any of us.'

'Then I'll have something to say about it,' Billy said angrily, and abruptly terminated the meeting by stalking out.

In Fleet Street he hired a hackney cab to take him to Sarah's house in Epping. He was not in the habit of going to this expense: in fact, it would be his first visit since the reaction of the girls had chased him away over four years ago. But Sarah's latest provocation had caught him at a sensitive moment. A critic had attacked his oil painting of a dewy morning at Petworth Park—commissioned by the owner, Lord Egremont—and dismissed his whole method as mere flimsy daubing. Smarting at the injustice of this, he was in the mood to vent his wrath on somebody or something, and Sarah's latest liberty provided him with just the butt he needed.

When he reached the cottage he kept the cab waiting at the gate, and pounded on the door. But when the door opened, the angry words that had been ready to spill out died on his lips. What checked him was not so much the demure and pleasant 'Good morning, sir' with which he was greeted as the general bearing and appearance of the person who said it—a small flaxen-haired young woman with disturbingly beautiful eyes, a charmingly tip-tilted nose and a conspicuous beauty-spot high on her right cheek. But what impressed him most was her quiet air of repose.

'Is—uh—Mrs Danby about?' he asked, flustered.

'No, sir. She's out walking with her daughters.'

There was a gentle nuance in the girl's speech that indicated to Billy a place of origin not very far from London; and while he was trying to pin it down more closely he stared at her with unconcealed fascination, until her obvious embarrassment made him realise what he was doing and he hastened to say, 'Oh, I see ... Well, then ... Very nice for her.'

'You've obviously come a long way,' she said, looking past him to the cab. 'Won't you come inside and wait?'

It occurred to him that even though he paid the rent for this cottage and had provided the furnishings he had never entered it. But he found himself restrained by the fear that there might be a repetition of what had happened the last time; and so he decided against it, saying, 'No, thank you all the same. I'll not wait.'

'Shall I tell Mrs Danby who called?'

'Yes, you could do that. Mr Turner.'

The girl's lips parted a little, shaping a tiny gasp, and something between awe and adoration shone in her eyes.

'I take it you're Miss Hannah,' he said.

With a nod, she answered, 'Yes, sir.'

'I'm happy to have met you,' he said, raising his hat to her. 'I'll say good-day for the present.'

He turned abruptly as Hannah curtsied to him, vaguely disturbed by her clear gaze with its undisguised admiration.

Back in the hackney cab again, jolted along as it started out on the return to London, he began to regret having left in such haste, until the cab rounded a corner and he spotted the redoubtable Sarah homeward bound, parasol swinging as she stepped out with her four youngest ducklings—now aged fifteen, thirteen, eleven and nine—in her wake. They were all exquisitely turned out and he was tempted to call on the cabman to stop; but the fear that the girls might turn and run the moment they recognised him was still too great for him to hazard. So he shrank into the corner of the cab as it trundled past them, and neither Sarah nor the girls saw who was half hidden inside it.

As the months passed, Billy thought of Hannah frequently. From the lawyers he gathered that she had been taken on by Sarah after paying a visit to Epping to see her aunt-by-marriage and the girls. He made no further protest about having to foot the bill for her wages; and he was often on the verge of going out to Epping to see her again. But before he did anything about this, she appeared one morning at the Harley Street gallery.

She handed him a letter as he asked her inside. 'Mrs Danby asked me to deliver this to you.'

He took it, thinking that here was another demand for something or other. 'And you were sent to London, alone, just for this?'

'Oh, no,' she replied, smiling shyly at his concern. 'I'm on my way to spend a week at home with my family.'

'Ah! Well—since you're passing through, you might care to take a look around the gallery. Officially I close at this time of the year, but there's still plenty to see.'

Hannah thanked him with an eagerness he was quick to note. And he would have been intrigued to know how much she had been thinking about him, reminded about him daily as Sarah carped against him to the girls for his alleged meanness. This, together with her growing dislike of Sarah and her domineering ways, had made Hannah increasingly sympathetic towards him.

Billy offered her a glass of sherry, and when she accepted he rummaged deep in a sideboard for his best crystal glasses. Hannah sipped the warming liquid as he opened Sarah's letter and read it. As he had guessed, Sarah wanted something—wording her request in such a way that it contained an element of threat; but for once he wasn't annoyed.

'Ah,' he said, unusually benevolent and unstinting, 'so she wants me to try to lay my hands on a harp, eh? Says Evelina's anxious to learn to play it.'

'Evelina really does have musical talent,' Hannah assured him.

'It could well be that she inherited that from her father,'

Billy said. 'I'll see what can be done. My Dad knows a man who deals in musical instruments—an old customer from his hairdressing days at Covent Garden. He's up the river at Hammersmith at present, but as soon as he's back in town I'll get him on to this.'

Billy put the letter on the table where he would see it and be reminded, placing it under the foot of a candlestick to keep it secure. He poured Hannah another sherry to carry with her and, after refilling his own glass, he escorted her from one picture to another. As he eyed her quiet reactions to his works he wanted to know more about this curiously self-contained young woman.

They passed from a dawn scene at a river ford to one of daybreak over tidal sands, then to another of the sun rising through a golden mist, and farther along to a fulminating sunset. Hannah's face remained solemn, her eyes large and steady, but as she went from picture to picture she was conscious of how wrong—how wicked—Sarah had been in saying that Billy's paintings were all mad, like their creator. When she came to the sunset, she gasped at the ferocious beauty of it.

'Ever seen a sunset like that?' Billy asked, pleased.

Hannah, still enthralled, shook her head without taking her eyes from the painting. 'No. Never.'

'But wouldn't you like to?'

'Oh, *yes*!' she assured him.

Elated by her enthusiasm, Billy moved her along to the next picture—a rather formal street scene.

'I've been there!' Hannah said excitedly, pointing at it.

'Are you sure about that?' Billy asked teasingly, challenging her to name the place.

'That's Oxford. I know it is.'

'Right first go,' he said. 'The High Street. How is it you come to recognise it so well?'

'I was in service there.'

Billy let her find her own way now, noting with growing pleasure that she had become more relaxed and consequently more open in her reactions. She stopped in front of a picture of an avalanche—a scene so vivid and real that something of its fury rumbled out of the frame: carrying trees with it, a massive slab of rock was about to crush a mountain cottage. As Hannah looked into it, a detail caught her eye.

'Oh, look!' she cried, pointing at a tiny cat racing away from the doomed cottage.

'Don't worry,' Billy said. 'That cat got away unscathed.'

'I do hope so,' she said earnestly.

He laughed and asked, 'You like cats?'

'Oh, yes. I'm very fond of them.'

Walking jauntily now, Billy ushered her from the gallery into his painting-room, where a large canvas measuring almost eight feet in width by five feet in height loomed on a big easel—a white and dark green storm curling over to form a cavernous wave above a mountain pass.

'This is going to be a picture of the great Hannibal crossing the Italian Alps,' he explained. 'I'm basing that snowstorm on a thunderstorm I saw recently when I was staying with friends in Yorkshire.'

Even though still at an early stage, the storm threatened to break away from the canvas that held it and crash down on them. Entering into the fun of being shown around, Hannah pretended to be a little afraid and cowered away from it.

Billy laughed, exhilarated by the effect of his work on her—but quite unprepared for her swift change of mood when she turned and found herself looking into the chaos of a much more frightening storm scene.

This was a finished canvas, already sold to a gallery. It depicted a large troop-transport heeled over on its side, its masts gone, the sea around it a boiling cauldron littered with men, rafts and wreckage while the crews of fishing smacks tried to rescue survivors.

Billy explained that this was the wreck of the *Minotaur*. Two hundred soldiers, marines and seamen had met death by drowning, and a number of the fishing smacks had also gone down. As he spoke, he noticed Hannah wiping tears from her eyes. He was dismayed as she suddenly broke down and wept uncontrollably. Through her sobs he gathered that the picture reminded her of a great personal tragedy, and as he tried to comfort her the full story came out. She had hoped to marry a young soldier on his return from service with Sir John Moore's army in Spain, but he had been killed in the fighting at Corunna. Billy's heart went out to her—another victim of the long Napoleonic struggle which had already been settled at sea by the Battle of Trafalgar but not yet on land. But it was more than sympathy that moved him as she dried her eyes.

Two days were to pass before Hannah got home to her people near Wendover in leafy Buckinghamshire. Billy had to be sure that Hannah wanted him as much as he wanted her, and he did not try to persuade her on that first night at Harley Street. He had a sense of real love flowering; a sense of something sweet, calm and enduring entering his life at long last—and this alone was enough to quell his impatience.

Before Hannah left Harley Street for the country, Billy arranged for them to meet at an isolated inn that he knew, in the hills some miles from Hannah's home, where they could stay with each other for another two days before her return to Sarah at Epping.

As they parted, Hannah going to Epping and Billy returning to Harley Street, they planned to meet again in two weeks when Hannah would ask Sarah for permission to go to London for the day on the pretext of meeting a friend from her home village. Consequently, when Billy found Hannah at Harley Street less than a week later he was greatly surprised: and when he saw who was with her he was more than a little on his guard.

'We've come into London to do some shopping for things for the girls,' Sarah told him.

'Then who's taking care of the children while you're away?' he asked.

'Caroline. She can manage the younger ones for the day—it's good experience for her. Anyway ... since we're in London, I just thought we'd call by and say hello to you.'

Billy knew that Sarah was incapable of doing anything without some clear-cut motive. In his increased wariness he made an effort to be polite to her.

'Oh, about that harp you were wanting for Evelina. Got your letter here to remind me.' He pointed to where it still lay under the flange of the candlestick on the table. 'As I told Miss Hannah, I'll be getting Dad on to the job of tracking one down for you once he's back here from Hammersmith.'

Sarah was not deceived. Neither was she concerned about the harp. She had come here to play a scene and, with her customary sense of the dramatic, she was waiting for the right moment. If it came sooner than she would have liked, it was only because Hannah's eyes—though she was doing her best to appear not to know Billy any better than would be in keeping with having met him only twice—shone with adoration. It precipitated matters. The self-control which Sarah had managed to exercise since her chance discovery that something was going on between Billy and Hannah suddenly broke. From her handbag she produced the damning evidence—a pencil sketch of a reclining nude whose identity was obvious, even though the model's head was turned away to one side. She said nothing, but she held the sketch so that it could be clearly seen.

Hannah went white and whispered, 'That's mine ...'

'Yes, you slut!'

'Who the devil are you to be calling anyone that?' Billy shouted.

'As for you!' Sarah said, momentarily lost for a description that would do justice to what she thought of him.

'That's Hannah's,' Billy went on, unsuccessfully reaching for the sketch. 'I gave it to her—and I'd like to know how you got hold of it.'

'She made the mistake of leaving it in her dresser drawer.'

Hannah drew in her breath, appalled. 'But it was hidden away among my things ... You had no right to go through them ... That's spying!'

Sarah lifted a warning finger. 'Before you start making accusations, Hannah, you should be very careful that you're making them against the right person. I didn't go anywhere near the drawer in question. It so happens that it was one of the girls.'

'That's even worse,' Hannah whispered. 'Who was it?'

'That I do not intend to disclose. This drawing was brought to me—and rightly so. And you're in no position to complain—not after all your lies about having gone home to your family.'

'But I did go home!'

'Then how did he draw this?' Sarah asked, holding up the nude sketch as if it were an obscenity.

Billy snatched the sheet of paper from Sarah's hand. He strode across to a bank of drawers, wrenched one of them open, lifted out a sheaf of sketches, returned to Sarah and thrust them into her hands, saying, 'Seeing as how you're so damned interested, you might as well see the lot.'

Sarah found herself holding some two dozen sketches of Hannah—a few drawn in the gallery, others in the hills near Wendover—half of them nude studies.

'Disgusting!' she cried, throwing them back at Billy so that they scattered on the floor.

'You bitch!' Billy roared at her. 'I ought to make you get down on your knees and pick 'em up.'

'Please, no!' Hannah begged. She knelt down quickly to gather the sketches together.

Sarah stood over her. 'I hope you realise what you've done. I'm certainly not having you back in my house. And I'm sure your family won't want you either—not when they've heard about this.'

Hannah looked up, petrified. 'Sarah—*please* ... you don't have to tell them.'

'I'm afraid it's too late *not* to tell them.'

Hannah rose slowly, leaving the sketches strewn on the floor. Her face was pale and the mole on her cheek stood out starkly.

'They may even have my letter by now,' Sarah went on.

'Sarah,' Billy said in a voice quivering with cold anger, 'when all the sweet and charming things you've said and done are sorted out and strung together, this'll stand out as one of your greatest kindnesses ever.'

'I'll never be able to go home now,' Hannah whispered. 'Never.'

'No one's asking you to go home,' Billy said.

'She can't stay here with you,' Sarah said quickly, swinging round to face him.

'Why not? If she wants to, she's welcome.'

Sarah turned back to Hannah, alarmed that her plan of destruction might go awry. 'You can't *possibly* stay here with this man!' she said urgently.

'I'm asking her,' Billy thundered. 'You're not telling her.'

'She doesn't know what she'd be letting herself in for,' Sarah said wildly. 'She doesn't know what it's like trying to live with a man who chases out after fires and shipwrecks and sunsets—a man who leaves without a word of explanation and comes back a week or a month later and either refuses to say where he's been or gives you some incredible story; a man who sometimes doesn't even remember where he's been. She doesn't know that it's like trying to live with a—a *madman*!'

'Go on, then!' Billy shouted. 'Tell her. Tell her about my mother. Tell her about chasing the customers and neighbours with razors and pokers and the like—just as you told the girls. *Tell her!*'

'Stop—both of you,' Hannah pleaded. 'I don't want to hear all that. Not again ...'

'Again?' Billy said.

'The girls told me everything Sarah told them.'

'And every word of it was true,' Sarah said.

'I don't care.' Hannah faced Billy. 'And I don't care what Sarah says now, either. If you'll have me, I'll stay.'

'Stay, then,' said Sarah. 'Stay! But mark my words, you'll live to regret it.' And kicking the scattered drawings from her path, she marched imperiously out.

Chapter 8

Hannah settled down contentedly into the life at Harley Street. At first it worried Will that she and Billy were not married, but he had come to understand some of the fears that prevented his boy from taking such a binding and final step, so after a while he accepted the situation without questioning it. He liked Hannah and appreciated her help in the household and with business errands. Once she had grasped the routine she was able to take over the running of the gallery, leaving him free to go for short spells to the house at Hammersmith, and later to the lodge farther up the river at Isleworth that Billy had built to his own design on a plot of land bought as an investment.

Realising that Billy had to be alone while he was at work, Hannah left him in peace. She missed him when he set out on sketching tours, but she never protested or tried to go with him. And for his part, Billy was as thoughtful towards her as his obsessive temperament would allow, and he usually returned with some sort of present for her. Remembering her love of cats, he came back from the Isle of Man with two tailless Manx kittens which grew and mated and interbred with other cats she had taken under her wing—so that she came to have a small tribe to follow her around.

Billy also found time to make friends in London and in the country, although his true character did not emerge in their company. He shaped a different image of himself to match the sort of person he was expected to be. One of these friends was a man very much his senior in years and station—the third Lord Egremont, one of the first buyers of his more poetic works. They were introduced at an Academy opening by Dr

Monro. Billy had been intrigued by the spectacle of the sprightly nobleman, wearing a rakish hat, moving languidly from one exhibit to another with several exquisite women trailing serenely after him. Subsequently, Egremont visited the Harley Street gallery; and out of this came the commission for Billy to paint a number of pictures at Egremont's country seat, Petworth Park, in Sussex. In the course of the first stay at Petworth, the two men found each other's company agreeable. They discussed art, literature, commerce, women and the world at large and discovered that they were kindred spirits even though born at opposite ends of the social scale and a quarter of a century apart in time.

Some three years after Hannah's entry into the Harley Street household, Billy and Lord Egremont sat one night at a dinner at the Academy Club to which members occasionally invited guests. Over the brandy and port, Egremont encouraged Billy to tell one of his jokes. This Billy proceeded to do in an exaggerated Cockney accent that carried the full length of the long table to where Sir George Beaumont and his sycophants were seated.

'This ol' lady totters into the butchershop an' says, "Butcher, have you two nice pieces of steak?" "All I have left, missus," 'e says, "is whale." "Whale?" she says. "Oh," 'e says, "it's well 'ung an' very tasty. I give you me word. Try it." "Very well, then," she says. "Two nice pieces of whale—one for meself an' one for me husband—an' if you'd be so kind, butcher, could I have the 'ead to take home for me cat?"'

Egremont let rip with his hooting laugh and pounded the table with his fist, setting the crystal ringing and the flames flickering on the candelabras all the way down to where the faces of the Beaumont faction displayed mass incredulity and outrage. To them, Billy's joke was crude, vulgar and totally out of place at such a function—another proof of the boorish and ungentlemanly origins of its teller, and the time he spent in unsavoury localities with low company. Billy had, in fact, picked up the joke from a fisherman in a Wapping tavern only the night before.

'I'd love the ladies to hear you tell that one,' Egremont said. 'Why don't you come along home with me tonight?'

'Be honoured to accept, m'lord,' Billy replied.

'Splendid. Tell us another, Turner, and then we'll be on our way.'

Billy obliged, and presently he and Egremont bade farewell to the company and departed.

Billy had assumed that Egremont was inviting him to his town house, but he had meant Petworth Park; and so they set out by private coach on a journey through the moonlit countryside, pausing for rest and refreshments on the way and arriving at the estate as the sun began to sop up the overnight dew from the lawns and meadows. Beautiful women and children swarmed out of the house to greet them despite the hour. They smothered Egremont with kisses and fond hugs—more than enough, to Billy's way of thinking, to turn any man's head; but the nobleman remained calm under the crush of so much affection and told everyone precisely why he had brought his guest with him. There and then, Billy had to repeat the joke about the whale's head and the cat, and, to the accompaniment of delighted laughter from all, he and Egremont were escorted inside.

With its show-piece rooms—one all white and gold, another divinely carved—the house was a work of art. Egremont's benevolence extended to all who lived and stayed here—mistresses, children, guests, servants, estate workers. All were free to follow whatever leisurely or artistic pursuits took their fancy. The vast parklands were always open to them. Meals were minor banquets. Evenings were for billiards, backgammon or chamber music.

The beauty of the women was an entity in itself. Whether young or old, they all seemed to partake of a timeless femininity that was unique to this place—so much so that Billy sometimes found it difficult to identify one from another except by age. One of them came to his room on the next night. He was woken by a rustling. Then, silhouetted against the faint moonlight reflected through the high window from the lake, he saw her naked shape as she shed a flimsy robe. He sat up: but before he could speak, she pressed her fingers softly against his lips to silence and reassure him. Within the shadows of the canopy over the bed and in the jumble of bedclothes he was unable to see clearly which of the women this was; she spoke only in sighs and moans. When he awoke in the morning, he was alone and ready to believe that it had all been a dream—until the smell of her perfume rose from the pillows to confirm that she had been there.

On sketching tours at home and abroad—and during seafaring masquerades at Wapping, Rotherhithe, Stepney and other places on the Thames—he had shared his bed with women whose names he never came to know; but in such cases he was gone by the morning. This time he had to face the woman involved, whoever she was—and a woman of high birth too. He hung back in his room until a servant knocked to remind him that breakfast was being served on the terrace.

Deciding to brave it, he found Egremont still at the table with half a dozen of the ladies including a very young Italian Contessa and an Austrian Princess. He tried to avoid looking at any of them as he exchanged good-mornings, but was conscious that the others at the table had their eyes on him. He felt sure that his companion of the night must be among the ladies present—but which one?

'You slept well, I trust?' Egremont asked.

Billy glanced up; the nobleman was grinning. He felt sure that the activities of the night were an open secret.

A steamed fish was placed in front of him and he had to force himself to eat it. But the ladies, thank God, were taking their leave and slipping one by one into the house through the open terrace doors. Then Egremont excused himself.

Believing himself to be alone at the table now, Billy looked up, only to discover that one of the ladies still remained—the seventeen-year-old Contessa, who greeted his wary look with a conspiratorial smile that solved all mysteries.

The Contessa embodied the beauty of northern Italy, her hair tawny, her eyes blue-green. She had been stranded in England by wars on the Continent. Her husband had managed to return to Italy through neutral territories to play his part in affairs of state, and she could have used the same route to join him had she wished; but he was old and she found him dull, so she made the hostilities her excuse to remain in England. Billy was thirty-eight now, but still a youth in comparison with her husband. And at Petworth there were no conventions.

Thanks to the continuation of warfare, the Contessa was able to postpone her return for a further two years, until her excuse vanished with the peace that followed Wellington's defeat of Napoleon at Waterloo. In those two years Billy kept visiting Petworth, feeling that he was not betraying Hannah once he was within Egremont's magic circle of unreality.

The beauty-spot on Hannah's cheek—a tiny brown mole—was just below the corner of her right eye. It stood out conspicuously when she wore her hair sleeked back from a centre parting and wound into a bun at the nape of her neck.

As she was arranging her fine hair one morning in front of her looking-glass, she had a curious feeling that the mole had shifted position. Looking more closely, she realised what had happened: it had become larger.

She thought little of it at first, but with the passing of the weeks she noticed that it was continuing to grow. When it reached the size of a farthing she became disturbed; then it turned a livid purple and darkened, and began to wrinkle and crack. In an attempt to conceal it, she first applied thick powder and changed her hair style. Then she made herself a bonnet that came well down on either side of her face. While this kept it hidden, it did nothing to retard its growth; and the secret steps she took to try to remedy it only made it worse.

Billy was away a great deal at this time. During his few days back at Harley Street he was far too busy to pay much attention to Hannah, and so he didn't notice anything different about her. Will, however, had been aware of a change. Hannah seemed to have become withdrawn—afraid, even. But of what? Whereas she had always enjoyed a walk and was ready for any errand, now she was reluctant to leave the house. For some strange reason, she seemed to keep herself at a distance from the candlelight at night. And he couldn't understand why she should have taken to wearing that unbecoming bonnet all the time.

For much of that year Billy roved the countryside, either working on commissioned oil paintings and drawings or gathering material for them. It was in this year that he visited Venice for the first time and experienced its light. Here, secretly reunited with the Contessa, in an enchanted city that seemed to float on air and water, it was as if he had come to the place where the sun shed the purest light on earth, yet where everything it touched took on an unearthly luminous buoyancy. Back in England, he would be at Queen Anne Street for as little as half a day sometimes—just long enough to check progress with etchers and publishers and attend to a few letters and other urgent matters. If he did stay longer, he would get down to work, from time to time keeping in his hand with figure drawing, even though he was doing less and less involving the human form in the anatomical sense. Hannah acted as his model.

She had always been willing to pose for him; so when she first said she didn't feel well enough he left it at that. When next he asked her, she wasn't keen but she didn't refuse—except that she posed wearing what was to him, as to Will, an unattractive cloth bonnet.

He put up with this once. But the second time he said, irritated, 'Do you really have to keep wearing that headgear?'

To his consternation, Hannah gave a tiny cry of distress, broke out of the pose and ran naked from the studio.

Billy stood astonished at his easel as he tried to find some reason for her behaviour. What had he said to upset her like that? He began to remember other things. For the past two mornings he had woken to find Hannah up and dressed and, moreover, wearing that damned bonnet. Come to think of it, she'd been wearing it ever since his return.

He put down his stick of charcoal and the lump of bread he had been using as a rubber and hurried upstairs to Hannah's room. The door was locked against him. He called out to her to open it and let him in. She didn't reply: but he could hear her sobbing.

'Hannah!' he insisted, thumping the door. 'Open up. I want to talk to you.'

Her sobs sounded muffled, as though she was burying her face in the pillow, but there was no reply.

He rattled the door handle. 'Hannah! Open up, d'you hear? Otherwise I'll fetch an axe and chop m'way inside.'

For some moments he listened, and then the key clicked in the lock. He grabbed the handle again, twisted it sharply and thrust the door inward. When he saw Hannah, still naked, waiting to confront him he let the door swing right back on creaking hinges. He took several steps towards her.

Without a word, she began to execute a graceful movement over her head with her right hand, full of femininity. Her fingers flared out to the full above the bonnet and then she brought them down and slowly clenched them so that she had a wad of the cloth in her hand. She lifted the bonnet up vertically from her head. As it rose, so too did her hair, exposing her cheeks—on one of which was a large putrid malignance.

In the convulsions that followed, as Hannah collapsed into his arms, Billy learned what she had done. She had gone in desperation to a quack doctor who had cauterised the growth with a red-hot iron stump and given her a potion to rub into it —all of which had made it even more hideous and malignant.

Not for the first time in his life, Billy sought help from Dr Monro. After examining Hannah he called in a surgeon of his acquaintance. But it was the latter's expert opinion that it was too late to do anything for her except resort to brutal surgery which would in any event leave her grossly disfigured.

As she withdrew from the outside world, Hannah came to believe—and Sarah encouraged the belief—that the growth was some sort of divine retribution, some punishment, for her illicit affaire with Billy. Nothing Billy said could shift this notion, and inevitably a dark barrier rose between them. Hannah sensed that he found her disfigurement so repellent that he avoided her because of it; and she came to harbour a deep resentment towards him because of this, as though the canker had also crept into her soul.

When Billy moved his gallery to better premises in Queen Anne Street, just around the corner from Harley Street, Hannah went with him. Where else could she go? Her cats moved with her; and as Billy slipped away to Petworth or Wapping with increasing frequency, she turned more and more to her pets—and to sherry and gin.

Chapter 9

As the genial thick-set seaman became better known in waterfront haunts down the river to the fishermen, watermen, smugglers, deep-sea sailors, hawkers, scavengers, women and others who also frequented them, Sarah Danby maintained her forays into London. Over the years she had effectively kept Billy from the girls—not even inviting him to the wedding of his own Evelina or letting him know about it until well after the event. In addition to the gallery, she carried her campaign against the enemy into the chambers of his legal representatives in Clement's Inn. Here George Cobb always heard her out with unfailing courtesy; but after assuring her that he would bring her complaints to his client's attention he did little. However, on Cobb's junior partner Sarah's ploys and wiles had a different effect.

Gascoigne was of the opinion that nature had perpetrated a grave injustice by endowing a man of lowly origin and ill manners, such as their client Turner, with money-making talents. And the senior clerk, Morley, had been persuaded to share this view. Sensing their resentful attitude Billy was often deliberately rude, although from time to time he confounded the pair of them with bursts of good humour.

On one occasion he dipped into his travelling-box and turned to Gascoigne, holding a small watercolour—a fresh impression of the Thames at daybreak—saying, 'My dear Gascoigne, I'd like you to have this.'

The lawyer, who grew more portly and pompous with his rising status in the firm, recalled how the artist had settled payments in a number of cases in the past and at first was not at all eager to accept it. He went so far as to murmur audibly, 'Not in lieu of fees, I trust.'

At another time such base ingratitude might well have provoked Billy into outraged anger, but he was in no mood to be discouraged by it now. 'Good gracious, no!' he cried. 'A gift. A mark of my esteem. With my very best compliments.'

And so Gascoigne took it and had it framed and hung it on his office wall—not so much out of appreciation of its artistic merits as the desire not to offend a valued if unpredictable client. But such demonstrations of high spirits and generosity failed to alter the lawyer's opinion of Billy, and it was on his dislike—and Morley's too—that Sarah cunningly played and won herself two allies.

While Billy knew that she still called at the gallery in his absence, for some time he remained unaware of the way in which she got at Hannah with her insinuations. But Will was an unhappy witness to some of this. He was, of course, appalled at what had happened to Hannah and how it had infiltrated and destroyed the bond of affection between her and Billy. It was a reminder of the way in which the life of his wife Mary had been taken over and ruined by an evil beyond the control of herself or others; and it disturbed him greatly to see Sarah maliciously adding to poor Hannah's distress. But he was afraid of the consequences should Billy come to hear of it, so he said nothing.

The truth came out, however, when Billy returned to the gallery one day to find Hannah in a state of extreme upset. He insisted on an explanation and, after he had wormed the facts out of her and Will, he left at once for Clement's Inn.

'Mr Cobb about?' Billy demanded as he burst into the outer office of the lawyers' chambers, nearly toppling Morley off his high stool with fright.

'Alas, no, Mr Turner,' Morley said nervously, stooped and servile. 'He's decided to remain in Brighton all this week.'

'Must be coining a hatful of money if he can afford to live the life of a seaside squire,' Billy said, striding across to the door to the inner office. 'I'll see Gascoigne instead.'

'I'll tell him you're here,' Morley said, trying to reach the door first to warn his superior that trouble had descended upon them.

'Save yourself the bother.' Billy slipped past him and thrust the door open.

Gascoigne glared up from a large desk stacked with papers and documents, stifling his anger when he saw who had burst in on him.

'Ah, Mr Turner.' He lifted his bulk up out of a chair that was slowly being crushed under his ever-increasing weight. 'Do come in. I'd been hoping you might drop by. We have the papers relating to the sale of your Paddington land to the railway company ready for signature.'

'I'll come to that,' Billy said tightly, intent on getting straight to the point of his visit. 'Am I right in believing that Mrs Danby's been in town again?'

'Won't you sit down, sir?' Gascoigne suggested, anticipating an outburst of some sort and preferring his client less mobile.

'I don't expect to be staying long enough. Was she here?'

'She did make a brief call,' Gascoigne admitted, lowering himself back into his chair.

'Well, I'm putting a stop to it. And high time too. Been lenient too long.' Billy cleared his throat and launched into formal instruction, using the high-flown diction that made his lapses, whether of grammar or speech, all the more noticeable. 'I'd be most deeply obliged, therefore, if you'd be so good as to inform Mrs Danby, on my behalf, that in future she's to refrain from calling at my gallery and acquitting herself in such a manner as to cause mischief. Furthermore, and likewise, she's to stop coming to this address and pestering you and Morley.'

'Oh, but that's not so, Mr Turner,' Gascoigne hastened to assure him. 'She doesn't *pester* us here, sir.'

'No, of course she don't,' Billy said, looking the lawyer hard in the eye and letting him know that he was well aware whose side Gascoigne and Morley were on—and why. 'But whatever it is she does when she's here, it's to end. Kindly warn Mrs Danby that if she don't abide by my instructions I'll have to review the matter of her allowance. As it is, I'm docking it by the sum of one pound per month.'

'Reducing it?'

'That *is* what I believe I was intimating. And why not?'

'In order to answer that, sir, all I need do is simply refer to why Mrs Danby was here. Her allowance, as it stands, would not appear to be sufficient for her present needs.'

'Never was and never will be,' Billy said.

Gascoigne was more dismayed at the prospect of having to deal with Sarah on the matter of a reduced income than of trying to stand up to Billy on her behalf. 'Wars and unrest have resulted in soaring prices,' he argued. 'Take, for instance, a loaf of bread. As Mrs Danby pointed out earlier today, this one essential item of sustenance alone is now treble the price it was at the time her allowance was first allotted. We all need more money for the necessities of life.'

'P'rhaps so. But Mrs Danby don't.'

'Don't?' Gascoigne repeated, his echoing of the other's faulty grammar sounding like a reprimand.

'Her household expenses are down, surely.'

'Pray, sir, in what respect?' Gascoigne asked, trying to make it a meek plea for clarification.

'Evelina's married, ain't she?'

After clicking his tongue to indicate that he considered this a poor justification, Gascoigne explained why. 'Mr Turner, sir —it must be all of *five years* now since Miss Evelina married.'

'Well, there you are, then. I should've docked the allowance five years ago, shouldn't I?' Billy said, not only totally unrepentant but also suggesting that thanks to his infinite kindness Sarah had already enjoyed a five-year bonus. 'And now, if you don't mind, I'll have them papers to sign.'

Gascoigne was so confused that he couldn't lay his hands on the relevant document and had to call Morley in to locate it for him. Billy occupied himself during the delay by stepping over to the wall and examining the watercolour he had presented to Gascoigne. Hoping that a little flattery might ease the tension Gascoigne said, 'That picture is greatly admired.'

'And so it ought to be,' Billy said, squinting into it. 'Had m'eye in trim the day I did it, all right.'

'Indeed,' Gascoigne intoned. 'Less than a week ago a client offered to purchase it from me.'

Billy wheeled around, demanding, 'How much?'

'Twenty guineas.'

'Twenty?' Billy said with curdling disdain.

'On the spot, sir—cash,' Gascoigne explained, trying to make the offer sound more attractive.

'I don't wonder. At twenty it's a bargain. That painting's worth three times as much. Sixty, at the very least. Take a word of advice, Gascoigne, and keep an eye on that client. Sounds to me like a prime scoundrel.'

Gascoigne swallowed hard and tried to extricate himself. 'In that case, I'm very glad I mentioned it. Now I know.'

'Don't go selling it, neither,' Billy warned him.

'Sell it?' Gascoigne said, sorry now that he had commented at all on the damned painting. 'But how could I even contemplate such a thing? After all, it was a gift ...'

But Billy had already dismissed the painting and was reaching for the document. 'Where do you want me to sign?' he asked without a glance at it, although on most occasions he would insist on going through each clause as if suspecting a sinister trap in every line.

Gascoigne heaved himself up again and leaned across the desk to help Billy turn the pages of the document to the final sheet, and then he inked a quill and put it in Billy's hand. With a quick dip of his own into the inkwell, Billy appended his signature in an impatient spidery scrawl and handed the quill and the document back to the lawyer.

'I'll be under way,' he said, going to the door. 'But I'll be dropping by again in a day or two with details of another investment. I'm drawing up some plans for the conversion of them cottages of mine at Wapping. There'll be full instructions with 'em.' He turned in the doorway. 'And don't forget what I said about Mrs Danby.'

When the plans came to hand a few days later, Gascoigne and Morley were amazed to see what sort of investment this was to be: the cottages were to be converted into a public house which was to be called The Ship and Bladebone. The plans went into some detail and included the design of the tavern sign—the hull of a ship on the stocks and the tool used by shipwrights to shape the ribs and timbers; and the accompanying instructions were also detailed. It was emphasised in them that the owner was to remain absolutely anonymous. Gascoigne was to find and appoint a suitable tenant-landlord and, once the public house was open for business, Morley was to pay weekly visits to collect the takings, check the accounts and pay the staff.

In his role of a seaman ashore between voyages, Billy was able to see the building operations at various stages; and when the tavern opened, he made sure he was among the first of its customers.

Gascoigne, meanwhile, had written to Sarah; and as he fully expected, she had promptly ignored the instructions not to call at Clement's Inn.

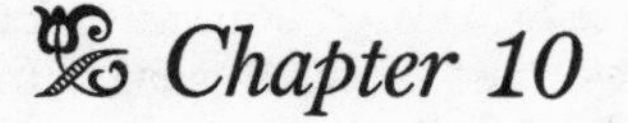

Chapter 10

'I starts 'em and I finishes 'em,' Will Turner used to say when talking about his son's paintings. It was a proud claim and not without some truth since he stretched the canvases before Billy started work on them and then applied the final coats of varnish once they had been completed.

As the years went by, Will kept on doing this—even when into his eighties. He remained remarkably alert and active for his age and still packed his striped apron and old tools of trade to pay his regular visits to Dr Monro in Adelphi Terrace, his one remaining customer.

Monro was also a great age now, and he looked forward to Will's visits. After his hair had been trimmed, Will would sit down with him and the two old friends would discuss Billy and his career—almost always as if the now acknowledged master of landscape and marine subjects was still some distance from the ultimate peak of his achievements but steadily climbing.

'Just look at that!' Dr Monro exclaimed to Will at one of these meetings, pointing to a watercolour Billy had given him of a storm at sunrise over the lagoon of Venice. Hanging alongside a Canaletto of the same scene, the contrast was breathtaking. The Canaletto was very exact and clear—a frozen image beside Turner's wild rhapsodic dream. 'This is an age of discovery—and William has discovered a new way of seeing things and putting them down. Art will never be quite the same again.'

'There be plenty who don't agree with 'ee on that, doctor,' Will reminded him ruefully.

'Oh, yes, indeed. And now that Sir George is no longer with us, we seem to have a very able detractor in his place in the person of the Reverend John Eagles.'

Will nodded heavily. He had heard about the new man spearheading the crusade against his son after the comparatively early death of Sir George Beaumont. Eagles, of Wadham College, Oxford, was also a wealthy man, free to indulge his artistic tastes and prejudices. He had tried his hand as a painter, failed, and turned to writing about art, displaying a notable flair for ridicule and invective: and he had taken up the tirade against Billy where Beaumont had left off. It was beyond Will how a man of God could play such a part, but he made no comment.

'And when the Reverend Eagles also passes on,' Dr Monro continued, 'you can be sure that some other blind prophet will arise to take his place. In a way, of course, William is an inventor too—and this is an age of invention as well as discovery. The greater the inventor's vision, the greater the outcry. Look at what the Brunels are having to endure with their tunnel.'

Again Will nodded. Before giving up the house at Isleworth, Billy had owned a sail boat in which he had taken his father on trips down the Thames, often past the site where the Brunels, father and son, were driving the first tunnel under the riverbed in the face of great public and political opposition and predictions of disaster.

Thinking of this reminded Will of the rumours that both he and Dr Monro had heard linking Billy with unsavoury neighbourhoods down the river; and neither of them had been able to ignore the fact that he tended to dress himself like a seaman rather than as an artist, and that his speech had acquired an even stronger nautical tang over the years.

On another visit, when Will found himself able to mention this, Dr Monro hastened to assure him that there was nothing in it to be unduly concerned about. It was just a minor eccentricity. Having said this, the doctor had his own thoughts on the matter. His years of practice and study of mental illness led him to believe that in Billy's odd behaviour he could see a symptom of the affliction which had blighted Mary Turner's life.

At Queen Anne Street, Hannah tried to play her part in the

running of the household and the gallery; but more often than not she was tired and befuddled. Consequently Will, despite his age, still handled a large proportion of the sales. The years began to tell and he found it increasingly difficult to cope with an especially hard or shrewd bargainer.

One such was a Manchester man called Murchison—a manufacturer of cooking utensils—who came to the gallery with his wife. The Murchisons typified the vulgarity of the *nouveau riche* of the industrial age; and negotiations with them had not got very far before Will decided that he needed Billy's support. Excusing himself, he went through into the painting-room where Billy was putting the finishing touches to his big picture *Ulysses Deriding Polyphemus* in readiness for the forthcoming Academy exhibition.

Will almost forgot why he had come here as he found himself facing a sunrise of astonishing beauty. The freshly-painted canvas blazoned so strongly that Will, with old age misting his eyes, had to blink and adjust his vision to it.

Although this picture was one that marked a point where Billy began to move farther from reality and deeper into the realms of his imagination, he had done a study for it over twenty years earlier and this was propped up for reference on a small easel nearby.

Will apologised for the interruption and listed the three paintings the manufacturer wanted and their prices. 'One be the 200 guinea size, and the others be 250 apiece.'

'That's right. And they're all for sale.'

'That I know, son. And I wouldn't be troubling 'ee if he'd just buy according to our prices an' sizes.'

'What's he proposing, then?' Billy asked, still not greatly interested. With *Ulysses* almost ready to put aside for drying and varnishing, he was thinking about starting another of the pictures he intended including in the same exhibition.

'He wants to buy according to the square inch.'

'The square inch?'

'Yes, son. Just like he be purchasing copper by the sheet for pots and pans.'

Billy chuckled. No one had ever before tried this as a basis for bargaining.

'Must be a catch in it somewhere,' Will said.

'How much is he offering?'

'Half a crown.'

'They'll be wanting to pay by the brush-stroke next. Push him up to three shillings.'

'Do 'ee think that's enough?'

'If I could get that much per square inch for everything that's stacked and rolled up in this place, I'd put the Bank of England out of business.'

Will scratched the thin white hair above his ear. 'I still have the feeling he's putting something over on us. I'll try him at three shillings, but at that price we can't let him have the frames at cost. There'll need to be an extra ten per cent going on to cover them. What say 'ee, son?'

'All right, Dad. Ten per cent extra for the frames, if it'll make you any happier.'

Will shuffled out, muttering under his breath. Neither he nor Billy realised just how frail he had become.

Later that year Will collapsed at Adelphi Terrace while trimming Dr Monro's hair and was brought back to Queen Anne Street to die. He lay in his room, sinking slowly and peacefully. On the walls were treasures from the early days of his boy's career at Maiden Lane—a few of the very first sketches and drawings he had placed in his barbershop windows, now discoloured, blotched and speckled with fly spots.

Billy could not contemplate life without his father—his sheet-anchor, his touchstone with sanity. It was true that the father-and-son relationship had become almost one of master and servant; but it had been based on pride and loyalty, never in the slightest way tainted with servility. All Billy's triumphs and successes they had openly enjoyed together. And some of their misfortunes—Mary Ann and Mary—had been shared more or less openly. Other misfortunes too, such as the virulence of the critics. But Billy's disastrous entanglements with women, in which his frustration at being trapped vied with his sense of responsibility, had reached Will only in a roundabout way—although he had come to understand what it was all about and to silently share his boy's torment. Will's whole life, after the death of Mary, had been his son; and only now did Billy realise that without Will to share his life he couldn't see any real purpose in striving on. Not yet.

In those last two weeks Billy was constantly at his side, with Dr Monro ready to be called from Adelphi Terrace. Will's mind tended to wander greatly. He would speak as if they were still in Maiden Lane with Mary. And several times, when Dr Monro was with him, he started to tell the doctor about his boy's successes, referring to achievements dating far back into the past—such as Billy's elevation to full R.A., which had been twenty-seven years ago.

As the end drew near, and Dr Monro softly warned Billy to be prepared for it, Will had a lucid spell.

'Murch ...' he whispered. 'Murch ...'

Dr Monro didn't understand, but Billy seized on it.

'Murchison? The manufacturer from Manchester? Is that it, Dad?'

Will closed the wrinkled parchment of his eyelids, and Billy quietly explained to Dr Monro that his father was referring to a customer who had purchased three pictures on the basis of so much per square inch of painted canvas.

'500 ...' Will whispered presently.

'Yes, Dad. 500. What about it?' Billy asked gently.

'Tricked me ...' Will's voice was barely audible.

For a moment Billy was mystified: then he understood. '500 square inches? Tricked you on the deal?'

Will's eyes didn't open again; and shortly after this, having made his attempt to apologise to his boy for bungling a sale, his chin sank down on to his chest and he quietly died.

Billy stood helplessly at the bedside as Dr Monro folded Will's arms across his chest. And then, after Billy had stooped down to press his lips to the little man's forehead, the doctor—old family friend, patron and customer—took him by the arm and led him from the room.

Hannah stood just outside the doorway, bent and silent, her once clear skin long since turned coarse. Some of her many cats sat about on the landing, tense and alert, as if knowing that death had come to this house.

'From now on, Hannah,' Billy said to her, 'you'll be in charge here on your own.'

He saw the dull look in her eyes, all her feeling numbed by her own misfortune. Those eyes rejected him, with their shocking revelation of her private hell. No wonder he painted the human face less and less as he went on—and then, more often than not, almost featureless on the head of a bubble.

He tried to put his arm round her shoulders to give her some consolation, but she shrank away from him with the quick, furtive movement of one of her jumpy cats; and all he could do was express something of his pity and despair for her in a murmured, 'Hannah ... Hannah ...'

Chapter 11

Billy stepped ashore on to the ooze from the boat that had brought him down the river to Wapping from the wharf at Westminster. The waterman handed him his travelling-box. In return, Billy obliged by giving the boat a shove to get it back out into the stream. Under a murky evening sky, the river was grey and flecked with white tongues brushed up by the wind.

Billy made his way between the shelter of tumbledown hovels and sheds to The Ship and Bladebone. He had been coming here more often, and staying longer, in the eighteen months since the death of his father. Other reasons drove him here too. Despite his instructions, Sarah had been in and out of the lawyers' chambers, stirring up trouble as only she could, and also trying to get at Hannah behind his back at the gallery. He hadn't been invited to the marriage of Georgiana—the younger of his two girls—yet Sarah had landed him with the wedding costs . . . which he had agreed to pay, at the same time docking her allowance again now that she had the last of the girls off her hands.

The tavern sign swung in the wind above the door. He glanced up at it and grinned to himself. It was always a source of private satisfaction to him that this was almost certainly the only tavern sign in the country that had been designed by a Royal Academician.

Entering the establishment, he went straight to the counter as he had done scores of times in the ten years in which he had secretly owned the place.

'Tot of the best rum!' he called to the publican, slapping some coins on to the counter.

He did not notice the unusual alacrity with which the

publican hastened to attend to his order; nor was he aware of the quiet, watchful looks of the regular tavern customers.

The publican set the glass of rum on the counter and pushed the money back towards Billy, saying, 'Really, sir—there's no reason why you should be payin'.'

Billy looked at him in surprise. 'Since when have you been giving away free drinks in this house?' he asked. His business interests were at stake. His instructions, passed on through Morley, forbade any such unprofitable gestures of hospitality. As he waited for an answer he became conscious of the change in the publican's attitude towards him. Where in the past this man had always treated him with a rough-and-ready familiarity—even rudeness—there was now a fawning servility that Billy found both curious and distasteful. Puzzled, he was about to ask if this was some sort of joke when the publican answered in no uncertain terms.

'Mr Turner, sir ...'

His own name descended like a great cleaver, splitting open the shell in which he had taken refuge, leaving him exposed and unable to move. 'Turner? Turner?' he blustered. 'Since when have I been Mr Turner?'

'Surely, sir,' the publican said, having sudden qualms, 'it's quite impossible there's been any mistake. Mr Morley paid his weekly call and—'

'Morley!' Billy cried, seizing on the name of the lawyers' clerk, so outraged that he could no longer keep up a pretence of mistaken identity. 'So Morley told you ...'

'No, no, sir. It was shortly after 'e'd departed, sir. A woman came in—lady with red 'air. She was makin' inquiries about a gentleman—an' it all added up to your good self, sir.'

'Sarah—oh, Sarah,' Billy muttered to himself. 'It was a Mrs Danby, was it?' he said to the publican, although he needed no confirmation.

'She omitted to give 'er name, sir.'

'But she didn't omit to give you mine—'

'Yes, sir. That is, no, sir. An' may we say, sir, 'ow honoured we are to know who you are, an' to 'ave 'ad the pleasure of your company all this time.'

Billy swung around from the bar counter. Among the local men and women gathered here—those with whom he had spent so many cheerful evenings—he saw the old fisherman who almost always had a new story for him and the woman with whom he sang duets of sea shanties. Now they were all as subservient as the landlord.

Also present were several men he hadn't seen before, all sailors.

'Does anyone know of a ship weighing anchor?' he asked them. 'Any ship, going anywhere...'

'We're on a collier bound back to Newcastle,' one of them said. 'We're leavin' with the tide.'

'That'll suit.'

'There's heavy weather outside, sir. It'll be a wild trip.'

'The wilder the better.'

The collier—a lumbering, broad-beamed three-master—staggered on short sail through a heavy sea under jagged masses of black cloud and fitful bursts of moonlight. Seas swept its decks. And a man clung, alone, to the forward mast, drenched and drenched again: Billy Turner.

One of the seamen he had met in The Ship and Bladebone fought his way forward along the storm ropes and shouted through the wind into Billy's ear, 'Master's compliments! The weather's growin' worse, so it's time to be below decks!'

'I'll ride it out!' Billy shouted back.

'You'll be swept overboard!'

'Lash me to the mast!'

The seaman stared incredulously. Waves buried them, and when the water cleared Billy shouted again:

'I mean what I say!'

It wasn't the first time he had done this—and it wasn't to be the last. Some years before, roped to a stanchion at the end of the old Chain Pier at Brighton, he had seen out the height of a fierce channel gale. Only by taking some drastic action could he calm his mind. The therapy had worked then, so he tried to repeat it now, remaining lashed to the mast for three long hours as the storm raged on and the empty collier shuddered up watery slopes, shivered on high crests and then plunged down into gaping black troughs, sheets cracking, shrouds shrieking. A wrecked ship, a victim of the storm, turned over like some great abandoned carcase and rolled by as the collier drove on past it. In its wake, the sea threw up a drowned sailor and the wind pinioned him momentarily in the air with outflung arms, leaving Billy with an image of his mother with the anchor.

As almost all physical sensation was pounded out of him, his mind cleared. Out of the past loomed the loss of his father, his link with so much that was sane. The little man was in Billy's thoughts at some time on every single day of his life. He had managed to find some relief from his grief in Wapping; but now that Sarah had struck there, that escape was lost to him.

Under the influence of the wind and the water he found himself calmer and able to come to terms with the loss of his hideaway. He looked to his future and saw that he must keep on along the path he had taken since his boyhood if he was to remain true to his vocation and vision—and to Will's faith in him.

The storm itself became a challenge. It wore a bold—a brutal—face; but he stared back into it, as he had looked into the hearts of fires, volcanoes, avalanches, searching out the secrets of light and motion and freezing them in his mind. Man seemed insignificant and transient against the might of creation.

Back at Queen Anne Street, in his painting-room, Billy created a scene full of spume and stormlight and hung it in the upstairs room of his gallery along with other pictures—a number of which were due to be sent in for hanging at the next Academy exhibition.

Among those who came to view them at Queen Anne Street was the Reverend John Eagles, who not only echoed the views of Sir George Beaumont but also bore a curious physical resemblance to the late baronet. He didn't stay long, nor did he have much to say: but his comment was loud and filled with venom.

'Moonshine and madness!' he said, his voice reverberating in the room and carrying down the stairs. 'What man in his right mind ever saw a sea like that!'

Billy, half way up the stairs from the lower room, heard and suddenly wondered whether, when lashed to the mast, he had been looking into his own mind rather than out on a stormy sea at night. '*Moonshine and madness . . . madness . . . madness . . .*'

He gripped the banister for support. Eagles's attack suddenly drained him. All his suppressed fears came flooding to the fore.

He couldn't remember backing down the stairs and dashing from the gallery. And he had no clear recollection of how he came to be at Tower Wharf—except that some sort of homing instinct must have brought him to the river. The only thing he knew was that he must keep moving—as far as possible from the voice that seemed to be echoing in his ears: '*Moonshine and madness . . .*'

There was no question of choosing a destination. The first boat to pull out was the one he boarded, and it was just chance that it was the paddlewheel steamer recently introduced on the Margate run. He was in no mood to appreciate the irony of the situation—that in his attempt to escape from himself he was bound for the place that contained his most searing childhood memory.

PART TWO

Chapter 12

This was not Billy Turner's first visit since the incident with his mother in the rowing boat over forty years earlier; but he had never been back in his present frame of mind.

He waited until all the other passengers had disembarked, and then stepped ashore and ambled along the curved stone breakwater—an inconspicuous stocky figure, wearing dark, durable, workmanlike clothing, with a beaver hat crammed over a large head of thick greying hair.

He was filled with an undefinable dread as he made his way to the beach and along the sand; walking became so exhausting that when he saw a gnarled driftwood log he had to sit down on it.

As he gazed listlessly around, he realised that the breakwater directly across the water from him had been erected where the 98-gun fighting ship had floated at its moorings on the evening that his mother had raised the anchor against the sun.

At his feet now the sand was a rich yellow, but he did not notice it; nor did he see the shades of blue in the water and the sky. He saw only what matched his sense of futility: a rotting fish; a drab bundle of decaying feathers; the twisted and contorted pieces of driftwood and grotesquely fragmented shells littering the beach down to where the tide crept in. As he sat hunched on the log in the chill of the advancing afternoon, the air was jarred and buffeted by the sound of coal being shovelled by the paddlewheeler's crew from the breakwater on to the steamer in readiness for the return journey to London. Presently the vessel signalled its imminent departure with the sudden appearance of a white plume of steam from the whistle by its tall funnel, and a shrill shriek that echoed around the bay. The paddle wheels began to turn over slowly. Thick black smoke belched out of the funnel and, as flakes of soot reached the beach and fell where Billy sat, the steamer pulled away from the breakwater and started out with paddlewheels thrashing the water.

Billy watched its progress until it was well out in the stream, then he stood up and looked about him. A path led up to the top of the white clay cliffs, passing a number of houses that, he thought, might take in lodgers. He headed in that direction.

A placard in the front window of one of the houses stated that there was a vacancy for a respectable guest. He wasn't sure that he would qualify in his present state, but he decided to try and gave the knocker on the door a polite rap. The front-window curtains parted slightly and an eye peered out; some moments later a key turned in the lock and, as the door creaked inwards, a small sharp-faced woman appeared.

'Yes? What is it?' she asked impatiently.

'I'm looking for a berth,' Billy said.

'Berth?' she repeated, as if plucking the nautical term out of his speech between thumb and forefinger to hold up with suspicion and disdain.

'Just for tonight, ma'am.'

She looked him up and down, ferrety eyes taking in the unstylish cut of his coat, the grubby white cravat bundled at his throat, and his tanned, rugged face in which prominent eyes were underlined with heavy bags and the lower lip protruded a little: and she obviously didn't like what she saw.

'That notice in my window says a vacancy for a *respectable* lodger. I never take in sailors.'

'Don't blame you, missus,' he said, turning away.

She slammed the door behind him and he heard the key grind over in the lock.

After following the cliff path for a short distance, the same crushing exhaustion that he had experienced on the beach overtook him again and he made for a wooden bench and sat down with his boots ankle-deep in grass and wild primroses. His gloom and depression blinded him to their freshness and colour. In the distance he glimpsed the receding paddle-wheeler with a smoky mane streaming from its funnel as it made good time back up the river, the tide rolling in behind it, and he wondered whether he might not have been better off to have gone back with it.

When at length he rose from the bench to move on again and try his luck elsewhere, he discovered that he had been sitting in front of another house that took in guests. A neat notice hung by the door, proclaiming in black lettering on white: 'Mrs S. Booth, Board & Lodgings.' He was reluctant to expose himself to a further rebuff, but the pleasant appearance of this house—a well-proportioned building of three storeys, with a bay window on the middle floor—encouraged him to try. The knocker on the door was a cheerful omen in itself—a smiling lion cast in gunmetal—and when he used it the rap echoed warmly within, as if the wood on which it sounded were part of some mellow instrument. As he waited, he glanced to one side and saw that the next-door building was an inn with a public room; but it only vaguely registered.

When he looked back to the doorway of the house it was open and occupied by a full-figured but shapely woman of about thirty. If she was critical of Billy's appearance he could see no indication of it.

'Good afternoon,' she began, a melodious Scottish accent and a smile adding to the warmth of the welcome that seemed to radiate naturally from her.

'Afternoon,' Billy said, his hand going to the brim of his hat in a sort of nautical salute. 'I don't suppose you take in sailors.'

The woman gasped in a mildly startled way that seemed to strike a balance between the fact that she should have been shocked but really wasn't.

'Now that's a curious thing to be saying, surely,' she said.

Gesturing back from the cliff path, Billy told her, 'I tried another landlady. She made it plain that she wouldn't touch 'em with a barge pole.'

'Oh, I know the sort you mean,' she said, with a hint of raillery. 'Pour souls—they're all the time wanting nothing less than a judge or an archbishop under their roofs. As for myself, I've no objection that I know of to seafaring gentlemen. Indeed, when I come to think of it, I've enjoyed some of the best times of my life in their company.'

As she paused, Billy quite suddenly came to life again, noting the deep aquamarine of her eyes, which seemed to capture the light coming in off the sea, and appreciating their clear, unclouded good humour. He felt warmth beginning to seep back into him, and he could have laughed with the pleasure of it. Thanks to this woman, he was seeing the external world again.

'Yes,' she went on, 'I'm always delighted to take in sailors.' And she added, with an exaggerated haughtiness that jokingly corrected any false impressions, 'As guests, mind. And provided, of course, that they can afford their keep.'

Billy reacted to this with rough-cast gallantry, shoving his hand in his pocket and bringing out a fistful of silver and copper coins which he thrust in his open palm under the woman's nose.

'What a beautiful sight!' she cried, clapping her hands together. 'I hope you'll no' be getting the idea that I'm an avaricious woman, but I'll be only too happy to relieve you of a little of that.' She paused. 'My name's Sophie Booth, by the way.' And when he failed to respond with his name, she stepped back into the hallway, giving him a little bow to usher him in. 'Will you no' step inside?'

'It's more a matter of trying to keep me out,' he laughed.

As Sophie Booth showed him up the stairs to the first floor, he gathered an impression of clean white walls, polished mirrors, shiny brass lamps; and then, inside the sitting-room, coloured vases and bowls, needlework cushions and covers. Through the bay window there was a fine view out over the estuary and up the river.

In a voice that suggested that no positive answer was expected, Sophie asked, 'I wonder would you have any references, sir?'

'References?' Billy said, turning away from the window. Still wearing his hat, he shook his head. 'Not likely.'

'You'd have no difficulty in obtaining them, I'm sure.'

'I wouldn't guarantee to that,' he said, straight-faced.

'We'll no' go into that, then,' she said. 'It was but a roundabout way of learning your name, you see.'

'My name? Oh, yes.' He hadn't prepared himself for this, and he hesitated as he groped in his mind for something suitable. 'It's—' And then, with a humour to match her own, he said, 'Just call me Mr Booth.'

'Mr Booth!' she exclaimed, momentarily taken in. 'Why, isn't that a coincidence!' And then she realised, and laughed. 'The cheek!' She laughed again and said warningly, 'That's no' the sort of thing you should be saying to a scheming widow.'

'Don't you worry,' he assured her. 'I can take good care of m'self.' He had been holding the money in his hand and he opened it again and said, 'How much of this do you want?'

'That depends on how long you propose to stay. I charge one shilling and threepence a day all found—or six shillings and sixpence for a full week.'

'I'll have a week for a start,' he said, counting out two florins and a half-crown and handing them to her.

'But you've no' seen your room yet,' she said, accepting the money.

'Time enough for that,' he replied, looking around at the seating and then settling for an armchair angled towards the window and the view.

'Ah, now that's what I like to see,' Sophie said as he lowered himself into the armchair. 'A man making himself at home. Would you fancy some refreshment? It so happens that I have some cakes baking in the oven.'

'I can smell 'em,' Billy said with a sharp, satisfying sniff. It was as if with the dispersal of his depression no sight, sound or smell could escape him.

'And some sherry, perhaps?' Sophie suggested.

'Thank you kindly.'

'Sherry and cakes, then,' she said, making them seem delectable just by the shape of her mouth as she spoke.

As she left the room and descended the stairs Billy shut his eyes—partly from weariness and partly to gather together his impressions of Sophie Booth for a quieter appraisal: face with high cheekbones; laughing mouth; those aquamarine eyes; and dark brown hair bursting with a high gloss out of an attractive house-cap with a bow in front. He worked himself deeper into the armchair, a stray tomcat that had stumbled into a good home, swiftly becoming enmeshed in the tendrils of a soothing lethargy.

By the time Sophie came back and set down a tray with a plate of warm oat cakes and a decanter of sherry beside him he was having difficulty in staying awake. She took a glass from the sideboard, poured a full measure of sherry into it and placed it on the tray, saying, 'There you are, sir. Whenever you're ready to go to your room, just give a call and I'll come at once.'

But he didn't call. After half the glass of sherry and one oat cake, he dozed right off: and when Sophie returned to the sitting-room she found him with his chin on his chest, breathing heavily.

Very gently, without disturbing him, she removed his hat. But before she took it down into the hallway to hang it on the stand there, she tilted the inside towards the light from the window to read the maker's name and address on the inner band. The lettering was worn away and she could not decipher it, but the hat was of good quality with a crimson lining—a hat that seemed to indicate that its owner must be a person of some standing. In her eyes that meant that he must be a sea captain at the very least. And thus was J. M. W. Turner, Royal Academician and the greatest marine and landscape painter of the day, raised from the lower deck.

Chapter 13

Nearly two hours later, when he awoke much refreshed from his sound sleep, it took Billy Turner some moments to realise where he was.

Through the bay window he could see the sun going down behind serrated lines of cloud. Instinctively, he broke down the scene into its integral parts, allotting colour notes to each as he would have done had he been jotting details in a sketchbook. Sun, sky, cloud, water, land. Deep orange, feathery pink, warm grey, streaky russet, dark green.

The odour of spiced fruit-pies drifted up to him from the kitchen and as he savoured it he became aware of a curious, wet, whispering sound in the room. He looked around to locate its source and discovered that he was not alone. In a corner, beside a lit oil lamp, sat a bald, rubicund ball of a man of about forty, holding up a black-covered Bible in plump fingers and mouthing the words as he read. He kept licking his lips to keep them moist. When he sensed that he was being watched, he lowered his copy of the good book and fixed the recent sleeper with a righteous stare, addressing him as if delivering a sermon.

'Ah, I understand from our mutual landlady that you are by way of being a sea captain.' He made it sound as though there just might be something lower than this, but if so he had yet to hear of it.

The sea captain role appealed to Billy. He was grateful to Sophie Booth for the promotion after so many years as an ordinary seaman, and he decided not to disillusion her. But even so, he doubted whether he would see out the full week here in the company of the man opposite him, so ecclesiastically attired in buttoned gaiters and parson's grey. The antipathy between the two men was instant and mutual.

'It's my belief,' the fellow-lodger announced, 'that there'd be fewer storms at sea and less shipwrecks if seafarers were to pay greater heed to this.' And he raised his Bible at Billy as if the sight of it should bring this obviously sinful seafarer to his knees.

'Are you suggesting we should take on Bibles instead of oil, and scatter Psalms and Proverbs out on the water to calm it down?'

The man drew the Bible in to the protection of his chest as if to guard it against blasphemy and said, 'Do I detect a heretic?'

'It wouldn't be the first time that's been said of me,' Billy admitted.

The lodger expelled a long, low growl of disgust.

At this point Sophie Booth entered the room, the hair over her eyes white with flour.

'So you're becoming acquainted with each other, gentlemen,' she said; and to Billy she went on, 'Mr Hark is a commercial traveller. Holy Bibles.'

'You sell 'em, eh?' Billy said, turning to the other man.

'If you are able to name a more honourable calling, sir, I'd be obliged if you'd tell me.'

Billy shrugged. 'Offhand, I can't. Except, of course, writing the whole thing in the first place.'

Sophie intervened before verbal hostilities could begin. 'Captain,' she said—and Billy basked in the sound of his new title—'I'm sorry to have to tell you this, but you'll no' be having the pleasure of so much of Mr Hark's enlightening company as you might wish. He's back for a night, but then he's gone for weeks at a time. It's his work, you know—it takes him all over the country.' She turned a smile on Hark, who was confirming what she said with vigorous nods. Then her eyes came back to meet Billy's, and she raised an eyebrow slightly. 'It's a great pity, because I find myself so uplifted by his knowledge. I'm always very sad for to see him depart.'

Billy had to drag out a large red handkerchief to cover his amusement at her cool impudence.

'If you'll come away in, the both of you,' she went on, 'I'll serve your supper.'

Hark and Billy followed her through into the dining-room, where candles in shiny brass candlesticks were alight on the table. She asked them to be seated while she brought in the soup; and when she had done so, Hark asked Billy, hoping to embarrass him, 'As the newcomer, would you care to have the honour of saying grace for us?'

'Grace?' Billy responded. 'Well, why not?' He paused to think. 'The best I can do at short notice is a mariners' grace—one that was composed for use during a storm at sea.'

'It might well be appropriate,' Hark said. 'Proceed.'

Billy plunged into a grace he had picked up on one of his coastal sketching tours:

> 'We thank thee, Lord, as we now sup;
> And we'll thank thee again
> If we don't bring it up.'

A jolt of silent laughter shook Sophie Booth.

Hark looked horrified.

'You were warned,' Billy reminded him.

Throughout the meal, as Billy joked and Sophie laughed, Hark's resentment against the new lodger increased. Towards the end he asked, 'Would your ship, sir, be one that we'd know anything of?'

Having been asked this sort of thing before at places where he had been taken for a sailor, Billy had developed a prompt, pat answer. The name of the ship was no problem—he simply used that of the street where he lived in London.

'The *Queen Anne*,' he said. 'Three-master, square-rigged, Thames-built, 340 tons, gentle as a baby lamb in a fair sea but bucks about like a drunken whore when a wind gets up—' shocked affront on Hark's face; a barely suppressed laugh from Sophie—'in a manner of speaking.'

A glance at Hark's tight features and then at Sophie was enough to encourage Billy to extemporise. 'So happens I'm just back from a long voyage,' he continued. 'Naples and Venice. Shipped out coal. Loaded wines and glassware for the return. Nearly lost the lot. And the ship, too. Storm in the Bay of Biscay. Got cast up on the French coast. Spring tides, fortunately, so we floated off. No harm done all round.'

After this Sophie urged him to relate more about his voyages and experiences on the high seas and in foreign parts, and he obliged by describing strange coastlines he had skirted and fabulous anchorages where the imaginary *Queen Anne* had swung on the tides. For some of this he exaggerated his travels at home and abroad, but in the main he drew on completed paintings and others planned in his mind. It was all very real to his two listeners, although it did little to endear him to Hark. In fact, the way in which Sophie Booth was drinking it all in made Hark regret having started the reminiscences flowing.

Finally, Billy told them about what he claimed to have been quite the very worst shipwreck he had ever seen—the foundering of the *Minotaur*—describing it as if he had been on board a ship standing by but helpless to assist, carrying it off with such conviction that both Sophie and Hark fully believed him to have been there.

When he had finished, Hark—moved in spite of himself—bowed his head and solemnly pronounced, 'God rest their spirits.'

Sophie shuddered and said, 'Aye, Captain—it's a perilous life you lead.'

Billy shrugged as if to say that it was all part of the job, and then an imp in him prompted him to try to take another rise out of his fellow lodger. 'I'm sure it's not anywhere near as dangerous as trying to sell Bibles to heretics.'

'It would do *you* no harm to resort to the good book for guidance,' Hark said testily.

'And it's only a penny-farthing a week,' Sophie put in, much too innocently for it to be a chance comment.

'A penny-farthing for what?' Billy asked.

'The loan of a Bible.' Sophie turned to Hark. 'Is that not so?'

Hark looked angry at having his operations reduced to such bald commercial terms. 'I am afraid my scheme is available only to persons of fixed abode. In the captain's case it would have to be a matter of outright purchase.'

But Billy was interested in what Hark was getting out of the scheme. 'You mean to say you supply the Bible on loan and then collect at a penny-farthing per book per person per week?'

'That is the basis of it,' Hark admitted, at the same time resenting the way it had been put. 'It enables a person who might otherwise be deprived to receive the light of the Lord.'

Billy gave a grunt of admiration for what seemed to him a clever business notion. 'So that's what keeps you trotting around the country, eh? Collecting five farthings here, five there. All mounts up, I'll be bound.'

Hark had endured enough. He rose from the table, bowed to Sophie and politely wished her good-night, and then presented a cold mask of a face to Billy, saying, 'You'll consider my offer, I trust.'

'Many thanks all the same,' Billy replied. 'I'm amply provided with reading matter for the present.' And from a pocket he produced a small volume, its leather binding very well worn, and held it up. 'The *Iliad*. From the Greek. By a fellow called Homer.'

Hark compressed his lips in disapproval; and as he left the room he muttered 'Pagan', meaning both the author of the work and the owner of the copy just shown to him.

Sophie sighed. 'Poor Hark! He takes his work to heart, you know.'

'And no wonder,' Billy snorted. 'With a money-making scheme like the one I've just been hearing about, he can't be short of a sovereign or two. Indeed, I've half a mind to try it m'self.'

Thinking that he meant selling Bibles, Sophie gave him a quick questioning look; but Billy was imagining himself finding homes for his paintings in the town and country houses of patrons, treating himself to plenty of fresh air and scenery in the process of doing the rounds and collecting so much each week for the loan of them. Not penny-farthings for him, though—guineas at least. But it was just a notion, and he dismissed it, saying, 'Never mind. Time now I was having a look at that room you promised me.'

Carrying one of the candlesticks from the table, Sophie climbed the staircase ahead of him. She led him into a small cosy room, using the candle to light the wick of an oil lamp. Billy looked about him, taking in the tiny window, the washstand with a basin and a jug of water, and the night shirt spread out on the bed cover.

Sophie waited until the flame of the oil lamp bloomed, adjusted the wick to a steady glow and then went to the door, saying, 'Sleep well, Captain—Booth ...' They both laughed, admitting that the name had been chosen on the spur of the moment; but Billy made no attempt to provide an alternative.

'Don't be in too much of a hurry to come down in the morning,' she told him, slowly drawing the door shut. 'Just take your time.'

She closed the door, and Billy was left with an image of her smile—a symbol of the warmth he had found here. He crossed to the half-open window and peered down on to the sea below the cliffs, lights from the windows of houses at the other end of the bay reflecting in its dark shine. He thought about what she had said. 'Just take your time.' She was urging him to relax and enjoy himself now that he was here for a week, yet perhaps cautioning him not to rush things where she was concerned. Clearly, she had taken to him; she had left him in no doubt as to whose side she was on in the encounter with Hark. Or was he reading too much into it—lulled into romantic imaginings by the sense of comfort he felt here and the presentiment of what could lie in store for him at this place in terms of contentment and escape? It was too soon to think about it. He had an instinct about Sophie Booth, but if he tried to consolidate his position too quickly he might spoil everything. 'Just take your time,' he told himself.

As he leaned at the window, the lights in the bay went out one by one, leaving only a few floating in the darkness that reached up the river to London and beyond. He felt a long way now from the city and what had driven him away earlier in the day.

Turning, he went to the side of the bed and undressed, pulling the nightshirt over his head before slipping into bed. And with the sea whispering in through the window he fell into a peaceful sleep.

Ezra Hark's early morning departure created a brief disturbance below Billy's bedroom. Woken by it, he threw back the bedclothes and crossed the room to peer down. While Sophie steadied his pony, Hark loaded several boxes of Bibles on to the back of his trap; then he mounted to the seat at the front and took over the reins. He touched the pony's hide with the whip, the animal jolted forward and the trap rocked away over the uneven ground. Sophie waved goodbye and went back into the house, and Billy returned to his bed to doze off with her singing down below faint in his ears. An hour or so later he got up to dress and found that Sophie had left a set of razors on the washstand, so he was able to go down shaved.

'Good morning, Captain,' Sophie greeted him, coming from the kitchen as he descended the stairs. 'You slept well, I trust?'

'Like the ship's cat in the Master's bed,' he said, the seafarer once again.

Later in the morning, still playing the part, he sauntered along the sea-front, adopting the gait of a man savouring the solid feel of dry land after a long spell with pitching decks under his boots. He gave nautical half-salutes to the local folk who greeted him, paid his first call at The Boat Inn next door to Sophie's house, and waved to his first clusters of local urchins. Before the week was out, he was drawing ships for them. And he made tiny models for them too, shaping the hulls and masts from scraps of driftwood with a penknife and using bits of paper to make the sails.

Despite his masquerade, however, he could never really stop being Turner the artist. If he was sure he was not being watched, he would take a small sketchbook from his pocket to make notes, especially if he spotted a subject suitable for one of his current commissions—a series of engravings of scenes in England and Wales.

After extending his stay for a second week the need to get down to a bout of solid work again became strong, but not so strong as his desire to be in Sophie Booth's company. He was, in fact, planning on a third week when Ezra Hark returned. That decided it for Billy. He told Sophie that it was time for him to return to his ship; but he made it plain that the next time the *Queen Anne* dropped her hook in a Thames anchorage her captain would come straight back to Margate.

Chapter 14

Back in London after his stay with Sophie Booth, Billy's spirits ran so high that they carried him safely through what might otherwise have caused him great distress.

On his way to Clement's Inn—where he still had to deal with the matter involving Morley and The Ship and Bladebone—he bought a copy of a monthly journal containing a review of the recent exhibition at the British Institution, where he had hung a number of pictures. His name jumped out at him from the printed page and he read on to discover that the journal's critic was still after his blood, describing his works as caprices more wild and ridiculous than even a man out of Bedlam would dare to indulge in...

At any other time he would have recoiled at the sight of the name of that horrific place where his mother had first been incarcerated; but now he ignored it, and crushed the journal into a ball, kicking it into the gutter as if applying his boot to the backside of the offending critic—another confounded lunatic trying to make out that he was a madman.

His appearance in the lawyers' chambers reduced Morley instantly to a quivering wreck. On his weekly business trip to Wapping, the hapless clerk had been told of what had happened there as a consequence of Mrs Danby's visit, and since then he had been waiting with increasing trepidation for the injured client to arrive at Clement's Inn. Now that the client was here, he began to stammer out an apology—only to be cut short with an effusive 'Morning, Morley' and led by the cloth of his coat-sleeve into Gascoigne's office.

Gascoigne, who was in conference with his senior partner, was so unnerved by this sudden entry that he barely had the strength to lever himself to his feet as Billy treated him and

George Cobb to a breezy, 'Morning, both.'

Releasing Morley's sleeve, Billy put his hands on his hips and looked from one face to another, shaking his head in mock despair. Gascoigne and Morley could not hide their guilt; but Cobb, who was leaving more and more of the firm's affairs to the junior partner, had the attitude of a bemused spectator to something that didn't involve him.

'Well, now, gentlemen,' Billy began benignly. 'I trust that you're starting to appreciate just what you're all up against as regards Mrs Danby and the lengths to which she'll go to pursue her ends. I imagine, by the way, that she's been paying you further calls despite my instructions.'

'Mr Turner, sir,' Gascoigne pleaded, 'we do our best. We carry out your instructions. But she is a most determined woman.'

'I'm glad you're starting to understand that, Mr Gascoigne. I didn't think for a minute she'd keep away.'

Like Morley, Gascoigne had prepared himself for a scene and was quite overcome by Billy's unexpected mildness. In his relief, he became almost gushing.

'It was most unfortunate, sir—most unfortunate indeed. Mr Morley, of course, had no intimation whatsoever—absolutely none—that he was being followed to Wapping.'

Billy refrained from asking what snippet of information had been dropped in Sarah's presence that had prompted her to follow Morley in the first place. 'That's just it,' he said. 'With Mrs Danby you never know what's afoot. It's not enough to have your eyes skinned port and starboard—you need 'em in the back of your head.'

'Mr Morley shan't be followed again,' Gascoigne promised. Oh, no. Indeed he shan't.'

'You won't have to concern yourself about that no more. The cat's out of the bag as far as I'm concerned at The Ship and Bladebone.' Billy paused. Then, as though to himself, he went on, 'Although it may well be that Mrs Danby's done me a good turn for a change.'

Gascoigne and Morley looked mystified, leaving it to Cobb to ask, 'What, precisely, are we to infer from that, Mr Turner?'

But Billy ignored Cobb and the question, a faraway look in his eyes and a contemplative smile on his lips.

When it was clear that no reply was forthcoming, Cobb gave a little laugh and hobbled to the door, using a stick to support a gouty leg. 'Ah, well,' he said, 'I can see I'm not going to be needed here, so I'll leave the three of you to sort it all out. Good-day, Mr Turner.'

Billy's reply was a genial wave; he was about to turn back to the junior partner and the clerk when the watercolour on the wall caught his eye. He pointed to it, suddenly excited, and exclaimed, 'Hah! See that! Just what that damned Constable meant when he said I painted with tinted steam!'

'A constable? Which constable?' Gascoigne inquired.

'John, of course.'

'Oh yes, indeed. *John* Constable—of course,' Gascoigne hastened to say, looking foolish. 'But—tinted steam, sir?'

'Oh, I'll use mud from the gutter, if needs be, to get my effects. Constable didn't mean no insult.'

As Billy continued to scrutinise the painting, peering so closely that he seemed to be trying to see right behind the flimsy washes of colour, he might have been looking at the work of a stranger. Presently he said, 'You know something? I'm not so sure I could do it up to that standard if I was out there on the river today. And what I was attempting in watercolour all that time back is what I'm just really getting down to now in oil.' He gave a loud appreciative grunt and turned to the others at last, saying to Gascoigne, 'Anyone been making any offers for this picture of late?'

'It's constantly admired,' Gascoigne said. 'And the client who made me that offer I mentioned to you some years ago assured me that he'd be only too pleased to give me sixty guineas for it any time I cared to accept. Not that—'

'No, eighty!' Billy cut in. 'It's gone up in value since then. Although you're not thinking of selling, I trust.'

'Indeed not, sir. That's just what I was about to say.'

'Except to me, of course,' Billy said, cocking a thumb and jerking it back into the middle of his own chest. 'Some day I might want to buy it back.'

He started to pat the outside of his coat with his hands until he located the pocket where he had the sketchbook he wanted. From it he read out a number of business matters for Gascoigne to attend to, and then he tore out a sheet covered with notes, saying, 'Another likely bit of property caught m'eye. Here's all I know about it so far. Would you kindly have it looked into, like a good fellow?'

The business had until now been conducted with such politeness and good humour that Gascoigne decided to put forward Sarah Danby's case for an increased allowance once again. While this brought on a serious outbreak of twitching from Morley, who thought it was tempting providence to broach this matter now, there was no outward change in Billy, except for a faint tightening about the lips, as he heard the lawyer out. Inwardly, he was still far too detached to be concerned; and when Gascoigne had finished, he mumbled, 'I'll give it some serious thought and let you know.'

It was already forgotten, however, as he set off for Marylebone, hailing a hackney cab in the Strand to take him to Queen Anne Street, his sense of well-being unshaken.

As Billy passed through the bottom room of the Queen Anne Street gallery, black and dark grey shapes vanished behind the pictures stacked against the walls, and dozens of pairs of eyes peered out at him. It seemed to him that the cats had become more numerous since his father's death. Not that they bothered him now. He paused to stroke a friendly member of the tribe on the head, and went so far as to mutter an apology when he caught another asleep on the stairs and nearly trod on it. The mood he had carried with him from Margate still swept all normal aggravations and irritations before it.

Under the skylights in the upstairs room, his pictures shone like blazing torches. One of them was a glowing classical scene similar to the British Institution exhibit which had been abused in the monthly journal. Passing it, he muttered, 'Caprice, indeed!' and snorted his disdain for the critic in question.

Hearing footsteps and expecting to find a customer, Hannah came out of the painting-room followed by a man who was a stranger to Billy. Both Hannah and the stranger stopped and stared guiltily. Then Hannah seemed to shrink, almost cringe; and Billy suffered a sharp twinge of conscience for having allowed their relationship to drift to the point that he could cause her such distress. But that didn't account for the furtive look of the man. Who was he and what was he doing here? Was he, in fact, a stranger? Billy sifted through faces in his mind to try to place this one.

The man suddenly burst into a fast bolting walk, but as he came closer Billy remembered having seen him at a crowded exhibition where he had been pointed out as someone to watch—a dealer suspected of handling stolen paintings and drawings.

'Hey, you!' Billy bawled. 'Wait a minute!'

As the dealer tried to dive past, Billy lunged forward and grabbed hold of his coat. As they scuffled, several proof copies of Billy's engravings fell from the dealer's coat to the floor.

There was a moment of stunned silence, and then Billy said thickly, 'So that's your game, is it?'

The dealer tried to wrench away but Billy tightened his hold; and all the good humour built up during his two weeks at Margate collapsed.

The two men rolled on the floor—one pummelling wildly, the other trying to break free—as Hannah attempted to drag Billy away, but it was useless until his rage began to expend itself. When it did, it was only because of the sheer physical impossibility of maintaining an attack at such a pitch; and when at last the battered dealer was able to crawl free and limp out of the gallery and down the stairs, Billy could not get back to his feet. From the gallery walls, dawn suns, midnight moons, evening stars, the eyes of storms and other orbs and effulgences took flight from the canvases and spun around his head. He tried again to get up but it still defeated him, so he lay on the floor and waited for the whirling beacons to come to a stop and settle back in their frames.

He tried to speak. At first nothing came. Then he managed a croaking whisper. 'Get Dr Monro.'

'I can't,' Hannah said, a shape looming over him—a reminder of an earlier apparition he could never forget.

'Get Dr Monro,' he whispered again. His mother's madness and violence, which he had struggled so long to suppress, had broken out in him and he knew that only Monro could help him now. 'Please get him.'

'No one can get him now,' Hannah said. 'His family wanted you to be at his funeral, but I couldn't tell them where to find you—I didn't know where you were. He died two weeks ago.'

Billy stared at her, then covered his face with his arm, not wanting her to see the fear in his eyes. If Dr Monro was dead, then all hope was dead. Who could help him now?

Hannah looked down at him uncertainly as he continued to lie there. She wanted to help him but she didn't know how. Certainly she didn't have the strength to get him to his feet. She stood there helplessly, looking from him to her prowling cats and doing nothing.

After some minutes, Billy stirred. He reached out to one of the legs of the big table which stood in the middle of the room. Using it for support, he hauled himself to his feet. It took him a little time to recover his breath as he leaned heavily against the table. When he could speak he said to Hannah, 'Don't ever sell my proofs again.'

Hannah had retired into herself once more. 'I had to do something,' she replied in a voice totally devoid of emotion. 'You went off without leaving me enough money.'

Billy fought to suppress a new surge of anger. He had heard this complaint often enough before, but from another source.

'Sarah put you up to this, didn't she?' he said in a controlled way. 'She used to sell proofs behind my back. It *was* her, wasn't it?'

Hannah refused to answer this. 'You left me without enough money,' she repeated. 'It's not myself I care about—it's the cats.'

'To hell with your cats!'

With a shaking hand he fumbled in his pocket, dragged out some money and spewed it across the top of the table. And as Hannah impassively gathered the coins, he saw that the baggy bonnet had slipped away from the side of her face, exposing the malignance which had made him believe that in man there was a certain madness of the flesh, a parallel to that of the mind. This monstrous thing had eaten away Hannah's youth, and now it somehow contrived to exist on her despair. But the worst and cruellest thing of all was that it made her abhorrent to him, however much he might try or wish to feel otherwise. Hannah realised this and it provoked her at this moment into flaunting it at him as a reproof for his neglect before she moved off into the shadows.

Billy shut himself away and refused to see visitors, leaving all the gallery business to Hannah. Forcing himself to work, he became immersed in a large brown and purple storm in an effort to paint the tumult out of himself. While he grieved over the passing of Dr Monro, he remembered the doctor's dictum that his work would be his salvation—and so he kept at it.

That advice still held good. After three days he was calmer and able to come to terms with his problem. His main desire was to get away again from the oppressive atmosphere in Queen Anne Street. But it was too soon to make for Margate without endangering the credibility of his masquerade; so he made his way out to his other retreat, Petworth Park.

Chapter 15

The peace that Billy found at Petworth entered all the work he did there—and he worked well. Soon after his arrival, he was out taking notes for a big picture of the house with the lake in the foreground. Back in the studio that had been put at his disposal on the first floor he made it clear that he did not want to be disturbed by anyone. Only Egremont was excepted from this ban. Between them, the nobleman and Billy devised a secret knock.

Egremont had turned eighty, but his zest for elegant living remained undiminished. Beautiful women still surrounded him, young and old, together with girls and boys in silks and velvets—all of whom seemed to Billy to have floated out of the creations of Gainsborough and Reynolds to congregate for what was one long unbroken house-party.

At least once a day Egremont would give the pre-arranged knock on the door and Billy would let him into the studio. The nobleman never ceased to be amazed at Billy's shrewd grasp of the workings of stocks and shares and property investment, and he frequently asked for opinions and advice. He always found Billy up to date in the latest developments: he would hear that steam had come to stay, that propulsion by sail alone was doomed, and that the canals had no alternative but to surrender to the spread of the railways. As for the various wars and border skirmishes on the Continent, Billy had them all well tabulated—if only because they affected his plans for tours abroad.

At the same time, Egremont kept his eye on the progress of the new painting he had commissioned.

'No second thoughts about the price as yet?' he inquired one morning.

'We settled for 500 guineas, m'lord. I'll make it higher if you want me to,' Billy said.

'I think I'll get it for less when the time comes.'

'I don't know how you can think that, m'lord. I drive a hard bargain—even with the best of patrons.'

'It's just a feeling I have,' Egremont said with an odd smile.

'We'll see, then, won't we?' Billy said. He couldn't fathom what Egremont was up to this time, except that he knew the old man loved a sporting wager and this somehow had that air about it.

On the day the picture was finished, Egremont brought in several of the ladies to inspect it. They all loved it—but then they always approved of anything Billy did, especially at Petworth.

Egremont withheld his opinion until pressed for it, and then he said that he liked it as a work of art though he believed that there was an error of detail in the foreground. 'What's this, here?' he asked, pointing at several small objects floating in the lake.

'Carrots, m'lord,' Billy told him.

'Floating?'

'Yes, m'lord.'

'You're painting better and better as time goes by, Turner—but I'm damned if I'm going to accept what I see there. Carrots don't float.'

'They were in your lake, m'lord, so I imagine they must've been your carrots—and floating they were.'

'No, no, no. You've slipped up this time.'

'Do you really think so, m'lord?'

'Yes, Turner, I do. I've caught you out at long last.'

'I wonder, could I hold a fish to blame?'

'A fish?'

'A loyal pike, m'lord—swimming just under them carrots to keep their heads up out of the water.'

The ladies giggled and Egremont smiled.

Billy went on, 'There are some very crafty fish out there, you know. After all my efforts to catch 'em, I can vouch for that.'

'Fish or no fish, carrots do *not* float.'

'Then there's where our opinions differ.'

'Shall we put it to the test?'

'As you please m'lord. How do you propose we go about it?'

Egremont replied to this by sending for a pail of water and a carrot; and as they waited, he said to Billy, 'I take it you're prepared to back up your claim.'

'What did you have in mind, m'lord?'

'Your price still 500 guineas?'

'I warned you I wouldn't come down.'

'Very well, then. If the carrot floats, I'll pay you double—and I'll be delighted to do so. If it doesn't—nothing.'

'Done,' said Billy.

The footmen arrived—one with a large gilded bucket of clear water, the other carrying a scrubbed carrot on a silver tray.

'Kindly do the honours, my dear,' said Egremont, handing the carrot to the youngest woman present, a Lady Charlotte.

A great admirer of Billy's, she gave him a sweet smile of encouragement. She lowered the carrot very gently towards the water, doing all she could to make it float.

Egremont spotted this. 'No monkey business,' he said. 'Into the bucket with it.'

With a helpless shrug to Billy, Lady Charlotte let the carrot slip from her fingers. It plunged down deep into the water, then slid up and down and kept bobbing about, alternately raising and lowering hopes until it settled upright with its green tuft and scrubbed red head floating clear of the surface.

'Floating, dammit!' Egremont exclaimed.

The ladies laughed mockingly at him and clapped their hands to applaud Billy for his win.

'That'll be 1,000 guineas now, m'lord,' Billy said.

'I should've known better than to gamble against a wily coot like you, Turner—'specially on a matter like this.' Egremont appraised the painting again. 'Ah, well—I'm getting something in return for my loss. That picture's worth every penny. Well done.'

The ladies retired to their chamber-music lessons and practice; the footmen removed the bucket of water and the carrot; and the painter and his patron were left together. To Egremont it seemed an opportune moment for a little probing. It was accepted that Billy led some sort of secret life, quite apart from his curious relationship with the strange little woman at Queen Anne Street, and the nobleman never gave up trying to coax something out of him.

'What news of the Contessa?' he asked, leading the conversation in the appropriate direction.

'None,' Billy replied. Egremont, the old rascal, had never received any confidences about that particular interlude and was not going to now. By way of an apology for his bluntness he went on, 'I'm planning another visit to Venice, so I expect I'll be calling on her.'

'Do give her our love.'

'I'll try to remember that.'

This too was dismissive, but Egremont tried again. 'Tell me —whatever became of the dear lady who wrote me those letters saying what an outrageously mean and irresponsible fellow you were?'

'Oh—her. She's still out on patrol and ready for action; but I don't think you'll be hearing from her again, m'lord. After you failed to respond to her complaints, she decided that you were much the same as me—a bad lot.'

'That's a great pity. The ladies did adore those letters of hers.'

'So they told me,' said Billy wryly, remembering the ribbing they had given him about the accusations made against him in the letters that Egremont had read aloud to them.

Egremont laughed at the recollection, and Billy laughed with him—although nothing to do with Sarah was a joking matter, even if her attempts to blacken his name by writing to the nobleman had failed.

'You're still a great mystery to us, you know,' Egremont mused. 'Just where do you hide yourself away?'

'Ah-ha!' Billy chuckled.

After Egremont had left him to add a few final touches to the picture containing the disputed carrots, Billy kept thinking back to that last question. He totted up how many weeks had passed since he had taken leave of Sophie Booth at Margate. Almost four. As long as he made sure when telling about his voyage to say that the winds had all been favourable and the sailing swift, it seemed to him that this should be enough time to have made a round trip to somewhere such as Gibraltar or Cadiz.

To be on the safe side, and reminding himself that he mustn't rush things with Sophie, he lingered another week at Petworth—still painting but with a gradual decline in interest. Then he returned to London for a brief call at Queen Anne Street before heading down river again.

Chapter 16

'Glory be!' Sophie cried when she answered the door and discovered who was there. 'So you're no' drowned after all.'

'Drowned?' Billy said. 'I'm damned sure I'm not.'

'Old Hark was positive you'd gone to your death.'

'Sorry to disappoint him. You'll have to tell him you've got a fairly substantial ghost on your doorstep.' The prospect of Hark's company did not appeal to him, but if it was the price he had to pay for seeing Sophie again he was prepared to endure it.

Sophie laughed. 'Oh, he's away gathering his penny-farthings at present,' she said. 'It's grand to have you back.'

'I'll be here a week or so,' he said. 'And I'd like that same room, if possible.'

'It's ready and waiting.'

After hanging his hat on the stand in the hallway, he went upstairs to leave his travelling-box in his room. A broad fiery sky up the river was squeezed into the tiny window, and he hurried to the sitting-room where he could see it better through the big bay window. As he made himself comfortable in the armchair to which he had become attached during his previous stay, Sophie came in with a tray of home-baked biscuits and a decanter of sherry.

'The weather was murder here,' she said, pouring him a glass of sherry and placing it at his side. 'Hark said that out at sea there'd be waves descending upon you twice as high as this house.'

'And he was praying for my deliverance, I don't doubt.'

'That I cannot say I recall,' Sophie said with a laugh.

'Well, he was wrong again. Had a stormy passage for a start,' he told her, thinking of what had happened on his return to London, 'but after that it was all plain sailing.'

During the following few days he fell into the easy routine he had established on his first visit, taking walks and getting to know the local people and children even better. After almost a week, Ezra Hark came back. If he was surprised to see the sea captain in residence again, he made no mention of it. His attitude towards Billy was that of a saint forced to cohabit with a disciple of the Devil.

From this time on, and despite the Bible salesman's intermittent presence at Sophie Booth's house, Margate became a substitute for the hideaway Billy had lost at Wapping—one that was infinitely more satisfying to him thanks to Sophie. His stays were irregular both in the time he spent there and in the intervals between one visit and another. He would arrive either by the fast paddlewheel packet now on the run from London or by the coach via Chatham, sometimes staying just for a day or two and sometimes for a week, but rarely for longer than a fortnight. He became well known in the locality as Captain Booth, said to be some sort of relative of his landlady. In the public room of The Boat Inn, and in a number of other neighbouring taverns, he frequently joined in the evening's entertainment, singing a sea shanty or taking along his flute and playing a hornpipe.

During the day he became a target for the urchins, who swarmed around him clamouring for accounts of his voyages and begging him to do sketches of ships and make models for them. His capacious pockets were crammed with bits and pieces that these boys found fascinating, the most popular item being the precious object which contained his own private rainbow.

'Got that piece o' magic glass wi' ye today, Cap'n?' one or other of them might ask.

Billy would make a show of searching through his pockets, sometimes deciding that the object was there and sometimes not. When it was, he would say, 'So happens I have,' and he would bring it out concealed in a grubby white silk handkerchief. Then he would slowly peel back the folds until he exposed a superb glass prism, its polished surfaces needing to be moved only a fraction to flash in the sunlight. One after another, the ragged mudlarks would be allowed to hold the jewel in their hands, passing it on with the very greatest care and awe. It was, they believed, something that the captain had brought home to England with him after a voyage to India, where he and his crew had carried out a raid on a temple choked with treasure. And presently, after the prism had passed from hand to hand, there would be another request from the small-fry—but usually a silent one made with breathtaking politeness, all those bright young eyes focusing on Billy's headgear as if in league to make it remove itself from its wearer's head by the sheer force of their wills.

Knowing only too well what this was all about, Billy would say, 'You'll be wanting m'hat too, I expect ...'

Grinning widely, the urchins would nod their verminous little heads; and so Billy would hand them his seaman-style beaver and then a small sheet of white paper.

After this, they knew what to do—turning the hat on its side, placing the sheet of paper inside it, and then sitting the prism on the paper. Next they got themselves under one of their coats, at the same time keeping the end of the hat exposed. Tilting and twisting the hat very gently, they positioned it so that the tiny hole bored in the crown caught the sun and aimed it at the prism inside. As the prism broke up the light into the colours of the spectrum and spread them out in seven beautiful bands on the paper, there would invariably be the utter hush of pure wonder; and then, as Billy had taught them, they would chant in a spellbound chorus what they could see.

'Red, orange, yellow, green, blue, indigo, violet.'

Sometimes they put it in reverse order; and if one of the smallest urchins determined to get through the litany on his own, Billy would hear, 'Wylet, innigo, boo, gween, yella, owange, wed.' And it was poetry to his ears.

Sophie took to strolling with him on some of his local walks smiling to neighbours as the captain made his half salutes. Each of his visits brought them a little closer. Sometimes he came down to Margate exhausted and passed days slumped in his chair in the sitting-room, sleeping heavily or gazing out through the bay window on to the estuary and up the river. At other times he would be full of restless energy; and once when he arrived to find Sophie whitewashing her kitchen he took over the brush and bucket.

She marvelled at his expertise with the brush, saying, 'My! You're a master at it.'

'And so I should be,' he said. 'Painted whole ships in m'day.'

'That I can well believe.'

Sometimes he read aloud to her, using his magnifying glass or tiny spectacles to decipher the print in the miniature volumes which he carried in his pockets of tales from Greek and Roman mythology—especially those he had used or planned to use as subjects for paintings. Included in these was the tale that had been the basis for one of his earliest mythological paintings and one of the first of his works purchased by Lord Egremont—that of the nymph Echo, who had the power of speech taken from her except for being able to repeat another's voice; of how she fell in love with Narcissus and pined away until only her voice remained; and of how Narcissus was punished in his turn and made to fall in love with his own reflection in a pool and was turned into a flower after taking his own life. He told, too, the story behind a more recent picture—that of the sorceress Medea who, after being deserted by Jason, sent his new bride a garment which consumed her in flames. And he also told her of the doomed love of Hero for Leander, the youth who swam across the Hellespont every night to be with his beloved: how Hero threw herself into the sea after Leander was drowned when swimming back from a nocturnal rendezvous. Billy already had in his mind a picture of their final parting.

It did not escape Sophie's notice that the tales he chose were for the most part connected with tragic love, and she wondered about this. But she adored these interludes, sighing at all the magic and romance—even weeping a tear or two at times.

One evening, when he put the book aside because the dusk swamping into the room made it too difficult to read, Sophie said, 'You've a wonderful way of telling a tale, Captain.'

'That makes a change,' he said, thinking of Sarah and how she had reacted to this sort of thing. 'I once knew a woman who used to interrupt me every time I opened my mouth, to pick me up on my accent.'

'Oh, but it's a lovely accent.'

'It's straight Cockney. I was born plumb in the heart of Covent Garden. My old Dad was a hairdresser there—and barber.'

Sophie was excited by this unexpected revelation of his past life and was ready to hear more, but Billy did not proceed. Even so, he often felt the urge to confide in her—especially when she revealed something of her own background. He gathered that she had been widowed twice and had a son John by her first husband, Henry Pound. The boy, who was eight years old when Billy came to stay with Sophie, lived with relatives at Deal. It puzzled Billy why the lad was not with his mother until she explained how his parental aunts had started to look after him following the death of Henry Pound and had continued to do so while she settled down at Margate with her second husband. As John seemed happy with his aunts—and they wanted to keep him and see to his education—she had allowed the matter to rest there; but the boy stayed with her from time to time.

It wasn't until two years after his initial stay at Margate as a sea captain, however, that Billy first met him. He took a liking to the lad—as he did to most young people—making special drawings and ship models for him and, as a particular treat, handing him his hat and the prism.

As the time since his first meeting with Sophie stretched from two years to three, Billy became increasingly reluctant to reveal the truth about himself. If he was going to speak at all, he thought, he should have done it earlier. There was no knowing what Sophie's reaction would be if she discovered that he had been deceiving her for so long. And if he unmasked himself now, he feared that he might destroy this haven. It was part of the caution he seemed to have been urged to exercise from his first meeting with Sophie—although he now felt that he had made something of a mockery of the gentle warning implied in her 'Just take your time'. But it inhibited him against making any physical advances towards her, even though he knew it was inevitable.

When it happened, it came about quite without plan or premeditation one evening as Billy sat facing the bay window, watching the sun going down. Sophie stood at his side, sharing the spectacle with him. They were alone in the house, free from Hark or any other lodgers.

As Sophie played idly with the coils of her thick hair about her neck, Billy reached up and grasped her wrist—not to stop her from cupping her hair but to draw her down to him. No more than the hint of this was necessary. Sophie sank on to his lap, sighing with relief as she said, 'Thank goodness for that. I was beginning to fear that I might have to wait until after yet another of your voyages.'

In the first flush of excitement over her new relationship with Billy, Sophie was content to thank God for her good fortune. If there were times when she wondered what to make of her sea captain, she was wise enough still to ask no questions. That there was more to him than appeared on the surface had always been apparent, but in a way she enjoyed the air of secrecy that surrounded him and was loth to disturb it. It added a piquancy to her feelings for him and heightened those moments when she was given a sudden and surprising glimpse of another side to his character.

There was, for instance, the time when he returned after an absence of two months, silently entering the house and creeping on tiptoe through to the kitchen, where she was blacking the stove. His hand slipped down the front of her dress to fondle her breast.

'You devil!' she gasped.

His laughter bounced under the low ceiling; and Sophie, almost losing her balance, slapped an open palm against the nearby wall, leaving the black imprint of her palm and her outstretched fingers on the whitewash.

'Well, now,' she said, so glad to see him that she couldn't even pretend to be angry. 'What's to be done about that?'

'Easy fixed,' he said, getting to work at once with his fingers and a cloth to spread the lampblack into the shape of a thick-boled tree. He seized on the flowers in a vase on a shelf above the stove to provide him with makeshift materials, taking his red from squashed rose petals, green from crushed leaves, and yellow and orange from other blooms in the random cluster that Sophie had bunched together from the garden at the back of the house. Squeezing the coloured juices into the whitewash, he kept rubbing and spreading until a misty dawn scene emerged, with the tree standing out in silhouette. As a finishing touch, he licked the backs of two pink Michaelmas daisy petals and stuck them on to the sky, making a bird in flight through the sunrise. Then he stood back from it to watch Sophie and enjoy her amazement.

For a moment, she gazed at the scene in open-eyed wonder; then she turned and gave him a penetrating look. 'I have known sailors to be very clever,' she said. 'Models of ships ... needlework ... carvings on sea shells ... But I've never known one who did the like of this. Never.'

Billy merely gave one of his secretive chuckles and said, 'Ah-ha!'

The love-making was perfect for both of them—passionate, tender, occasionally humorous. As they embraced in bed one morning, he murmured:

'Within you, dear Sophie,
Within you I be,
Like a boy in a cave
Full of sweet ecstasy.'

'Rabbie Burns?' she said.

'Burns, my stormy eye! Made it up m'self.'

Verse, now, on top of the vision he had created on her kitchen wall. Never mind what sort of a sea captain he was: what sort of a man was he?

Ezra Hark had been asking himself much the same question. Unlike Sophie he couldn't keep it to himself. He waited until the captain had left, presumably for another spell at sea, before raising one or two points with his landlady. What, for instance, was the relationship—the blood tie—between them?

Sophie fobbed him off with, 'Distant cousins. Quite a coincidence his coming here, don't you think?'

Hark thought it a most unfortunate coincidence. Meanwhile he had been doing some sums. The sea captain's last voyage had been, according to the man himself, to Genoa. But by Hark's humble calculations, it would have been impossible for the *Queen Anne* or any other ship—unless fitted overnight with steam engines and paddles capable of racing a ship along at fifty knots at least—to have made the round trip in the specified time. And concerning the last lot of presents the captain had brought back for Mrs Booth—decorated glass bottles for mustard, sugar and salt—they were manufactured in Bristol and, to the best of Hark's knowledge, obtainable nowhere else.

But Sophie refused to be drawn.

Chapter 17

Outwardly, at least, Sophie Booth continued to accept Billy for what he pretended to be—although some of his voyages sounded curiously like the Greek and Roman myths he had read or related to her.

While things like this gave her further cause to wonder about her sea captain, she was careful to accept only such lodgers who minded their own business. In this way, without realising it, she provided what Billy needed—the right atmosphere in which to mull over work in progress and think ahead as he started out on the most visionary—and the most vulnerable—stage of his career. As he sat with her in the sitting-room near the bay window, or took the air with her along the seafront, or half listened to the uninhibited chatter of the mudlarks, he was mentally at work. And so at Margate, without putting a pencil to paper or brush to canvas, he began to fashion what were to be some of his greatest pictures.

His only problem here was the confounded Bible salesman, who had been lodging with Sophie for so long that she hadn't the heart to send him packing. Hark was an increasing annoyance to her, too. Not that he doubted that Billy was a genuine sea captain. It was the nature of Billy's seafaring activities which he suspected, hinting to Sophie that the captain's inconsistent and chronologically inaccurate accounts of his voyages might arise from his need to conceal the true nature of his activities, which were undoubtedly nefarious and certainly illegal—smuggling, perhaps ... or, worse still, trafficking in slaves.

But Sophie still would not be baited.

Billy was well aware that Hark would dearly love to discover something that would discredit him: and while he got some satisfaction from putting the pest off the scent and taking a rise or two out of him, for the most part the man just irritated him—until an incident occurred involving the waterfront urchins.

It began when one of the urchins held up a Bible one afternoon and asked, 'Please, Cap'n, will ye read us a story out o' this?'

As Billy took the Bible from the child, he recognised it at once as one of Hark's. He smiled to himself, wondering if these ragamuffins had stolen it, until a quick run through its pages showed that it was a reject of the worst kind. Chunks of the Old Testament were reversed or completely missing, with thick wads of blank pages in their place.

'How'd you come by this?' he demanded.

'Mister 'ark,' the urchins chorused.

'Y'mean—he *gave* it to you?'

The urchins hesitated, looking at one another. Then one shook his head, and the others followed suit.

'You *bought* it?'

There was another hesitant shaking of heads.

'I trust you're not going to tell me that you've entered into an arrangement to pay him a penny-farthing per week. Not for this.'

The urchins again shook their heads.

'Then will you kindly tell me what you did?'

'We swopped,' said one of them.

'This,' asked Billy, holding up the faulty volume, 'you swopped for what?'

'A salmon,' another of the grubby youngsters explained.

Billy's face became thunderous. 'Damn his holy hide!'

Two nights earlier, on the evening before leaving on one of his rounds, Hark—who had always tried to ingratiate himself with his landlady—had made a big thing of presenting Sophie with a fine salmon. Receiving it with thanks, she had baked it for the evening meal, serving Billy a generous portion, every mouthful of which he had enjoyed. Now he wished that it was still in his stomach so that he could puke it up.

'Will ye draw us a ship on one o' them empty pages?' an urchin asked.

But Billy was too angry. 'I'll do you a ship or two another

time,' he said. 'Just don't let me catch you swopping salmon —or anything else—with Ezra Hark again.'

Back in the house, he exploded about it to Sophie; but she cooled him down, trying to make him see the funny side of it. She said she would make sure that Hark replaced the reject with a Bible containing the full text. And she did. Billy put the matter in the back of his mind but he didn't forget it.

His tolerance towards the Bible salesman, at a minimum after this, finally gave out altogether one morning when he came down to the sitting-room before breakfast and found Hark planted there. The previous night, Hark had let himself into the house and gone to his room while Billy and Sophie were out at a nearby tavern.

Throughout breakfast, Hark maintained an icy silence towards Billy. He was, however, punctiliously polite to his landlady and curiously solicitous—as if she might be in need of his protection. Billy was amused by the performance. Sophie, too. She caught Billy's eye when she passed behind Hark's back after removing his empty plate and pulled a comic face.

Shortly after breakfast, Sophie set out on her morning visit to market, leaving her two lodgers to relax in the sitting-room.

'Something's bothering you, Hark,' Billy began. 'What is it? Sales of the good book turned sour? Penny-farthings proving hard to collect?'

Hark scowled at him. 'I've said it before, and now I say it again: you, sir, shall burn!'

'I know,' Billy said, quoting the rest of a pronouncement on himself that he had heard before. 'Where the sinners are blackest and the fires of hell hottest.'

'I am more certain of it than ever I was.'

'You once said I'd drown, but I didn't,' Billy reminded him, with a grin at the spectacle of so much indignant righteousness emanating from one small man. 'Come on—you've got sparks flying off you. What's it all about?'

'I'll tell you what it's all about, if you're so greatly concerned,' Hark said coldly. 'Last night, sir, as I lay in my bed, I was woken by the sound of your uproarious return to this house.'

'Ah, that. We were three sheets to the wind.'

'I beg your pardon?'

'Three parts drunk.'

Hark grimaced in disgust.

'Both of us,' Billy emphasised.

With increased outrage Hark continued, 'I couldn't sleep. My ears were assailed by the sound of your—your—indecent cavorting.'

Billy was no longer amused. 'So that's it, is it? You were straining your ears and you didn't like what you heard. Well, let me tell you—it was all clean, normal and healthy.'

'Are you without shame?'

'Apparently.'

'Do you realise what you have done? You have mesmerised the good Mrs Booth with your insidious and foul seafaring ways. You have taken advantage of her hospitality—led her into vile temptation—dishonoured her.'

'Oh, lord!' Billy groaned. 'Can I believe my ears?'

But Hark ignored this, now fully wound up. 'Yes. Dishonoured her—that's what you've done. You are a ravisher of women, sir. A rogue and a villain.'

'Which would put me in league with them that take salmon from poor children in exchange for damaged Bibles.'

Hark gave Billy a quick sharp look but ground on. 'You cannot be allowed to continue your evil habits among decent folk.'

'I see,' Billy said with dangerous calm. 'And what are you proposing to do about it?'

'The remedy's quite simple.'

'Is it, now?'

'Yes, it is. You will gather your belongings and leave this house.'

'Ah!' Billy tried not to show his rising temper. 'And you will help me on my way, no doubt ...'

'I shall be delighted to,' Hark assured him.

'All right, Hark,' Billy said in a deceptively soft tone. 'You've had your say—now I'll have mine. First and foremost, I've had a bellyful of your high-minded spouting, and so—'

'You'll leave at once,' Hark said.

'No, Hark!' Billy roared. '*You'll* leave at once.'

Hark was flabbergasted. 'Me? Leave?' He looked at Billy with scorn. 'You don't know what you're saying. I have been boarding with Mrs Booth for many years and I shall continue to do so. It is *her* house, you know.'

'It is, is it?' Billy started for the door, suddenly in high good humour. 'Well, you just wait there a moment, Hark, old shipmate. I've got a little secret I'd like to share with you.' He went out of the room, calling back, 'Don't go away.'

Up in his room, Billy opened his travelling-box and took out two documents, one of which he placed in an inside pocket of his jacket. The other he rolled up and brandished in the air like a cudgel as he bounded down the stairs and back into the sitting-room.

Hark still sat there, now looking slightly apprehensive.

'It so happens,' Billy said, 'that I've been thinking of giving you the push for some time now.' And when Hark merely stared at him in silence: 'I'll leave you to glance through these papers while I take a walk.' He dropped the document into Hark's lap, where it began to unfurl of its own accord. 'You'll find the firm "Cobb and Gascoigne" mentioned. In case you can't work it out for yourself, they're my lawyers and they represent me in this matter.'

'What is all this?' Hark blustered. 'I demand to know.'

'You'll know soon enough when you've read that. I want you gone—you and your Bibles—before I get back in this house ... let's say half an hour. If you're still here, I'll have no hesitation in calling in a constable to remove you.'

Billy strode from the room and out of the house, making his way down to a low wall near the jetty where he could sit and keep an eye on the house and also be in a position to intercept Sophie on her return from the market.

He had expected Hark to make a fairly quick departure but he was not prepared for the swift and complete surrender of the Bible-hirer, who soon rushed out of the house and ran with coat-tails flying to the field to catch his pony, working feverishly to hitch the animal to the trap and then dashing in and out of the house with pieces of luggage and boxes of Bibles, all of which he piled haphazardly into the trap before scrambling up to the seat and getting the pony started.

When Sophie came along the path and joined Billy at the low wall, she was only just in time to glimpse Hark whipping the pony into a fast trot and vanishing over the curve of the hill in the bumping trap.

'Will you look at that!' she gasped. 'Hark didn't tell me he was going off so soon.'

'When you left the house, he didn't know himself. Wave him goodbye. You won't be seeing him again.'

Sophie didn't understand.

'I've booted him out,' Billy told her. 'Bibles an' all.'

She stared at him, farther than ever from understanding what had been going on in her absence.

'I came out here leaving him something to think about. You'll see for yourself when we get in.'

Back in the sitting-room, Billy picked up the document and gave it to Sophie to examine.

'It's deeds,' she said, after a quick look. 'The deeds of this house. What are they doing here?'

'See if you can work it out.'

Searching the document for some clue, she said, 'The owner informed me some time ago that the property would be changing hands over my head. But he said it was to be of no concern to me. There would be no change, he said—and he was right. The agent has been collecting the rent as usual.' She looked at the document again. 'I don't know how you got hold of this.' And then she found something. 'Cobb and Gascoigne ... Are they the new owners, then?'

'Not really. They're my lawyers. Nominees for me in the purchase. No more rent now, Sophie. And no more lodgers—unless you want 'em. Except the owner, of course. It's a surprise I'd been saving up.'

She stared at him for several long astonished moments, and then she burst out laughing. 'Oh, you wonderful man! What surprise will you be springing on me next?'

'I do have another, as a matter of fact,' he said, trying to look straight-faced, his eyelids heavy and his mouth drooping a little.

'I'm not sure I can stand another just now,' she said.

'Are you prepared to try?'

'I'll do my very best.'

He took the other document from inside his frock coat and held it up.

'More deeds. The tenant of The Boat Inn don't know it, but he's also got a new owner. Amongst other things, it struck me as being a good investment.'

It was too much for Sophie. She sat down in the nearest chair and shook her head in wonder.

Chapter 18

Lord Egremont's death brought the peaceful sojourns at Petworth to an end, and the haven at Margate became all-important. The inspiration Turner found there was reflected in the work he did in the painting-room back at his gallery. He began to advance farther into those private forests of light where his visions lurked and beckoned, waiting to be captured.

In the evenings, at Margate, Sophie loved to drop into the public room of The Boat Inn with her seafaring lodger; and it was a source of great delight to her when Billy got the tenant-landlord going on his pet obsession—the mean-minded tyranny of the mysterious owner of the establishment.

Billy would ask whether the landlord was any nearer learning the owner's identity, and the conversation would go much the same way every time.

'No—not a solitary inklin'. I've 'ad another of me monthly meetings with Mr Morley, but he still don't give nothin' away,' the landlord would complain. 'The owner wants every pint pot an' drop o' ale accounted for.'

'Sounds a very miserly person to me,' Billy would observe.

'That's it—miserly!' the landlord would say.

'I trust you'll tell him, if ever you get the chance.'

'I'll tell him all right. To his face, too.'

'I can just see you doing it. Can't you, Mrs Booth?'

But Sophie would be speechless trying to stop herself from laughing.

The atmosphere was usually lively, and it grew distinctly boisterous one night when some sailors from a ship moored in the harbour came ashore and joined the company. Billy was up on the table, conducting the community singing of sea shanties, when one of the legs gave way. As the table collapsed, he tumbled down into the crowd, the singing disintegrating into laughter as he lay sprawled on the floor.

Pushing his way through the hilarious customers, the landlord finally reached Billy and stood over him grimly. He normally treated him with the respect due to his standing as a sea captain, but he was not prepared to tolerate any nonsense from him, particularly as he'd had experience of this sort of over-exuberance in the past.

'You've been warned before, Captain,' he said.

Billy gave him a glazed smile of unconcern as he was helped to his feet.

'The owner don't stand for this sort of thing,' the landlord went on, shifting the responsibility for being so strict on to this higher and unseen authority.

'To hell with the owner!' Billy cried.

The customers cheered to that.

'Let me tell you something, mate,' Billy said, breathing into the landlord's red and angry face. 'You're probably working your fingers to the bone and breaking your back just to keep some drunken ol' misery in grog. So to hell with him!'

The customers cheered again.

But the landlord was adamant. 'That'll be enough, Captain. You'll 'ave to pay for the damage. Owner's orders. Otherwise you don't never set foot in 'ere again.'

'Ain't this just normal wear and tear?'

The customers thought it was, and said so, but the landlord had received his instructions and was not going to deviate from them.

'I'm sorry,' he said firmly. 'The owner don't allow for nothin' like that. You'll 'ave to pay.'

It was a shame and a disgrace, the customers claimed, as Billy swayed about and searched through the change in his pocket, eventually thrusting a coin into the landlord's hand.

'Here. Take this. I hope it makes the ol' skinflint happy.'

The landlord gulped in astonishment as he gazed at the sovereign in the palm of his hand.

'Make very sure he gets it, too,' Billy added; and the landlord found himself looking into a pair of unexpectedly sober eyes.

Sophie was still laughing about it half an hour later as she held Billy's arm and steered him the short distance home.

'Come along, you old skinflint,' she whispered into his ear. 'Time you were abed.'

Chapter 19

For a short time now, life ran relatively smoothly. The critics had, for the most part, been either perceptively kind or entirely silent—although there had been an injured howl from John Eagles after Billy had allowed himself a little dramatic licence in one of his paintings, removing Shakespeare's Juliet and her Nurse from Verona and putting them on a balcony overlooking St Mark's Square in Venice instead. Sarah had not been sighted, nor had a shot been fired from that direction. And Billy had managed to turn a blind eye to the situation with Hannah and the state into which the Queen Anne Street gallery was falling.

All of these things, and the success of the hideaway at Margate, combined to bring about a dangerous mood of exuberance and optimism which coincided with the annual exhibition at the Royal Academy. Billy sent in three entries; and then, on the last of the Varnishing Days—when the artists were free to add finishing touches to their paintings—he arrived by horse-cab from Queen Anne Street with a fourth. It was three feet by two and a half feet in size, and it was entirely concealed in a cloth wrapping.

Billy's appearance anywhere in the art world always created a stir, especially among the young painters. On this occasion, it was with the rolling gait of a seaman that he entered the Academy and waved vaguely in reply to all the greetings. He held the picture by its frame through the cloth and treated it to a jaunty swing as he set about locating the space that had been allotted to him.

'Over this way, Billy!' someone called.

It was little William Etty, R.A., who was pointing to a space close to one of his own entries—a nude.

'What have you got.hidden there?' Etty asked as Billy came over and stopped beside him.

'Ah-ha!'

Billy placed his mystery entry against the wall, still within its cloth wrapping, then opened up his travelling-box and took out a palette, brushes, gallipots, jars of powder, small bottles of oils and spirits, bladders of colour and—most essential for such a social occasion—a bottle of sherry. Finally, he dipped into the box for two small tumblers and proceeded to pour two drinks, one of which he handed to his fellow Academician.

'Good health,' he said to Etty as they raised their glasses to each other.

'Good health, Billy,' Etty replied, taking a quick sip. 'But don't keep us in suspense. Hurry up and let's see what you have there.' He spoke on behalf of himself and a group of young artists and older contemporaries who had gathered in the wake of Billy's arrival and were now joined by a number of prowling critics and sundry official busybodies.

As Billy put his tumbler on to the floor and unhurriedly peeled back the cloth covering the picture, the onlookers pressed in closer to see what the most adventurous painter of the age was unveiling this time. But when the cloth finally came away, all they saw was a handsome gilt frame containing nothing more than a blank canvas. Except for a grounding of white, it was quite bare.

While there were exclamations of amazement from others, Etty gave a loud shout of delight and cried, 'What's the name of this one, Billy?'

'I'll have to get it done before I can decide that, won't I?' Billy said. As Etty and the others realised that Billy intended to paint his entry on the spot—something no one to their knowledge had even attempted—they watched in disbelief.

Billy hung the blank canvas in his space and then backed away from the wall so that he could look over the paintings already in position around it. Etty's nude glowed on the left, a touch of gold rippling through the ripe greengage of her flesh tints; on the right was a darkly composed view of St Paul's Cathedral; above his space was a fox-hunting scene; and below it, a riotous flower piece.

Having sized up the immediate opposition, Billy set his

palette with his beloved yellow and other hues from the warm end of the spectrum.

Before getting down to the task, he refilled the two tumblers with sherry; then he tilted his beaver back off his forehead and set to work swiftly. Something in his performance defied the eye. The colours could be seen to be applied to the surface, yet they took root and bloomed so quickly that it was as if part of their iridescence had sprung straight out of the stuff of the canvas itself at the touch of his brush: drifts of sheer colour, the first hints of a meadow with a rising sun, and then a dawn scene full of delicately muted lambence that began to steal the sparkle out of all the pictures on the wall.

Etty made several attempts to get on with his own work, managing to apply a little more of the final bloom to the skin of his nude; but presently he gave up and watched. Although he held certain reservations about Billy's work, for the most part he thought it miraculous—and this was impudent magic.

'I'll borrow a dab of that orange you've got there, if you don't mind,' Billy said, his eye catching the colour on Etty's palette; and without waiting for permission, he whipped the orange away and fixed it on his own picture.

To the majority of the onlookers, what Billy was doing was a wonderful prank—as it was to Etty. Not only was he openly matching his skill against the opposition, but he was also quite obviously cocking a snook at tradition—and that meant at the members of the strait-laced 'old guard'.

A number of these esteemed persons were drawn to the scene by the excitement of the crowd. And among those horrified to see what was to them a public act of artistic sacrilege was the Reverend John Eagles.

'I've always said it,' he murmured to two of his disciples. 'There's insanity in that fellow's work—and now you see it in the man himself.'

This was said too far away for Billy to hear, but he had keyed himself to the reactions of his audience and he sensed the change in the atmosphere behind him. Swinging around, he sighted the enemy.

As Eagles started to move on, registering his low opinion of what was happening with a look of infinite contempt, Billy —in his present over-stimulated, almost manic, state an easy prey to impulse—cried, 'One moment, your Reverence!'

Eagles stopped, and Billy adopted the flowery and somewhat incongruously gracious manner of speech that went with his sorties into the higher levels of society. 'Here am I, the "over-Turner", willy-nilly defying the rules and upsetting all the cherished conventions, while it is left to truly responsible lovers of art, such as yourself, to uphold and defend the great traditions. I'd like to drink a toast to you, and I'd be highly honoured if you'd join me.'

The onlookers were amazed at Billy's friendly overture to a man who had always attacked him so savagely, and Eagles found himself unable to refuse without seeming churlish. He indicated that he accepted the offer—but his attitude was one of monumental wariness.

Billy dipped into his travelling-box for another tumbler and, fumbling about as he filled it, he rose and thrust it into the clergyman's hand. 'May this,' he said, raising his own tumbler, 'pour, as it were, a little oil on troubled waters.' He downed his drink.

Anxious to get this unpleasant business over and done with, Eagles did likewise with his. Only part of it went down his throat before he spluttered and began to spit the liquid out.

'Gone down the wrong way, your Reverence?' Billy inquired with a ludicrously exaggerated air of innocence.

In something between a croak and a whisper, Eagles gasped, 'Linseed oil!'

'How very clumsy of me,' Billy said, glancing down in mock dismay at the sherry and linseed oil bottles as if they had deliberately deceived him.

An explosive burst of laughter from the crowd and a wild whoop of joy from Etty echoed through all the other rooms, bringing more people hurrying in to see what the uproar was about.

Eagles coughed into a handkerchief and wiped his mouth, and as it became evident that he was going to say something everyone grew quiet for him—but no one was prepared for the outburst that followed.

'You despicable lout!' he began as his two companions tried to draw him away. He knocked their hands aside and went on, 'You desecrate our art, you corrupt the young with your hideous muck—you'll stop at nothing!' And then, as his friends secured a stronger hold on him and started to move him, he shouted 'What else can be expected of a congenital lunatic who leads a shady double-life with whores!'

A shocked silence followed. Then the crowd melted away in embarrassment. Etty alone hovered on, almost in tears.

Billy stood with a defiant grin on his face, but the outburst had left him numb. He slowly turned his attention to the dawn scene on the wall—and in his eyes the soft incandescence turned into a sulphurous seething, as if it had become the open door of a furnace. Through it all a shape loomed—that of his mother with the anchor raised to strike—and he clamped his eyes shut to destroy the image.

Taking up his brushes and palette again, he attacked the painting feverishly, applying harsh and lurid purples. The picture underwent a swift and vast change, becoming a violent storm at sunrise—a scene similar to one that had been stored away in his visual memory since seeing it at sunset on his last visit to Venice. Once again he tried to face up to his mother's madness, to pin it down and dispel it by painting its symbolic image in the form of an outline of a tree, making it black and setting it starkly in the foreground, caught in a tortured pose.

He exhausted himself. Etty carried over a stool and made him sit on it and replenished his tumbler with the last of the sherry; then he took a closer look at what had become of the blank canvas since it had been placed here. The present painting was the sort of work by Billy which Etty had disliked and called fiery abominations; but now that he had seen something of how such a painting came into existence his opinion was undergoing a rapid change.

'Don't let it bother you, Billy,' he said. 'Eagles had it coming to him—every drop of it.'

At first, confusion showed in Billy's eyes. He seemed to be working out why he was here and what he had been doing. Then, when it caught up with him, he jumped up and crammed his materials in a jumble back into his travelling-box. He lifted the wet canvas off the wall and began to wrap the cloth around it.

'That's a marvellous piece of work,' Etty protested. 'Surely you're leaving it to hang.'

'I've got three pictures hanging in the great room already. That ought to be enough for Eagles and the rest of 'em to blaze away at.'

He returned, dazed, by horse-cab to Queen Anne Street and dumped the wet canvas in the bottom room of the gallery; and for the next few days he remained in the house, powerless to do anything. Hannah brought him food, but he only picked at it then pushed it away. Newspapers and journals with reviews of the exhibition were delivered, but there was little joy in them for him. The critic of one of the leading art magazines mounted a patronising attack, calling his works frenzies and claiming that his talent was running riot.

He was so low in fighting spirit by now that he was ready to believe that the critic was right; and it was in this frame of mind that he eventually made his way to the steamer wharf and went back down the river.

Chapter 20

Billy's original plan had been to leave on a sketching tour of France immediately after the Academy exhibition. This would have meant a month or two away, so he had told Sophie that he was going on a lengthy voyage. But now, after little more than a week, he was back.

'Ran into some sticky weather,' he said by way of explanation.

Sophie would have been prepared to believe from his appearance that he had been shipwrecked. It wasn't the first time he had come back beaten and defeated, but he had never been as bad as this. Just to speak seemed to involve him in a great physical effort, and even his facial expression seemed to have undergone a change. That he was suffering was obvious, and it upset her not to be able to do anything positive about it. But she had always accepted him as she found him, without asking questions, and she could ask none now. She simply did the best she could for him by being on hand to provide the care and companionship he needed, but it took a week before he showed signs of beginning to shake off his lethargy and despondency. It began with a stroll outdoors, and after that his recovery hastened to the extent that several mornings later he offered to go to the market for Sophie.

There was a fine drizzle, so he took his umbrella. He enjoyed walking under it, as it seemed to add to the protection he sought in his seafaring disguise. The day was grey, but his eyes seized on touches of colour: the breast of a robin matched the rust-red sails of a yawl bucketing along out in the bay; the blooms of a laburnum glowed as if soaked with wax distilled from clean yellow candlelight; and the market itself he found a feast of colour, with all the fruit and vegetables glistening with wetness.

On the way back with a laden basket he dipped his umbrella to the urchins peering out from under upturned boats and the locals standing back in doorways out of the weather. It wasn't until he was back in the house that he realised he had not received a single greeting in return. Not so much as a solitary wave. He hadn't given it conscious thought at the time because he had been aware that everyone was sheltering from the rain. But now, in retrospect, he could see and recognise the looks they had all given him: still and tense, restrained and respectful, even servile—the same sort of looks that he had received when he had swaggered into The Ship and Bladebone at Wapping only to learn that Sarah Danby had been there.

As he planted his umbrella in a big earthenware jar in the hallway to drain, he saw that there was another wet umbrella in it already. A woman's umbrella. And it wasn't Sophie's. He knew then with a chill sense of foreboding that Sarah was in the house.

He found her in the little-used parlour with Sophie, her eyes greeting him with a bold gleam as he entered. She was still remarkably handsome and robust, and the excitement of tracking him down had brought a healthy flush to her cheeks.

Sophie watched them eyeing each other and said with a flat formality, 'This lady introduced herself as Mrs Danby. She assured me you would know her.'

'What else has she been telling you?' Billy asked.

'Virtually nothing—except that I would receive a full explanation on your return to the house.'

Billy realised then what Sarah was up to. She had been talking to the local people and the urchins already—that was why they had looked at him as they did—but she had saved Sophie till last so that she could rip his masquerade to shreds in her presence.

'Well, I'm here,' he said, trapped and admitting it. 'What's she waiting for?'

Sarah draped the airs of the grand lady about herself and began in the stagey voice that had so often plagued Billy. 'I have been asking questions in the locality,' she said, addressing herself to Sophie. 'It would appear that this gentleman is known in the neighbourhood as a sailor.'

'A sea captain,' Sophie said, curtly correcting her.

'Forgive me, yes. Captain Booth, is it not? Some sort of relative of yours? And I expect you've been hearing all about his voyages and adventures.'

'The captain can be a most informative person,' Sophie replied, more aware than ever of imminent disaster. 'Now what is it you want, Mrs Danby? I've waited patiently long enough to hear.'

'How long have you known this man?'

'That is not the point. Why are you here?'

Sarah would have dearly loved to prolong the preliminaries, but she was astute enough to see that Sophie was not going to stand for much more.

'Very well, then, Mrs Booth: I'll put it to you this way.' She paused for dramatic effect. 'Have you ever, by chance, heard of a painter of sea and landscapes called Turner?'

Billy felt naked and sick, unable to look at Sophie even though her spirited reply surprised him.

'Are you suggesting that it would be unlikely for a person in my station to know of such things?'

'Certainly not,' Sarah said, but it was exactly what she had been trying to imply.

Something was crystallising in Sophie's mind—something she shied away from, wanted to reject; and so she found refuge in words, talking only to Sarah, going into careful detail to postpone the inevitable culmination of all this.

'As it so happens,' she said, 'I *have* heard of Turner. And not only that: I have seen something of his works. I came to London from Scotland as a young woman and I was employed for a time in the service of Sir John Leicester at his town house in Hill Street. Once every so often, as a special privilege, we were given leave to enter his gallery and look at the pictures hanging there. I recall that among those said to be most highly prized by Sir John were many paintings by Turner. Indeed, in my mind's eye I still see them to this day. Some were among the most beautiful things I have ever seen. Others—scenes of storm and wind—well, to be truthful, they rather terrified me ...'

Sophie's voice trailed off even before Sarah spoke.

'He can be a terrifying man.' With a limp theatrical gesture, Sarah allowed her hand to droop in Billy's direction.

And now Sophie could avoid it no longer. Her mind flew back. She could see Billy using leaves and flower petals to turn a blemish on her kitchen wall into a spontaneous vision. It was still there. Fresh coats of whitewash had worked around it and left it isolated, its colours faded to dingy browns and greys, a greasy film of cooking fumes all over it. This alone should have been a clue.

Much more that had puzzled her fell into place. For a long time she had been prepared to learn that her lodger, now her landlord, was someone rather out of the ordinary as far as seafarers went—but not a man whose name was a household word. It was too much to try to reconcile so quickly the man she had come to know with the public figure he really was. She felt she had been cheated. That a relationship such as theirs should have blossomed on lies somehow cheapened what had happened between them. She had an acute sense of something precious having been lost. Her main impulse was to get away and leave this virago Sarah Danby to settle whatever dispute she had with the artist, so that she could be alone to sort out the turmoil in her own mind; but it was not in her nature to surrender to any woman without some show of defiance—certainly not to anyone as hell-bent on trouble-making as this one. As for Billy, she couldn't even look at him.

When she spoke, however, she had her voice well under control. 'Would you be kind enough to explain, Mrs Danby, why it is you've gone to so much bother to tell me this about Mr Turner?'

It seemed to Billy that Sophie's formal use of his surname meant that the wonderful relationship that had existed between them had already been sealed off behind some door in the past.

'He's been deceiving you, surely,' Sarah said.

'And, pray, what concern is that of yours?'

This wasn't the reaction Sarah had been anticipating. 'Haven't you any idea of how he treats the unfortunate women who become involved with him?' she said, suddenly finding herself on the defensive.

'I know how he treats me,' Sophie replied coolly. 'Until now, I have had no cause to complain. But since you raise the matter, I must confess that I can now well imagine him being provoked into acting otherwise.' And as Sarah stiffened at the thrust, she pressed on. 'You were determined to push your way into this house and wait. It may be that there is some specific and valid reason for your visit, but it would appear to me that your sole purpose is to create mischief.'

'How dare you!' Sarah exploded. She searched for other words but could only repeat, 'How *dare* you!'

Sophie simply turned her back on Sarah and at last faced Billy. He searched desperately in her eyes for some understanding but found none.

'If this were my house,' she said—and she might have been talking to a complete stranger—'I would waste not one second in asking Mrs Danby to leave. But it's not; and that being the case, I must ask you to excuse me.'

And she left the room.

Billy swung on Sarah. 'So you've run me to earth again. If Gascoigne or Morley have slipped up once more, this time they're finished.'

Sarah laughed. 'Those two fools! They take infinite care to conceal every scrap of paper whenever I see them. I find it most insulting—and quite unnecessary. Once I made up my mind, I had little difficulty in tracing you. I happened to be at the gallery talking to that miserable Hannah when you were shut away in one of your moods, brooding over something or other. All I had to do was wait around and follow you to the wharf when you left. I saw you board the Margate steamer. I spoke to a seaman—a *genuine* seaman—and he told me where you went. A day or two later I came down here by coach, and since then I've been staying at a comfortable inn while looking around and finding out things.' She paused. 'I'm rather sorry for Mrs Booth.'

'Sorry for her?' Billy said in disbelief.

'Why not? Quite obviously she's fond and proud of her "sea captain"—although I have the feeling that she resents having been taken in by your impersonation.'

Billy held on to his temper with an effort. 'Look here, Sarah,' he said, 'you'd better get out of this house good and quick, or I'll be giving you a helping hand. You've done what you came for, so now get out.'

Sarah saw the anger in his eyes and became wary of it. She had heard about the violence of his attack on the shady dealer at his gallery, for which she had been largely responsible in encouraging Hannah to sell the proofs. And her own experience of his temper had convinced her that there was a good deal of his mad mother in him. She had no wish to stay any longer, having—as Billy had just said—accomplished what she had set out to do. Or almost accomplished it. As she reached the safety of the doorway, she turned to say, 'You're the owner of the inn next door, aren't you?'

Billy was thunderstruck. 'Who told you that?'

'No one said anything as such. It was just something I picked up when I spoke to the tenant-landlord. The owner he was complaining about sounded very much the same odious sort of person who was the owner of that disgusting place at Wapping.' Sarah's laugh was brittle. 'I'm afraid the landlord's petrified now that he finds he's been insulting you to your face all this time.'

'Out, out, damn you!' Billy yelled. 'Get out!'

But Sarah had already gone from the room and was moving along the hallway. In other circumstances her last piece of news would have devastated Billy, but now it was of only minor importance in comparison with his need to be alone with Sophie and try to make his peace with her.

He remained in the parlour until Sarah had collected her umbrella and left the house, slamming the door behind her. Then he went to the parlour door and called down the hallway, 'She's gone!', thinking that Sophie must be in the kitchen.

But there was no reply. And when he called again there was still no reply. So he started to look for her.

She wasn't in the kitchen. She wasn't in the house at all. And her hooded cloak was no longer on the stand in the hallway.

Chapter 21

Billy left the house hatless and without his umbrella. The drizzle had turned into a steady downpour, and the rain soaked his hair and ran down the crags of his face. He didn't know where to start looking. With rising panic, he tried the waterfront, then some of the alleys in the town, and finally the path along the cliff-tops. Perhaps Sophie had rushed off to young John and her first husband's family at Deal.

He sat on a bench to try to think. From here, with Sophie, he had watched the sun go down up the river; but now rain obscured the view and misty clouds sagged below the level of the cliffs. He was ready to believe that he had lost Sophie for all time and that he might never set eyes on her again.

As the raindrops sputtered down, bubbles appeared and vanished in a muddy puddle at his feet. Bubbles. He had filled his paintings with them. He had used them to represent men and women. After all, the life-spans of men—whether kings or scavengers, painters or urchins—were little more than so many bubbles when set against the infinite scale of the ages. He wondered now whether he was right to have reduced human life to anything so transient. This did not allow for all the disappointment and suffering that could be crammed into any one lifetime.

In his anxiety to heal the breach with Sophie, he was ready to tell her everything in the hope that she might understand and forgive. Everything. His boyhood over his father's shop. His first steps as an artist. His mother's madness. The entanglement with Sarah. The tragedy of Hannah. The loss of his father. And all the hounding—not just from a cast-off mistress and narrow-minded enemies but from his own inherent instability.

The rain seemed to stop falling directly on him, yet it was still seething down into the puddles around him. And he could still hear it, although it had taken on a hollow drone. Looking up, he saw a blurred menacing shadow above his head. He brushed the water that dripped from his hair away from his eyes and realised that what he had taken for the apparition of his mother with a raised anchor was a woman with an umbrella.

'Sophie!' he said.

'You went out without this,' she said quietly; and he saw that it was his umbrella she held.

'Where were you?' he asked.

'Back at the house, wondering what had become of you.'

'You vanished.'

'I went back.'

His coat was sodden, and Sophie saw the gleaming flecks of colour—dried paint—standing out sharply on the wet cloth. How was it she had never guessed what he was when he had been speckled with these dabs? They were on his hands too. She had seen them there before but without attaching any significance to them since she had believed him to be a seafarer—a man from a world where paint and boats went together.

'Your next-door neighbour knocked to tell me where you could be found,' she went on, drawing his attention to the man who stood back some fifteen yards from them. 'He was worried about you out here alone in the downpour.'

The tenant-landlord of The Boat Inn gave an anxious smile and bowed in Billy's direction.

'He's got nothing to worry about,' Billy said roughly. The landlord's servility made him cringe with embarrassment at the torment he must be causing the man. 'I asked for all I got from him.' He caught the searching look in Sophie's eyes. 'No need to look at me like that. I'm no different.'

'I'm sorry,' she said softly. 'That is not so. Indeed, I find that it is as if I had discovered I had been sharing my bed with —with a nobleman.'

'Sophie, for God's sake, I'm nobody. My Dad was a hairdresser, a common barber. M'mother ended her days in the madhouse. That's all I am.' And seeing bewilderment in her eyes now, if no actual forgiveness, he went on, 'I was afraid it would wreck everything if ever you got to know the truth. So I just let things sail along as they were. We were happy enough, weren't we?'

Avoiding a direct answer, she said, 'Look at you. You're soaked to the skin. This is no place for us to be talking. Come along back to the house.' She had to help him to rise as his legs had become weak.

They stopped to speak to the tenant-landlord, Sophie telling him that he wasn't to worry and assuring him that nothing he had said would be held against him. Billy nodded his confirmation of this.

Inside the house, she took him up to the sitting-room and made him remove his clothes in front of the fire. Then she helped dry him and wrapped him in a blanket. She made him sit down while she brought up some hot broth, and she insisted that he must sip some of it before he discussed anything further with her.

'Now,' she said at last, seating herself in the chair opposite him and folding her hands in her lap, 'if that overbearing female is called Mrs Danby, then she's no' your wife.'

'No, thank God,' he said. 'At least that's one torment I was spared.'

He stopped, realising that Sophie's expression was inviting him to explain; but suddenly the power of speech seemed to have deserted him.

'I'm a poor talker,' he said, trying to account for his hesitation.

'On the contrary!' Sophie replied with a short, tart laugh. 'I seem to recall many a voluble account of voyages and adventures at sea.'

'Yes, yes, I know what you mean,' he said heavily. 'The truth of the matter is I'm right enough when I'm just spouting what comes into m'head; but the moment I really start to *try* talking, I'm done. Ask 'em at the Academy. I was Professor of Perspective for more years than I can count before they drummed up the courage to give me the push. I got into hot water for failing to deliver the prescribed number of lectures. The fact was, I used to do m'best to dodge 'em. I was down here at Margate towards the end of m'term, walking the sea-front and passing the time o' day with all and sundry when I should've been up the river giving my lectures. I worked hard enough at what I wanted to put over, too. Got up whole stacks o' charts and the like to help me out—but it never came to much more than one long bumbling mumble. In fact, I'm told the only man who understood me was stone deaf.'

He grinned wryly, and Sophie had to smile. This was no stranger talking.

'That's better,' she said.

And suddenly he was telling her everything.

Chapter 22

By the time Billy had finished talking the weather had lifted. From where she sat, Sophie could see parts of the cliffs on the far side of the bay shining white where the sun had broken through on to them.

Even though Billy had been ready to tell all, it was not possible for him to cover everything in detail at once; but he managed to convey more than enough to answer the main questions Sophie had been asking herself—enough to make her realise that while he may have concocted some fearful storms to support his seafaring masquerade they were mild in comparison with the real-life tempests from which he had sought shelter and sanctuary both before and after discovering this Margate haven.

She was thinking about this as she gazed at the cliffs, hardly conscious that Billy had stopped. Worried by her silence and unable to interpret it, he made another effort to excuse his prolonged secrecy. 'It wasn't as if I never thought of telling you the truth ... or didn't want to ...'

'Please!' Sophie cut in, giving him her full attention now. 'I may have been taken in by the way you presented yourself to me, but I have no right to complain. After all, I started off by telling you a lie the very first time we met.' And as Billy looked puzzled, thinking back to their first meeting some seven years ago, she went on, 'Did I not say that I was a widow?'

'You did,' he said, still puzzled.

'As regards Henry Pound, that was true. But not, I fear, where Mr Booth was concerned. He was here with me from time to time but, as it so happened, only when you were away off on your voyages. He died two years ago on a visit to relatives of his in Scotland. So you see, Captain, I have done my share of deception in the past also.' Laughing at the recollection, she added, 'I often think about it. One moment there you were standing on my doorstep as miserable as a month of wet Sundays—the next as perky as you please. That, I am sure, was what brought out the devil in me and made me say I was a widow.'

A faint grin relieved the anxious expression on Billy's face, only to be replaced by a look of alarm as something struck the roof overhead with a sharp crack and rattled loudly as it rolled down and fell over the edge.

Sophie sprang from her chair and rushed to the window to see a small crowd of local men, women and children, including the tenant-landlord of The Boat Inn, gathered in front of the house—apparently in the hope of catching a glimpse of the great man they now knew to be within. And she realised what it was that had landed on the roof when she saw a young man stooping to pick up a stone from the ground; but as he prepared to hurl it, the tenant-landlord ran at him and knocked it out of his hand. At the same time, another man began to cavort about in a grotesque loping dance. Sophie asked loudly, 'What in the name of goodness does that grown male imagine he's about?'

Tightening the blanket around his shoulders, Billy left his chair and joined Sophie by the window. He said wearily, 'He's aping a madman, that's all.'

'Aping a madman?' Sophie echoed, not understanding.

'I'm the son of a woman who was put away in Bedlam, ain't I?'

'You mustn't say that!' she said. Then she realised that he wouldn't want the subject evaded after being so frank to her about it. 'What if you are? How on earth would that man down there know about it?'

'You've met Sarah, haven't you?'

'She told them?'

Billy nodded. 'With a parting shot like that in the barrel, can you imagine her leaving without firing it off?'

'What a wicked thing to be doing!' Sophie said fiercely. 'I should have torn out her red hair!' She moved swiftly back near the fire to drag her cloak off the back of the chair on which she had hung it to dry. 'It's just as well she's gone—but I'll no' stand for another second of the behaviour of those brutes out there!'

'No need to worry any more about 'em,' Billy murmured, still at the window.

'Don't worry,' Sophie said, coming back with her cloak. 'I said I'd put a stop to it—and I mean to do just that.'

'It seems to be over now,' Billy said, pointing through the blanket to where a group of men, women and children were brandishing folded umbrellas and sticks as they chased off the man who had been performing the mocking dance.

'Good for them!' Sophie said approvingly. She put down her cloak but kept watching until she was quite satisfied that there would be no more stone-throwing before turning to Billy and saying quietly, 'There'll be precious little peace for you here from now on.'

'Ah, well,' he sighed, taking refuge in seafaring phraseology, 'I'll just have to cast off m'mooring lines and set sail.'

'But where to?' she inquired with gentle understanding. 'You must have some place to go.'

He shrugged under the blanket and looked at her steadily for a moment before going back to his chair by the fire. Sophie remained where she was, waiting for him to reply. When he did, he spoke without looking at her. 'I'll put it to you simple an' straight, Sophie. I don't give a damn where I go—Timbuctoo, if you say so—as long as it's you an' me together.'

For once her control of her emotions very nearly crumbled. She turned back to the window so that he would not see her face and tried to compose herself.

'We've no secrets between us now—have we?' he asked.

She managed to steady her voice as she answered his question with a question of her own. 'But what would a man such as yourself be wanting with a woman the likes of me?'

'Sophie, Sophie,' he said. 'After that mud-slinging man of God threw all his moonshine and madness at me, what would've happened to me if I hadn't come down here on the steamer and found you?'

Still unable to look at him, she sneaked the knuckles of a hand up to the corner of her eye to brush away a tear. 'What about the house?' she said.

'You've got no other lodger at the present. Let's just shut it up and leave.'

'I suppose we could do that.'

'Then you'll come?'

She didn't answer immediately, and he watched her anxiously.

'Did you have anywhere in mind?' she asked presently, still with her back to him.

He heaved a sigh of relief. 'The state I'm in now, I hardly know who the devil I am, let alone where to go.'

'I know of a quiet place at Greenwich. We could be together there and work matters out.'

'Then that's where we go.'

She was now in control. 'Very well, then. We'll catch the early coach in the morning and avoid as many people as we can.'

And so on the following day at around noon they reached Greenwich and made for a cosy inn situated near the bank of the Thames at a point where the course of the river starts to swing to the north in a tall loop on its way to the sea.

There they took a room as husband and wife.

Chapter 23

If it had been left to him, Billy Turner would have remained indoors all day at Greenwich, just sitting around and brooding as he had done in the past after returning to Margate beaten and depressed. But Sophie managed to inveigle him into taking a walk at least once a day, although for most of the time he shambled along totally oblivious to his surroundings—even the closeness of the river failed to stir him out of his lethargy.

One late afternoon several days after their arrival, Billy responded to Sophie's tactful coaxing and set out with her along the river-path leading north to the top of the loop. On their left, the western sky was set with powerful pigments in readiness for a rich sunset.

Opposite a boatyard, where the air was filled with a clang of hammers on steel plates—a sound of the times now that iron hulls had begun to replace those of wood—a small rowing-boat had been hauled up on to the shingle and turned into a riverside shop to cater for the needs of the workmen, offering for sale oysters, winkles, cockles, mussels, crabs, lobsters, smoked herrings, shrimps and cooked prawns.

Sophie was well aware that when Billy was down in spirits his interest in food vanished, but she also knew that he had a special liking for cooked prawns. In the hope of stimulating his appetite and getting him interested again in life in general, she bought a pound of prawns and carried them off in a plaited rush basket. Billy dragged a big red handkerchief out of a pocket and tucked it firmly between his chin and cravat, and as long as Sophie kept handing him the prawns he peeled and ate them; but to her disappointment he showed no real taste or enthusiasm for them.

This was an evening without wind, and the sails of a

merchantman hung flat as it was towed upstream on the incoming tide by a team of oarsmen in a long boat. The light was now beginning to change over the river as the sun started to set.

Still peeling and munching the prawns, Billy and Sophie reached the top of the river loop near the marshes. When here before they'd had the place to themselves, but this time a young man was already there. He had a lightweight collapsible easel in front of him on which was propped a small canvas, and he was facing the gathering sunset and painting it.

Billy came to a halt the moment he saw what was happening; and Sophie at once sensed that something that had been rendered dormant by his depression had clicked into life again, the movement of his head becoming quicker as he glanced from the canvas on the easel to the sunset itself, then back again. Taking a sharp bite of the peeled prawn in his fingers, he chewed rapidly, throwing the remnant away and reaching out his hand for Sophie to put another in its place. This he peeled swiftly, tearing off the skin, biting hard and chewing even faster. The sight of someone painting—especially trying to pin down one of his favourite subjects—was reawakening the want to work. He moved closer to the easel; and as he saw what was going on to the canvas, he had to grapple with an overpowering urge to start here and now with the young painter's own materials.

Sophie remained a few yards behind Billy, watching his transformation with wonder.

When the young man—a mathematics tutor from the Royal Naval Academy at Greenwich—became aware that he was being observed, he interrupted his painting to take stock of the uninvited audience and found himself receiving a genial nod from a rather disreputable-looking man in his late fifties at least, while a little farther back a plumpish woman beamed a rosy smile. The young painter decided that the man must be some sort of worker from the boatyards in the locality and that the female was his woman. He had an intense dislike of prawns, the smell of them being enough to revolt him without the sight of one held up between thumb and forefinger in the man's left hand. To make matters worse, bits of flesh from prawns previously devoured stuck to the red handkerchief under the man's chin. The youth registered his lack of appreciation of the company with a cold glare and a pointed turning of his back.

The snub was wasted on Billy. In two quick bites he devoured the remaining flesh of the prawn as he moved to within reaching distance of the canvas.

Incensed by the increasing nearness of this spectator, the young man turned furiously towards Billy and found him striking an extraordinary pose, standing rigidly with his right hand held aloft and a piece of stiff coral prawn skin held in his fingers. Billy greeted him with a sublime smile, while Sophie quite innocently added to his fury by laughing with delight.

Billy's control now left him. After another glance at the sunset and another at the young man's canvas—making a lightning comparison between the splendour of the real and the crudeness of the copy—he reached forward, turning the prawn skin into a makeshift palette knife as he whisked an offending blob of scarlet off the canvas and then, with a swift return stroke, reapplied the paint elsewhere to better effect. The skill with which this was carried out, and the aptness and delicacy of the result, was as yet utterly lost on the would-be painter.

'Let me show you, lad!' Billy now cried, snatching the palette out of its owner's hands. After tossing the shred of prawn skin over his shoulder, Billy mixed the colours on the palette and applied them to the canvas with his fingers and the edge of his hand. Then he wiped his fingers on the red handkerchief and used the cloth itself to help spread the paint. Such an approach would have given the young man's art teacher apoplexy, if only because it seemed to show such contempt for the sanctity of art: but the youth found himself hypnotised by the display and reduced to a state of dazed awe by the result. However sacrilegious the manner of execution, what now showed on the canvas was by any standard a magnificent concept of a river sunset.

Sophie was ecstatic. Apart from the times Billy had made drawings of ships and rigging for the children at Margate, she had glimpsed Billy the artist in action only twice—the first time when limited to a big brush, a bucket of whitewash and a kitchen wall, and the second time he had created a picture on that same wall with improvised pigments. But she still couldn't bring herself to believe that those pictures in Sir John Leicester's house had been painted with such abandon.

'There, now,' Billy said, backing away a little from the canvas so that he could match it up better with the original up the river in the western sky. 'More like what it ought to be, ain't it?'

The young man couldn't speak for a moment. Then, in a reverent whisper, he said, 'You're Turner.'

Sophie groaned inwardly. To be recognised now, when he so needed to remain anonymous, could well plunge Billy back into the depths again.

But he merely laughed and shook his head, saying, 'Me, lad? You must be jesting. I'm just an old salt.'

The youth stared disbelievingly at him and then back at the canvas. Billy winked at Sophie.

Any dispute over his identity was suddenly forestalled by a piercing shriek which came from the top of the loop in the river. It swept past them, spreading out over the water—a sound monstrously alien to the soaring beauty of the sunset.

All three turned towards the source of this intrusion and saw two fiery devils—black and green tugs—dragging their captive—a noble spectre that was once a mighty ship of the line—into the reflection of the sunset. The aged derelict moved with quiet dignity, its spars bare, its three masts and timbers a ghostly silver-grey in the closing light of day, while the squat bodies of the tugs were slung low between the shoulders of busy paddlewheels and their tall, blackened funnels spat out gouts of dark smoke and flame.

At least, that was what two of the onlookers saw. To Billy it was something else: those funnels with their menacing plumes were twin versions of a familiar apparition, and now they had a helpless victim in tow.

The young man said, 'It's the old guard ship from the Nore at Sheerness, sir.'

'The ol' *Téméraire?*'

'Yes, sir.'

'The Fighting *Téméraire,*' Billy said, recognising her lines and using the name by which the man-of-war had come to be affectionately known. 'She was at Trafalgar,' he went on, for

Sophie's benefit. 'Second in line to Nelson's *Victory*. A 98-gunner; one of the greatest.'

'They're taking her up to Rotherhithe,' the young man explained. 'To a yard there to be broken up.'

'Broken up?'

'I fear so, sir.'

'Damn their hearts! Why ain't there a law to stop 'em putting a ship the like of this to such a death?'

From their viewpoint at the water's edge, the new and the old—the ugly energetic tugs and the stately veteran—began to pass; and as they did so, they crossed the blaze laid on the water by the sinking red-gold orb of the sun.

Billy rummaged in his pockets and took out a sketchbook and pencil and then began to sketch rapidly in a style that only he would be able to interpret later, gathering what were little more than scrawled signposts as aids to his visual notes. As he did so, he moved along the waterfront to try to keep pace with the old ship and the tugs.

As Sophie followed, the young man joined her.

'Surely I cannot be mistaken, madam,' he said. 'That gentleman *is* Turner the great R.A. He must be.'

Sophie just shrugged. 'He told you he was an old salt. The truth of the matter is that I have known him for a number of years, and always as a sea captain.'

'A sea captain?' The youth was incredulous.

'Aye. Master of a vessel called the *Queen Anne*. Perhaps you have heard of her.'

'No, I can't say that I have.'

Sophie shrugged again and, leaving the young man with his bewilderment, followed along just behind Billy until he gave up trying to keep pace with the gliding veteran and its two angry escorts. As he stood making his final notes, he said to her, 'I want to start work on this, so we'll be wasting no time now getting settled in.'

'Settled in?' she asked, revelling in the change in him.

'Yes,' he said, abrupt and breezy. 'I knew there was somewhere we could go, but I couldn't bring it to mind till now. Thought of purchasing a particular house there. Had m'lawyers investigate and make an opening offer. Must've guessed I'd be needing something like it.'

'Are we going somewhere else, then?'

'That's right. Up the river, past the heart of London. Known the spot since I was a boy. You can keep track of the sun from the time it gets up in the morning till it goes down at night. Chelsea.'

PART THREE

Chapter 24

To look out from the compact three-storeyed house at Chelsea was to Billy like being within a big eye commanding a sweeping view along the river and out across the green shimmer of Surrey. The house stood back from the north bank of the Thames, almost opposite a wooden jetty—a good spot for fishing judging by the numbers of local men and urchins who cast their lines from it. On one side of it was a blacksmith's forge and on the other a bakery shop. Along the front edge of its roof was a high ornamental grille which was partly overgrown with creepers, giving a concealed view.

Household goods and working materials were brought down in two main stages. After being taken to a drayman's yard in King's Road, they were picked up by another drayman for the second stage. In this way, direct deliveries were avoided. The reverse procedure operated when anything had to be sent up to town by cart, the garden gate at the back being used for all dispatches and deliveries.

As for the properties at Margate, Billy decided to hold on to them for the time being. While he was working at Queen Anne Street, or in the countryside or abroad, Sophie could go down there to the house and have young John over from Deal.

His painting-room in the Chelsea house was on the top floor, directly underneath his eyrie on the flat rooftop, its windows facing south over the river. As he had told Sophie at Greenwich, he didn't want to waste any time getting down to painting the *Téméraire*; so while she got the house in order and made her first attacks on the weeds and overgrown shrubs in the secluded walled garden at the back, he prepared a medium-sized canvas—one that his father would have called the 200 guinea size—and made his start.

Now that Sophie knew who he really was he could be himself when he was with her; it was a liberation. It was reflected in his work, and he didn't need anyone else to tell him in order to know that the picture was a gem.

When he called Sophie up to the painting-room to take a look at it, she stood with her hands clasped over her bosom for some moments without saying anything.

'Recognise it?' he asked.

'You've turned it into a dream,' she said quietly.

He liked that.

'And if my memory is correct, have you not sunk one of the tug-boats?'

He liked that too, and laughed. 'Yes—and I've put a bit of new moon up in the sky for luck.'

'So you have,' she said, and then studied the painting again in silence. One side was all sunset. On the other side was the one spiteful tug with the veteran in tow—still proud and erect, full of faded glory and undaunted by neglect. 'Most of all,' Sophie went on presently, 'I love the old ship itself. It's just as if it was all made of pearl and moonbeams.'

That pleased him more than anything. Some of the picture's symbolism was deliberate, some instinctive—such as the tug with its tall black funnel topped with a mass of dark smoke and flame, and the old ship still afloat to the last despite the hateful thing that had a grip on it. Sensing something of himself in it, he told her the title he was thinking about: *The Fighting Téméraire tugged to its last berth.*

'I won't worry it any more now,' he said. 'In due course, I'll get it up to the gallery and have Hannah arrange its framing.' He put down his palette and brushes. 'Come on, now. Let me show you some of the walks round about this part of the world.'

Sophie had been out many times on her own here at Chelsea, but this was their first stroll together. They took their time, exploring the bank and its paths up towards Hammersmith before turning back. As they approached the house, a lumbering waterman with a lantern jaw stumped off the jetty with his catch of fish and brought up his hand in a powerful salute. 'Evenin', Ma'am,' he said to Sophie, and to Billy, 'Best respects, Admiral.'

Billy returned the salute, but he was so startled by the title that he nearly missed his footing.

Sophie gripped his other arm to steady him and said close to his ear, 'Careful now, Admiral, or you'll be turning turtle on yourself.'

'Admiral, eh?' Billy said. 'Seems as if I've been promoted again.'

'Aye. You have.'

He took a closer look at her, realising from the way she spoke that she had played some part in this.

She laughed and explained. 'The baker next door was asking me what sort of a sea captain you were, and before I knew what I was doing I was saying "Not a captain—an admiral." Things like that soon get around the neighbourhood. Besides, "Admiral" suits you better.'

And so he became Admiral Booth to the local people, who added something of their own by nicknaming him Puggy because of his squat build and brisk manner.

Quite apart from the protection that Billy felt this disguise gave him, Sophie enjoyed the deception—an extension of the game she had learned to play with him at The Boat Inn at Margate, when only he and she knew the identity of the owner.

They settled into a harmonious routine. Several mornings a week Billy would get up very early, wrap himself in a heavy coat, climb through the trapdoor on to the roof and sit in a low cane chair to watch the miracle of another day breaking. If anyone happened to be out and about at this hour, the grille and the creeper screened him from prying eyes.

Billy would have liked to float dampened sheets of paper in the early morning skies, like kites, and let them soak themselves in the hues of the sunrises. In his mind, he could see this happening as clearly as if it were really possible; but since it wasn't, he would go below to his painting-room, where he settled for the next best thing with his colours and a pail of water.

It was a unique performance. He worked in sequence with four identical drawing boards, each having a grip—a sort of handle—screwed on to its back. Each board also had a sheet of drawing paper fastened to it. His procedure was to pick up each board in turn, dip it in the water and set it on the floor, leaning it back on its grip. When all four had been so treated, he would go back to the first and quickly wash in the main watercolour hues, repeating this with the other three. Then, going back to the first board again, he would work along, painting the next stage of each until four similar versions of the same sunrise or dawn scene emerged. There might be further dips back into the bucket, or he would dab the paper with a wet cloth or rub it with a dry cloth to obtain his effects. Once this first set of four sheets had been completed, he would remove them from the boards and lay them out to dry, after which four new sheets would be attached in readiness for the next round. Having finished this part of his day's work, he would go down to breakfast.

Later in the morning he might decide to potter at the end of the jetty, under the pretext of fishing. Here he frequently sat alongside Josh Mottram, the waterman who had first addressed him as 'Admiral', striking up a bantering friendship with him. Josh, a keen angler with a booming voice that could startle birds off the trees on the south side of the river, mixed religion and rum in strong measures—which led Billy to find a sort of justification for him in the works of Byron. After reading the relevant passage aloud to Sophie one evening, he repeated it to Josh the next time he saw him: 'There's nought, no doubt, so much the spirit calms as rum and true religion.'

Josh grunted. If he had heard of the notorious Lord Byron he would have been reluctant to accept such a man's philosophy. But the poet was unknown to him so he didn't dispute the observation even though, being sober at the time, he showed no great interest in accepting it.

There was a new set of urchins here to be introduced to the prism Billy still carried around in his pocket, and he sometimes took out his copy of Izaak Walton on the jetty and used his big magnifying glass, or fitted on his spectacles, to read out passages describing the ways and habits of the river's coveted inhabitants—the chub, the pike, the perch, the eel, the roach, the dace, and even the minnow and the stickleback.

Sophie was well satisfied with the way things were going

and felt that her vigilance could cope with anything that might happen at Chelsea; but when Billy went into town or down the river she could not completely quell her fears.

A few months after settling in at Chelsea, Billy decided to smuggle the canvas of *The Fighting Téméraire* to his gallery in a new item of travelling equipment—a long leather telescope-case. Before he fitted the leather lid over the end of the case that morning, he slipped a round bottle of rum down the middle of the rolled-up canvas.

At the sound of a loud knock on the front door, Sophie said, 'That will be Josh.'

Billy slung the leather case from his shoulder on its strong strap and picked up his travelling-box, which had become dented, scarred and stained from its many tours and voyages. Sophie helped him to the door to hand him over to the waterman. She had come to accept Josh as a staunch friend; he still had no glimmering whatsoever of Billy's real identity.

'Boat's awaitin', Admiral,' Josh said, with his usual big-handed salute.

'I'm under way,' Billy replied, acknowledging the salute.

Sophie gave him a warm peck on the cheek. 'Have a good time,' she said.

'I've a sneaking suspicion I might,' he answered, with a mischievous grin.

He tried to wave to Sophie from the front gate, but the combined weight of the leather case and the travelling-box made him unsteady.

'Help ye wi' the telescope, Admiral?' Josh offered.

But Billy declined. 'Never fear,' he said. 'The ol' ship's righted herself again.'

A number of urchins spotted the jocular Admiral Puggy emerging, and they crowded around to escort him to the boat tied up at the jetty steps.

'Can ye really see the man-in-the-moon wi' watcha got there, Admiral?' one of them asked.

'My boy, you'd be truly dumbfounded at the strange sights you'd see if I unpacked this long case,' Billy answered earnestly.

Josh helped him down into the stern of the boat, stowed the long case and the travelling-box, then took the oars. Billy waved to the urchins on the jetty and then across to Sophie, who stood in the doorway of the house, continuing to wave to her until she was lost to sight as the boat merged with the river traffic on its way downstream to the Westminster jetty.

Billy intended to return that night, so he arranged to meet Josh at a waterfront tavern called The Duck and Dolphin, near Blackfriars, in time to catch the tide.

Meanwhile, at Chelsea, Sophie busied herself about the house. But though she kept herself fully occupied, she couldn't throw off a feeling of unease. She sensed that the more Billy let his imagination go, the more vulnerable he grew —and that his vulnerability could well start him on the path taken by his mother. She felt that she could adequately protect him only by being with him. Her disquiet continued throughout the day and into the evening, when the tide started to flood up the river again under the cover of darkness. She sat up to wait but eventually fell asleep in her chair—until, towards midnight, she was woken by two lusty voices singing a shanty out on the river.

Smiling to herself and greatly relieved, she put on her cloak and picked up a lantern she had left burning on a low wick and hastened out and along the jetty.

As the boat started to emerge out of the darkness, she heard Josh issuing an order, his voice thick and slurred with rum. 'Eashy on yer shtarboard oar, Admiral.'

'Aye, aye, Josh,' came the dutiful reply.

Seeing Billy doing the rowing while Josh slumped on the boards at the boat's stern, his long arms hanging out over the side and one hand trailing a near empty bottle of rum in the water, Sophie burst out laughing—but it was more in relief than in amusement.

Chapter 25

When Billy decided to give *The Fighting Téméraire* an airing at the next Academy exhibition, Josh rowed him down to the Westminster jetty once again; and, as was usual now, they arranged to meet later in the day at The Duck and Dolphin.

As Billy bounced along Regent Street in a horse-cab on his way to his gallery, his thoughts were on what final touches he might add to his entries once he had them at the Academy; but he would have been less sanguine had he known at that very moment Sarah Danby was at Queen Anne Street in a room off the lower part of the gallery, complaining to Hannah and trying to discover his present whereabouts.

Sarah had to raise her voice to be heard above the mewing and growling of the many cats, and the wet, lascivious sound as they ate the liver which Hannah was slicing on the table and then scattering on the floor.

'He still won't give me back what he took away when Georgiana was married. And now he's cut my allowance *again*. By another pound a month. Just because I happened to go down to Margate and find him there. That man really must be as mad as they say he is.'

She loomed over the tiny, shrunken Hannah, who now looked the older of the two despite being so much younger.

'He's found himself another hideaway, I'm sure of it. And that appalling Scots woman must be with him. When I last took a look around at Margate, I was told that she spends a little time there, then she isn't seen for months. She's with him—obviously.' The sound of the cats eating and the smell of the liver revolted her, and she had to fight to wave of nausea as she persevered. 'He's altered his will again—Morley let that much slip this morning. We're still in it, I gather—but one day we could wake up and find that that common trollop has had everything made over to herself. She has a way with him. And you've only got to see how he looks at her to know that he just dotes on her.'

The years of withdrawal had placed Hannah beyond jealousy, and she made no comment.

'If you'd only keep your wits about you,' Sarah went on, 'you might find out where they are.'

Hannah spared Sarah a contemptuous glance. 'And if I did—would I tell you?'

'You'd be stupid not to.'

As Hannah made no response, Sarah took out her frustration on an oil painting leaning against the wall—an ethereal Roman scene in a chunky gilt frame. 'Look at that eyesore!' she said, indicating it with a wave of her hand. 'How much is he getting for this sort of thing?'

Hannah paused in her slicing to glance at the work. 'Up to 350 guineas,' she said listlessly.

'350 guineas—and he cuts my allowance by a pound a month! The money that man must have! How much is he worth now? You must know.'

Scraping the last pieces of liver off the table, Hannah gave a tired shrug but said nothing.

'Why don't you wake up and try to find out?' Sarah's patience was being strained beyond control. She nodded towards another picture—a pastoral landscape, smaller in size than the Roman scene and easily identifiable as an earlier work. 'He used to sell things like that for twenty guineas. What do they fetch now?'

Hannah looked briefly. 'He paid 250 for it.'

'He *paid*?' Sarah said in exasperation. 'Don't be absurd. That's one of his, surely.'

'He keeps buying them back.'

'What on earth are you talking about?'

'He says he has some plan in mind to give them to the nation.'

'The nation, indeed!' Sarah laughed harshly. 'That's *very* noble of him. But what about us?' She thumped the table with her fist. 'Oh, my God. That lunatic will be the ruin of us.'

The cats suddenly stopped their evil-sounding masticating. Heads rose. Ears sharpened. Eyes glittered. But not because Sarah had raised her voice. The cats had heard footsteps in the lower gallery, followed by Billy's voice. Now Sarah and Hannah heard them too.

'I've got five in all to be loaded,' he was saying to the cabman, who had come in with him. 'Here's the first of 'em.'

On the verge of sailing out to confront Billy, Sarah changed her mind. She might find out more by hiding and listening. With a warning to Hannah not to say anything, she moved behind the door, steeling herself as the cats arched their backs and hissed when she stepped too near unconsumed pieces of their food.

Hannah, vaguely aware that it would be in the best interests of her cats to play along with Sarah, passed through the open door to the lower room of the gallery where Billy was going through the accumulated letters and accounts stacked on the main table. There was also a list of messages Hannah had taken in his absence. He picked this up, giving it a brief glance before shoving it and the mail into his pockets.

'I'm only in town for today's varnishing,' he said, without looking up at her. 'I might be back in time for Opening Day—but then again, I might not.'

'I need some money,' Hannah said flatly.

It had become impossible for her to ask him for anything without making it a blunt demand, and because of this he could never part with a penny of his money to her without some show of ill grace or resentment. The accusation with which she habitually looked at him brought out the very worst in him.

He fumbled in his pocket and found two half-sovereigns which he dropped on the table, then he turned away and helped the cabman load the last of the paintings.

Sarah waited in the side room until the five paintings had been loaded on to the horse-cab, coming out only after it had moved off from the front of the house with Billy back on board.

'You little fool!' she raged at Hannah. 'Why didn't you ask him?'

'Ask him what?' Hannah said without interest, lifting a big pewter jug of milk from the table.

'Heaven give me strength! What do you think? Where he stays when he's not in London, of course.'

'Would he have told me?'

'He might have said something—given something away without realising it. He's not always as clever as he thinks he is.'

Refusing to be drawn into an argument, Hannah started a round of the bowls on the floor, filling them with the milk—but her hands shook so much from excessive drink that she splashed some of it over the frames of stacked paintings and rolled canvases.

Some of the cats began to lap the milk, filling the gallery now with another sound which Sarah found as distasteful as it was unnerving. Other cats began to wash and preen themselves. A few just sat staring at her.

She left the gallery in disgust, but with a determined glint in her eyes.

At the Trafalgar Square premises of the Academy, Billy handed his five entries to the porters for delivery to the hanging committee and was seized upon by Etty, who escorted him off to a luncheon around the corner in St Martin's Lane. Billy had been asked to this function but his invitation was unopened in his pocket along with the other letters he had picked up at the gallery.

The luncheon went on for hours, during which a great many bottles of wine and spirits were emptied. Half a dozen of those present were artists who were exhibiting, so it was a boisterous party that returned to the Academy to enliven the social proceedings on this the first of the three Varnishing Days.

Billy checked where his entries were hanging. He often complained about the committee's positionings, but this time he was quite satisfied. *The Fighting Téméraire* was on the wall at eye-level, below a space allotted to another artist's entry. While awaiting its arrival so that he could see how it affected his own picture, he went through into an adjoining room where he had two views of Rome hanging side by side for contrast—one ancient, one modern. He set his palette with scarlet, orange and yellow to add some final touches to them. Etty was at work nearby on one of his nudes and he had a bottle of sherry which he insisted on sharing with Billy.

Some time and a considerable number of sherries later, Billy sauntered back to see if anything had yet been hung above *The Fighting Téméraire*. A painting was now in position—a drawing-room scene of a mother and daughter by the Scottish painter Geddes—a muted picture that did nothing to distract the eye from the fires of his own sunset. Having satisfied himself on this point, he went back to potter about alongside Etty.

When Geddes himself arrived he was dismayed to see how insipid his painting looked above that light flaring underneath it. He set to work at once on the first stage of an attempt to heighten the colours in his picture by painting in an eye-catching Turkish carpet over what had been a subdued floor. Consequently, when Billy took another look at the picture after wandering through various rooms, he found that Geddes had overlaid the floor with a base of bright crimson.

As Geddes was nowhere to be seen, Billy asked a neighbouring artist where he was and was told, 'He's so anxious to make something strong out of that carpet of his, he's gone to Bond Street to borrow a really fiery one to copy.'

'Ah-ha!' Billy chuckled. This was just the sort of challenge he liked. He hurried back to where he had been working near Etty and then returned with some of his materials and equipment. Working and rubbing, he stood close to his picture as he built up the hues of both his sunset and its reflection on the water, using the colours already on his palette—scarlet, orange and yellow.

'There!' he said, only a few minutes later, standing back to survey the result. 'I'm very much afraid that when friend Geddes returns he'll have to raise his guns and shoot a lot higher if he's going to keep me within range.'

Pleased with himself, Billy left the other painters in this

room laughing and remarking on what he had achieved so swiftly. Back beside Etty, he helped polish off what was left in the sherry bottle; and then he and Etty packed up and started to leave.

As they passed rather unsteadily through the main vestibule on their way out, they met Geddes struggling in with a rolled carpet sagging fore and aft over his shoulder.

'This a magic carpet?' Billy inquired, giving it a sharp pat that jolted the carrier and set him momentarily off balance.

'It's Turkish—and a rare one, at that,' Geddes said with dour belligerence.

'Best of luck with it. But it'll need to have some hidden power if it's going to do the job you're wanting of it.'

Billy gave Geddes an airy wave, and he and Etty staggered out of the building and into the dusk, passing the Reverend Eagles as he entered. In the sherry glow of good humour, Billy gave him a wave too.

Back in front of his picture, Geddes discovered what Billy had meant. The final impromptu touches to *The Fighting Téméraire* may have been done in a matter of a few minutes, but they reduced the impact of Geddes's picture to a point where nothing could redeem it.

A single horse-cab waited in front of the Royal Academy, and a porter jogged away to fetch another.

Billy and Etty tried to focus on the one that stood there. In the chill evening air, their powers of vision seemed to have doubled and each played out a similar role in a brief pantomime—closing one eye, then the other, and squinting to get a good fix on the position of the real horse-cab of the two they could see. To Billy, it seemed to detach itself from its axles and float and split and divide and become two cabs again.

'You go first,' he said to Etty.

So Etty made the first attempt to get on board, but he veered badly, lost his balance and sprawled on the ground.

'Wrong cab!' Billy cried, squinting again before trying his luck. 'I always take the first one,' he said, referring to the front cab of his particular double image of horse and vehicle.

As Etty tried to focus on him from a prone position, Billy tumbled into the cab and struggled up on to the seat. An imperturbable footman closed the cab door and waved the cabman on his way.

Billy waved to Etty—two of him, in fact—who was being assisted to his feet by the footman. Then he shouted his instructions up to cabman. 'Blackfriars!'

'Where in Blackfriars, sir?'

'I'll tell you where in good time.'

'Very good, sir.'

As the cab trundled along the Strand, Billy poked his head out of the side and drank in the cool air. He tried to sort out the matter of his double vision by searching the early night sky for the evening star. But when at last he did manage to locate it, he got a blurred double twinkle. After trying to reduce this to the one point of light, but without success, he looked to the rear and used a cab that was following as an object to help him bring his vision back to normal focus.

Passing St Clement Danes and starting along Fleet Street, Billy began to feel that he was being deliberately followed by the other cab. Presently he became certain of this; and while his vision remained faulty, his thinking became clearer—particularly about the cab behind him. It was Etty, of course. At the luncheon the figure-painter had teased him about where he hid his mistresses. Now Etty was trying to find out.

'Ah-ha!' Billy said aloud.

'Beg pardon, sir?' the cabman called down.

Billy told him to whip the horse along and take a roundabout route towards the waterfront tavern The Duck and Dolphin; and as the cabman took him at his word, skidding around sharp corners and down alleys, Billy was thrown about.

Although the pursuing cab duly increased its speed, Billy's drew ahead into a slightly longer lead; but the other held on. It was just as Billy had expected: Etty could be a persistent little devil.

Enjoying it all, Billy shouted up his next instructions to the cabman and passed a crown up to him for his trouble. He was about to make a quick exit.

As the cab slowed down to take a sharp alley-corner, Billy opened the door and, grabbing his travelling-box, jumped. He rolled into the archway of a passage leading to The Duck and Dolphin and came to rest jarred but unhurt.

His cab sped on.

In the shadows Billy laughed. He had given his cabman directions and enough money to ensure that Etty had a long chase ahead of him.

Moments later, the other cab slowed down to take the same turning, the horse's hooves braking against the cobblestones. As it thundered past the archway, Billy saw someone leaning out of the window and peering ahead. Not Etty, but Sarah.

Chapter 26

After that glimpse of Sarah, Billy remained subdued at The Duck and Dolphin, waiting with Josh for the tide to turn so that it would be behind them on the way back to Chelsea.

The customers here accepted Billy as a minor admiral who had suffered some disaster in his career, and was content to pass his retirement in obscurity. As for what Josh believed, Sophie had encouraged him to think that the Admiral went down the river from Chelsea to see his legal advisers, and that the rolls of papers he sometimes carried in the long telescope case were charts; so Josh had come to assume that Billy was caught up in some Admiralty Court of Inquiry that might drag on for years.

Billy said nothing to Sophie of the Sarah incident upon his return, knowing that it would worry her; but it remained in the back of his mind as proof of Sarah's determination to root him out whenever and wherever she could.

Three days after the Varnishing Day, Billy went back into town for the Academy opening, paying particular attention to Geddes's Turkish carpet. It was well done, but the picture as a whole was still left in the shade by the torch that blazed below it. Billy spent an hour or so at the Academy before going to Queen Anne Street, where he stayed on to work on a set of drawings for which a publisher had been waiting patiently. At the same time, he made plans to visit Venice again, feeling the need to immerse himself in some of that city's peerless light for the work ahead.

Before returning to Chelsea, he collected some of the critics' reviews of the Academy exhibition. He expected to find the usual abuse aimed at the five targets he had left hanging there, but there was one exception. And so, on arrival at

Chelsea, he was able to say to Sophie, 'The old ship weathered the storm.'

The Fighting Téméraire had been acclaimed. It was described as a poem—which gratified Billy deeply, poetry being inherent in his whole approach. He had been consciously striving for such an effect. The painting was also likened to a symphony. And that pleased him too. One way and another, the favourable reactions to this one picture were so great and unanimous that he was able to ride out the attacks made on his other entries, which came in for the usual abuse; they were described as mad exaggerations, daubs, absurd antics, and caricatures —the man responsible for them, of course, being obviously out of his mind.

Sophie was relieved to have him home again. Although she didn't know about Sarah's most recent attempt to trace him, she was conscious of the threat that Sarah represented. And as Billy continued to play the part of the Admiral to the full, she intuitively grasped that a little madness, carefully controlled, was the key to keeping him going. It was up to her, she felt, to see that the balance was maintained—and that meant protecting him from Sarah.

In this, she increasingly felt the need of a loyal and dependable friend to help keep watch; and she thought she may have discovered just such a one in Josh Mottram. Certainly he seemed devoted to the 'Admiral'. Often, the more he drank the more fiercely religious he became, tending at such times to break out into inebriated declamations of Biblical texts. Partly as a change from this and partly out of fun, Billy had taught him some chunks of Milton's *Paradise Lost*, so that of an evening, as they fished and drank side by side at the end of the jetty, Sophie would hear the waterman thundering away about the battles between the powers of Darkness and Light. It was because of his strong religious convictions that she hesitated to take him into her confidence. Asking him to help protect Billy might mean having to reveal that they were not husband and wife—and Josh was liable to be so scandalised that he might find it impossible to have anything further to do with either of them. For the present, therefore, she merely asked him to tell her at once if he spotted any suspicious-looking person lurking in the neighbourhood. Josh asked no questions and agreed readily, assuming that he would be keeping a weather eye open for some sort of Admiralty spy.

Despite this precaution, one of the last people Sophie ever wanted to set eyes on again—here or anywhere else—was delivered to her doorstep in all good faith and innocence by Josh himself.

She answered a knock on the front door one day to find Josh and a familiar figure standing there, with a pony and trap in the background.

'This gentleman would like to have a word wi' ye, ma'am,' said Josh as Sophie faced Ezra Hark. 'He works for the Lord.'

'Aye, I know,' she replied, eyeing Hark, who stood there with a self-satisfied smirk. 'Selling Bibles—or loaning them, rather—at a penny-farthing a week.'

'No, ma'am,' Josh corrected her. 'A penny-ha'penny. Ain't that so, sir?'

Nodding curtly, Hark said, 'My work takes me farther afield these days. Costs are higher.'

'Well, I have all the Bibles I want today, thank you very much,' Sophie said, making it dismissive. But she knew that she wasn't going to be rid of Hark so easily. She was aware, too, that Josh realised that there was an undercurrent to this exchange and was puzzled by it.

What had happened was that Hark had approached Josh near the jetty and explained his business. Were there any potential customers in the locality? Josh had at once obliged by listing some of the residents. As soon as he mentioned the Admiral and Mrs Booth, Hark had shown great interest, saying that he had once known a Captain Booth and would be glad to call at the Admiral's house if Josh would take him there—even though the Admiral was away.

Sophie wanted to get Hark inside on his own. She knew of at least one way of trying to handle him; but the situation was complicated by the presence of Josh. A certain doubt had been planted in the waterman's mind, and he would have to be given some explanation.

Before she could come to any decision, Hark cunningly said, 'It would appear that, as at Margate, no one here realises what an illustrious person they have living amongst them.'

Greater bewilderment spread over Josh's expanse of weather-beaten face, and Sophie said hurriedly, 'You'd better step inside. Both of you.'

As she took them into the front room, where there was a hazy view of the jetty and the river through the gauze curtains, she could see that Hark was beside himself with delight at the situation he had created. He could scarcely wait to expose her, especially in the presence of a God-fearing man such as Josh.

Sophie decided to get in first. 'I can see you're all in a lather of excitement, Hark, with a proven sinner such as myself at your mercy.'

'Come now, Mrs Booth,' Hark remonstrated with oily charm. 'If I hold anything against anyone, it's not you. Although I must confess I was totally amazed when I returned to Margate and learned the true identity of the Captain.'

'Admiral,' Sophie corrected.

'Ah, yes. Now, how did that come about?'

'Never you mind. Just answer me this—is it purely by chance that you come to be here?'

'As it happens, I've been asking myself that very question. No, I do not think so. This isn't chance. I thought I was merely extending my work into another locality: but now I wonder ... Would it not be more in keeping to believe that it was divinely ordained that I should come here.'

'For what reason?'

'To bring you to your senses, perhaps.'

Sophie snorted her disdain and turned to Josh. 'Before I moved to this part of the world, Josh, I was a landlady at Margate. Mr Hark was a boarder with me for some considerable time. I'll no' bother you with the details now of how he came not to be a boarder any longer, but he left. The Admiral was also a boarder from time to time, and he stayed. Indeed, he became my landlord. He's a man of wealth and —as you'll discover presently—of great note.'

Before Josh could make any comment, Hark asked, 'Precisely where is he, now that we're talking about him?'

'Well out of earshot, I'm happy to say. He's gone to Venice.'

Josh gaped. Venice! A month ago he had taken the Admiral down the river with his travelling-box and a worn carpetbag:

and he had imagined that the Admiral would be staying in town for a time so that he could be on hand for the day-to-day wrangling with the Lords of the Admiralty. But Venice!

'In order to make it clear to you precisely who the Admiral is,' Sophie went on to Josh, 'I'd like you to come upstairs with me.'

She led the way out of the room, along the hall and up the staircase to Billy's painting-room with Josh following obediently. Hark came behind him, more than satisfied with the way the truth was coming out. He was looking forward to the shock that awaited the gangling waterman. And he was not disappointed.

Josh stood absolutely motionless, almost in fear of what confronted him. A half-finished canvas of a misty palace was on the easel, while scores of watercolours—river scenes, cloud studies, storms, vistas, sunsets and sunrises—beamed their beauty and iridescence at him from all parts of the room. It was as if he had entered some sort of Aladdin's cave; and as his eyes slowly took in more of what was here he saw open bundles of sketches which, rolled up, he had taken for charts, and the long leather telescope case with a bolt of unused canvas sticking out of it.

Hark, too, was lost for words. At Margate he had learned the true identity of the man who had been his fellow boarder, but he had never seen his work.

Sophie allowed them time to take it all in.

'Ma'am,' Josh said presently, speaking in a hushed voice, 'does this mean it was the Admiral 'imself as done all this?'

Sophie nodded. She picked up a sunrise painting and pointed to the signature, but Josh shook his head; then she remembered that he couldn't read, so she said what it was. 'J. M. W. Turner.'

'Turner ...' Josh echoed uneasily, knowing that the name was supposed to mean something to him.

'You've heard tell of him, perhaps,' Sophie suggested.

Josh hadn't, but he could well believe that the man who had created such wonderful pictures must be a great and famous person; and he didn't want to appear ignorant in front of Hark. 'Aye,' he said. 'It's a familiar name is Turner.' And then, to sort out things in his own mind, he added, 'So this

Turner, ma'am, an' Admiral Puggy are one an' the same, is that it?'

'Yes, Josh. As for myself, I am just plain Sophie Booth. I have been widowed twice, and I use the name of my last husband. I'll have to shock you: but if I do not, then Hark here will do it for me. The Admiral and I—well, we're no' husband and wife.'

Leaving Josh to come to terms with this as best he could, she turned to Hark, who exuded pious triumph. 'You're looking very pleased with yourself,' she said.

'I wouldn't say that, Mrs Booth. Pleased? No, no, indeed not.'

'Well, whether you are or no', it matters little either way. You've had all the rope you're getting from me.' She paused, and a faint crease of concern showed between the Bible-seller's dark, furry eyebrows. 'For a long time now,' she went on, 'I have been in possession of certain information which I chose to keep entirely to myself. I refer to the manner in which you came into possession of all those cases of Bibles.' Hark looked wary. 'Why did I keep it to myself? That is probably because of the sort of person I am. It rather amused me since it seemed that, unwittingly, you may well have done a service to a number of sailors and marines stationed around the globe. You saved them from having to study those Bibles ... I see you understand.'

Hark was white-faced and silent; and as Josh glared at him as if suddenly in the presence of one of Milton's Angels of Darkness, Sophie continued, 'Those Bibles you kept at my house—they'd gone mysteriously astray between the naval stores at Sheerness and the ship on which they were due to be loaded. You can't deny it, Hark—I know.'

The man was incapable of denying anything. He licked dry lips as Sophie put her proposition to him.

'In return for my silence concerning your Bibles, I want you to swear that you'll never disclose to a living soul anything whatsoever about who you discovered to be living here. It will be a pact between you and your Maker.'

'On yer knees, man!' Josh commanded. 'Down on yer knees!' He placed the flat of a palm on the top of Hark's head to force him down, but the mere touch was more than enough to hasten the other's adoption of a praying position.

'I swear, I swear!' Hark affirmed hoarsely.

But this wasn't good enough for Josh, either. 'Repeat after me: Before God and my Maker ... I do solemnly swear ... that what I 'ave discovered 'ere this day ... I'll never disclose in no manner whatsoever ... to no livin' person ... until I reach the day of my judgement.'

Hark repeated this word for word and remained on his knees.

'That will be all,' Sophie said.

'Can 'e go?' Josh asked her.

'The sooner the better,' she replied. And as Josh grasped the back of Hark's coat and hauled him to his feet, she added, 'I'm sure he'll be able to find his way out of the house on his own.'

Hark needed no second bidding, racing out and clattering down the stairs.

Sophie and Josh went to the window. They saw Ezra Hark reach his pony and trap, get up on to the seat, snatch up the reins and the whip, and frenziedly lash the pony on its rump to get it going.

As soon as Hark was out of sight, Josh turned back to the wonder of the paintings. Sophie watched him closely. It seemed to her that it now depended on him whether or not Billy would be able to come back here and find his haven still secure. She was dismayed when at first the waterman began to shake his head slowly from side to side.

'No,' he said, speaking his thoughts. But his next words reassured her. 'The Almighty would never 'and out a gift the like of this to a man if it were wrong the way 'e lived.' He swung around and faced Sophie. 'Ma'am, what sort of life will it be 'ere for the Admiral if it gets out who 'e is?'

Sophie gave him a clear, direct look. 'No life at all, Josh. We would have to go far from here and try again somewhere else. Billy ... that is, the Admiral would—' She broke off and shrugged. 'What am I to do, then?'

'You'll stay where you are—that's what you'll do,' Josh said gruffly. 'I'll not be tellin' anyone what I've 'eard an' seen 'ere this day. And certainly not the Admiral 'imself.'

Chapter 27

Sophie now took Josh completely into her confidence, making a special point of describing the appearance of Sarah Danby in detail so that he would not fail to recognise her if she happened to come their way. Josh acted as though he had been entrusted with a precious secret of state; but Sophie could not be absolutely certain that she had made the right decision until Billy had returned from Venice. Then, when she saw the two men together, she allowed herself to breathe easily. She had made no mistake in trusting Josh. He gave no inkling that he knew who his seafaring comrade really was; and when they shared a bottle of rum between them at the end of the jetty, he behaved in the same way towards his friend the Admiral as he had before.

The majestic flow of the Cockney visionary's greatest period was now in full flood. Billy's pictures vibrated with colour and mystery, yet more often than not his revolutionary works, after having been displayed briefly at exhibitions, were brought back unsold to Queen Anne Street to be stacked with other masterpieces cluttering the main galleries and storerooms. Enemies such as John Eagles tried to discourage people from buying them, as Sir George Beaumont had done. To them, the unruly Turner was still a corrupting influence on both young painters and art in general. He was no gentleman, nor was he ever likely to be one. Yet he prospered—and made money from his orthodox works and his drawings and engravings for publishers.

At the Academy exhibition the year following his return from Venice he showed three pictures set in that city, all of which were well received by the critics. But other exhibits were said to be the fruits of a diseased eye and a reckless hand; and his version of the German home of young Queen Victoria's new husband, Prince Albert, was described as looking like eggs and spinach. It was claimed by some critics that he painted his pictures with a mop and bucket or simply set up his canvases and pelted them with eggs.

Without his Chelsea hideaway, it was now becoming impossible for him to ride out his reactions to the jibes and insults —they were having a greater effect on him and he was taking longer to recover after them.

During an intense working spell at the gallery one morning, Hannah crept into Billy's painting-room to tell him that there was a customer outside who was very anxious to deal with him personally.

'Not seeing anyone today,' Billy said. 'Not even the Duke of Wellington.' He had a score to settle with that worthy after learning that the Duke had turned away in disdain from a number of his pictures a few years earlier.

'But it's a couple. They've come all the way from Manchester.'

'Let 'em go all the way back.'

'They're talking about how much they plan to spend.'

'Let 'em spend it somewhere else.'

He accompanied each reply with a dismissive stroke of his brush across the canvas. At that moment he was engrossed with the first zephyrs that were to fill out the painted sail of the boat in the picture he was to call *The Sun of Venice Going to Sea*, which wouldn't be ready to exhibit for a year or two yet.

Hannah persisted, knowing that what she had to tell him next would jolt him out of his indifference.

'It's that manufacturer,' she said. 'The one your father said had done him down. Remember?'

Billy's painting arm was arrested in mid-air. He remembered all right—even the name.

'Murchison ...' he said. 'Is that who it is?'

Hannah gave a small nod of her head within the baggy bonnet. 'Him and his wife.'

Through the peep-hole bored in the door, Billy squinted out. He had never seen the Murchisons before, but what he saw now did full justice to the picture he had built up of them—over-fed, over-dressed and resplendent with vulgarity.

'Show 'em around,' he said. 'Let 'em see all they want.

I'll be out presently to deal with 'em.'

As Hannah left the painting-room, he set down his palette on the table and slowly wiped his fingers on a cloth. He had an old score outstanding in memory of his father, and the settling of it would be a token of his respect.

Meanwhile, out in the gallery, the general dilapidation of the place, the splendour and neglect of the paintings, the bedraggled hag who had shown them in and the presence of so many cats combined to unsettle the usually insensitive Murchisons.

'Look at that, Martha,' George Murchison whispered to his wife, his fingers thick with dust after grasping the frame of one painting in order to lean it towards them so that they could see the one stacked behind it. 'The state of the place, this stuff must be going for a song.'

'They say he always drives a hard bargain,' his wife reminded him.

'Not with what's here, surely. It's like a scrap heap.'

When Billy came out into the big room, the manufacturer took his wife by the lard of her arm and helped her across to him.

'Mr Turner!' he said, his voice oozing goodwill and cordiality. He clasped Billy's right hand. 'The great man himself,' he announced to his wife; and then he introduced her. 'May I humbly present my better half?'

Martha Murchison proffered a clutch of podgy fingers choked with rings, and Billy had to force himself to grasp them, giving them a brief perfunctory squeeze.

He found himself looking at a couple who demonstrated that in this day and age fate exercised very little discretion in the rewards it meted out. Thanks to the export of pots and pans to a growing Empire, this pair had more money than they knew what to do with and absolutely no taste in the spending of it.

'We've been passing a few memorable days with our good friends Sir Benjamin and Lady Small at their new home in Kingston. He's the railway magnate, you know,' George Murchison explained, summing up the vast wealth of Small, the modern Midas, in a gesture in which his hand flew upwards as if towards the top of a pile of gold standing so high that it was out of sight: 'Millions!' He then went on to reveal why he was here. 'Before we return to our home pastures, so to speak, we thought we might avail ourselves of the opportunity of acquiring some more of your pictures.'

'Ah,' said Billy with a polite bow. 'Those first ones you purchased—three, wasn't it?—were to your liking, then.'

'Aye, they were that,' Martha Murchison said, her face a rosy rump with a smile puckered in the middle. 'We have known some of our guests occupy the entire evening talking about 'em.'

'If we weren't pleased,' her husband put in, 'we wouldn't have come back, now would we?'

'About how much were you thinking of laying out this time?' Billy asked him.

'On the basis that it would be three, we had in mind the sum of 600 guineas. How does that strike you?'

There was a broad smile on Billy's face and a gleam in his eyes which the Murchisons took to be a twinkle and found encouraging. Hannah, on the other hand, considered Billy's attitude highly disturbing. She recognised the prelude to a storm and remained in the background, checking on the whereabouts of her cats so that she could safeguard them when the period of calm ended.

'Three of your very best, mind,' George Murchison said as Billy went to where some of the pictures were stacked against the wall.

'I'll hand-pick 'em for you,' Billy assured him, stopping by a large framed picture covered with a grey cloth. He patted it, setting loose a cloud of the years of dust with which it was saturated, but not as yet removing the cloth. 'This here,' he began, 'is called *Ulysses Deriding Polyphemus*. Does that mean anything to you?' He looked first at one and then at the other.

The manufacturer shook his head, but his wife said, 'I do believe I've heard the name.'

'You might well have done, madam,' Billy said. 'It's one of the many tales in Homer's *Odyssey*. Homer, the Greek poet. The story's simple enough. On his travels, Ulysses went ashore on an island—Sicily, in fact. A giant—a one-eyed Cyclops—trapped him in a cave. To escape, Ulysses had to get the giant drunk on his own wine and then put his eye out. Here you have what I made of it.'

He pulled the sheet away and, through a swirl of dust, the colour and light gushed out from the picture, just as it had done at its one showing at the Academy when the critics had complained that it was far, far too rich and daring.

The Murchisons cocked their heads from side to side, playing at being connoisseurs.

'Just what is the sun supposed to be doing?' Martha Murchison inquired. 'Coming up or going down?'

'It was dawn when Ulysses escaped on that ship.'

'Of course—dawn,' she said. 'And look what's up here!' she exclaimed, making a sudden find. 'A giant in the clouds!'

'That's him—Polyphemus—blinded. And it's a mountain crag he's reclining on.'

'So it is,' Mrs Murchison hastened to say.

'At the time I painted this,' Billy said, 'it was the thing to choose subjects from classical myths and legends of the Greeks and Romans.'

'You picked a good 'un for this, Mr Turner. Quite a tale,' said Murchison. 'And look what we have here,' he went on, pointing excitedly to where he had discovered silvery sylph-like figures swimming under the ornate prow of the ship.

'Nymphs,' said his wife.

'Nereids,' Billy said, perverse in his growing irritation with this woman.

'Of course,' she agreed embarrassed, unsure what the difference was.

'As far as classical subjects go, this here is one of my finest pictures. At the same time, I was just as interested in doing a big sunrise. What you see there is one of my very best.'

George Murchison actually licked his lips before declaring, 'This is one we *must* have.'

'How about a sunset to go with it?' Billy suggested.

'Capital idea!'

Billy felt like an outfitter recommending a suitable hat to match the frock-coat he had just sold as he led the couple along the gallery to where *The Fighting Téméraire* had been propped up since its return from the Academy exhibition. Those last quick additions of scarlet, orange and yellow were still on it.

Billy told them about the ship, and Martha Murchison said, 'I'm sure this must be one of your best sunsets, too.'

'If I never do anything to match it, I'll not have cause to fret,' Billy admitted.

'Then that's two we've got,' George Murchison said with satisfaction.

'What'll you have to go with 'em? A storm or a calm?' Billy asked as he led them to another part of the gallery. 'I can fit you cut with either.'

He stopped, and they stopped with him, in front of a vast canvas hung on the wall. It was nearly eight feet wide and just over five feet in height; a golden harbour with pillared mansions rising on either side, a tree standing out very strongly near the foreground.

'The Building of Carthage,' Billy said. 'There were people who wanted to have me thrown out of the Academy for having the effrontery to exhibit this. One man in particular did his best to damn it, and he was successful to the point that it came back unsold. However, like the sunrise and the sunset that seem to have taken your eye, if there are any pictures I'll be remembered for, then this is one of 'em.' He peered around towards dark corners of the gallery. 'On the other hand, if it's a storm you want there's one of the biggest if not the greatest I've done. It's rolled up and lying about here somewhere.' He was thinking of *Hannibal and his Army Crossing the Alps.*

But the Murchisons were already more than satisfied. 'Don't bother,' said the manufacturer. 'We'll have this one here to make up our three. So let's get down to brass tacks and thrash out a price. How does my offer sound? 600 guineas for the three ...'

Billy affected not to hear, insisting on showing them another half dozen scenes of storm and calm, briefly describing the subjects and outlining the histories. 'Take this one, for instance,' he said, pulling the sheet from one of his most sublime calms—painted much earlier, *The Sun Rising Through Vapour.* 'Had it on m'hands for the best part of ten years before Sir John Leicester offered me 350 guineas for it. After his death it was put up for auction, so I got it back. But I had to bid nearly 500 guineas.'

'You mean—*you bought it back?*' said Martha Murchison incredulously.

'Yes, madam. I'm planning to leave a collection of my best works to the nation.'

Mrs Murchison glanced anxiously towards her husband, who had rapidly reassessed the situation in the light of what Billy was telling them.

'Look here, now, Mr Turner,' Murchison said heartily, 'I can see I started pitching a trifle on the light side. I'll make it 1,000 guineas for the three. 1,000. Does that sound better?'

Billy appeared to be deaf. He crossed back to the *Ulysses*, the Murchisons trotting along behind him, and as he stood in front of it said, 'This one never sold, so I didn't have to try buying it back.' Then he shook his head as a man might do at the recollection of some scene of his departed youth. 'I'll never manage the like of that again.'

This triggered off another frantic bid from the manufacturer.

'Let's not beat about the bush. 2,000 guineas. I'll make it 2,000 guineas for the three. What do you say to that, eh?'

'You've picked three of my favourite works.'

George Murchison was not going to be thwarted. The caution that had helped win him a fortune from pots and pans deserted him. 'I know what a thing's worth when I see it,' he said. 'I'll double up. Four. 4,000 guineas the three.'

'Four?' gasped his wife.

'Four,' he affirmed, slamming a fist into the palm of his other hand. 'I know what I'm about. 4,000 guineas. How's that feel for size now Turner?'

'Four, you say?' Billy said with a hint of uncertainty.

Murchison leapt in again.

'Five, then! Let me prove I'm not a man to quibble for the sake of a thousand. 5,000 guineas the three. You can't say no to that, can you now?'

Billy stood in silence, torn between what his business sense told him and what his heart demanded for the memory of his father. Hannah's interest was aroused for once. She had been present at many unusual bargainings and hagglings, and she knew how unpredictable and contrary Billy could be: he might suddenly surrender graciously and insist on a buyer having a picture for half the price in question, or he might double a sum already agreed upon—or decide against selling altogether. But in all her years here she had never witnessed a sale quite like this one.

At last Billy shook his head and said, 'No.'

'Name your price, then ...'

Billy hesitated.

'All right,' said George Murchison, desperate now to have the paintings at any price. 'I'll put it to you another way. I'll make you an offer for this whole room. Everything in it. 10,000 guineas.'

Billy shook his head again, partly out of disbelief at what he was hearing.

'15,000, then. Another five. 15,000 guineas for the contents of this room. Lump sum, prompt payment.'

'Sorry,' said Billy quietly. The man grated on his nerves with his overbearing money-can-buy-anything manner.

'Twenty!'

'Twenty?' said his wife.

'20,000 guineas ... that's my offer.'

'Do have a care,' she whispered.

'I'll even go to another 5,000 to close the bargain. How about that, then, Turner? Everything in the gallery—25,000 guineas.'

'That's a hatful of money.'

'Lump sum, prompt payment—like I said. Now, can you say no to that?'

Martha Murchison dragged out a lace handkerchief and mopped the perspiration from her face and from the folds in her neck.

'Tell me, Mr Murchison,' Billy said, now very cool. 'About how much would you say that'd work out per square inch?'

The manufacturer faltered for the first time, sharpening his look at Billy. His wife swallowed hard.

'How much by the square inch? Well, it's hard to say.' He gave a quick glance around the gallery. 'I dunno. I suppose it'd be something like—ooh, as much as half a guinea ... Certainly much more'n I gave for them first three I bought. Very much more.'

Billy took a magnifying glass from his pocket and, after

giving it a quick rub on his sleeve, placed it flat over the heart of the sunset in the picture of *The Fighting Téméraire*. 'That sun's about a square inch, give or take a little—and the price is 25,000 guineas.'

'For what—a square inch?'

'For *that* square inch, Murchison. Except that it ain't for sale. Not that, nor any square inch in this place. Not to you.'

George Murchison was confused by Billy's sudden change of mood and, feeling that his offer may have been misunderstood, he repeated his closing bid with great emphasis on the actual sum. 'But I'm making you an offer for everything here. I'm offering you 25,000 *guineas*!'

'And I'm saying no,' Billy replied. 'You can make it 100,000 guineas for all I care, but I'll still say no. Rather than let you have a single square inch of these paintings I'd see m'self wrapped up and buried in 'em.'

He spun away and headed back to his painting-room, saying to Hannah as he passed her, 'See the pair of 'em off the premises.' The slamming of the painting-room door punctuated the silence in which the stunned Murchisons stood.

After a moment, George Murchison shook his head in bewilderment. 'What do you make of that?' he asked his wife.

'We've heard often enough that he's daft, haven't we?' she said. 'People looking at them other paintings of his have said so. Well, now we know for ourselves.'

Although she was greatly relieved that the haggling had come to nothing in view of the astronomical sum her husband had ended up offering, Martha Murchison was put out by not getting what they had come for. It was a rare experience for both of them these days to find that their money could not secure for them whatever they set their hearts on.

As they descended the stairs and crossed the lower room, Hannah followed them. They had to pass the large table on which Billy had left a number of watercolours he had brought in for framing, one of which lay at an angle that gave Martha Murchison a clear view of it. It caught her eye, and she stopped and held her husband back so that she could point something out to him.

'George. Look here. Haven't we seen that place somewhere?'

He shrugged, wanting to get out of here now that he had been bettered in the bargaining. He felt uncomfortable with that crone slinking along behind them like a grey shadow and cats peering at him from all angles.

But Martha was determined to work out where she had seen this scene before, and within a few seconds she had it. 'I know! On the Thames. I'm sure of it. We passed by this spot in Sir Benjamin's barge. Don't you remember all the birds flying up out of the trees?'

George didn't, but he agreed that she could be right—if only to avoid delaying here any longer. And so, having satisfied herself that she had identified the place, Martha allowed him to lead her out into the street.

When they had gone, Hannah returned to the table thoughtfully. Cats seethed around her skirts, and she picked up a kitten and stroked it as she turned to her discovery. The painting Martha Murchison had examined was in a batch of watercolours that Billy had brought in rolled up in a long leather case. Putting the kitten down, Hannah sifted through them and saw that they were all of the same locality—a stretch of river bank with an occasional isolated building such as a mill or a boat-house. They had been done mainly for the skies and churning cloud effects, although where trees stood out they were very softly outlined and ethereal. Billy had brought in similar scenes for framing before this. Hannah had scarcely glanced at them; they were nebulous scenes that could have been anywhere. But now that the Murchison woman had given them a recognisable location, Hannah could see that they provided a valuable lead as to where Billy spent some of his time when absent from Queen Anne Street—something that Sarah would undoubtedly want to know about.

Hannah formulated no plan to use this information; she locked it away in the recesses of her mind. She had no love for Sarah and felt no compulsion to help her to hound Billy. So when Sarah next visited the gallery and took up her customary harassment for clues to Billy's whereabouts, Hannah held her tongue and determined never to share what she knew with any one. But when she was alone and dazed with sherry or gin, she would sometimes whisper her secret to the cats.

Chapter 28

Sarah Danby was wary of having any direct contact with Billy after unmasking him at Margate, and she took care to avoid coming face to face with him at Queen Anne Street. But one afternoon at the lawyers' offices in Clement's Inn, as Billy breezed in from the bustle of Fleet Street to be gaped at by Morley in the outer office, Sarah was being shown out of the inner office by Gascoigne. Billy took one swift look at her and was instantly consumed with white rage. 'What the devil are *you* doing here?' he shouted.

In the face of this, Sarah found it impossible to exercise any restraint and flared back at him. 'You, of all people, should know. If you weren't such a miser, I wouldn't have to come here begging.'

'Begging?' he yelled. 'My God! With all I provide, since when did you ever have to beg?'

'What you provide isn't enough.'

'It never was!'

'How right you are!' she shouted back. 'It *never* was. And it's not what you promised your father.'

They stood matching hostile looks, soaking up each other's rage and resentment. Gascoigne and Morley waited nervously —both all too conscious that they had been caught red-handed in the act of extending courtesy to someone they had been instructed to keep off the premises.

Billy had come here with the intention of spending a quarter of an hour or so dealing with a number of business matters, but he now had something quite different in mind. Looking away from Sarah, he turned to Gascoigne and said, 'If you'd be so kind, Mr Gascoigne—get this damned harpie out of my sight and join me in your office.'

'Harpie, am I?' Sarah cried, outraged. 'How *dare* you!'

She held up a tightly clenched fist as if to strike him.

She bore only a faint resemblance to the figure of his mother with the raised anchor; but the suggestion of it shook him. His legs felt weak as he pushed past her and entered the inner office, where he slid into a chair.

As Gascoigne whispered pleadingly to Sarah to leave at once and avoid further unpleasantness, she glared in through the open doorway to the inner office where Billy slumped in the chair. He looked harmless enough now; but she had seen the terror and helplessness in his eyes a moment before, and she knew from experience what might follow if she tried to argue further. So she allowed herself to be escorted to the street door and shown out.

When Gascoigne joined him in the inner office, Billy asked for a glass of water and took several minutes sipping it as he recovered his composure. Then he began mildly enough, saying, 'Tell me, Gascoigne—how often have I said to you and Morley that Mrs Danby wasn't to come here pestering?'

'I'm not in a position to give you an exact figure, sir, but you have conveyed your wish to us in no uncertain terms. We've done our best to carry it out but, unfortunately, that has been extremely difficult. If Mrs Danby decides of her own volition to pay us a visit—short of stationing someone permanently at the door to turn her away, how are we to stop her coming?'

'I'll tell you one way that would help. Cut out all your bowing and scraping. If you treat her as if she is some kind of duchess, she's bound to keep coming back for more of your pandering.'

What infuriated Billy was the knowledge that Gascoigne and Morley were really in sympathy with Sarah. He was sure that they regarded him as no more than a jumped-up Cockney and resented being in the position of either taking his instructions or losing a valuable client. And there was much truth in this.

Pausing for some moments to allow his point to sink in, Billy went on, 'This will not happen again.'

'You may rest assured that we'll do everything in our power to see that it doesn't—believe me,' said Gascoigne with genuine feeling.

Gascoigne had a lot at stake. The artist's private and business affairs had become increasingly complex, involving more people and other legal firms. The intricacies of his will, for instance—now prominently mentioning one Sophia Caroline Booth as a beneficiary—a long document that he kept altering and redrafting, had been taken over by an astute younger solicitor, Henry Harpur, who also dealt with some of his investments. George Cobb had not yet completely severed his connection with the partnership that bore his name, but the firm still handled most of Billy's dealings in land and property, as well as the matter of the allowance to his one remaining dependant other than Hannah.

As he rose back on to his feet now, Billy came to the crux of what he had decided—not only about that one dependant, Sarah, but also the legal firm.

Replying to Gascoigne's reassurance at last he said, 'I'm relieving you of the worry that it doesn't happen again. As you know, I have a number of people acting for me in various capacities, and I have in fact frequently contemplated making arrangements which would put an end to my association with this firm. I have stayed on out of my long regard for Mr Cobb; but this is the parting of the ways. So if you'll be good enough to open up your safe, I'll have all m'boxes.'

After a dumbfounded moment, Gascoigne managed, 'Mr Turner, sir—you cannot mean ...' His voice petered out in the face of the unthinkable.

'Deeds, bonds, shares, letters—everything,' Billy said.

'But sir—' Gascoigne began feebly.

'I ain't prepared to argue,' Billy said roughly. 'Are you going to hand 'em over or do I have to get a charge of gunpowder and blow that safe open m'self?'

Morley had been a woebegone witness to all this from the outer office. As Gascoigne produced a bunch of keys from his pocket and fumbled with them, Billy spotted the clerk through the doorway and called to him, 'I'll be needing a horse-cab. See to it.'

Morley went off promptly; and as Gascoigne found the key to the safe Billy glanced around the inner office, where his framed watercolour took his eye. He had never forgotten or forgiven the way in which Gascoigne had accepted that spontaneous present, intoning suspiciously, 'Not in lieu of payment, I trust.' Now he decided that the picture had been subjected quite long enough to the indignity of being on this wall. Choosing a moment when Gascoigne was down at the opened safe with his back turned, he slid the picture upwards off its hook and slipped it under his coat.

At Chelsea, Sophie came to the door and held it open as the cabman helped Billy carry the deed-boxes into the ground-floor sitting-room facing the river, where they were stacked beside his desk with the rescued watercolour on top of them. To her, the look of these ugly boxes was disturbing enough without the taut expression on Billy's face. He offered no explanation and she asked for none; it had been a day of glorious autumn sunshine from dawn till dusk in Chelsea, but she knew that there had been another storm down the river.

After picking at his supper, Billy went to his desk to work on a new draft of his will from notes provided by Henry Harpur; but it entailed referring to several property deeds that were somewhere in the boxes beside him. Gascoigne or Morley would have found them in an instant, but he didn't even know where to begin and had to abandon the idea for the time being.

In the course of the ensuing week he tried again and again to get to grips with the will, only to be frustrated by being unable to find the right documents. He made starts at work up in his painting-room—and Sophie was disturbed to see that the subject was darker and stormier than usual, with the trees in it sharper in outline and starker—but his concentration was weak. He went up to the rooftop but had barely settled down in his chair before he was back on his feet and downstairs again. Things that he normally accepted or enjoyed—the hammering from the blacksmith's forge and the smell of hot bread wafting in from the bakery—now irritated him.

One evening, though, he agreed to go for a walk with Sophie. She helped him on with his new blue coat with silver buttons—a splendid garment which matched the role he played here—and out they went, Billy trudging along beside her through shoals of fallen leaves on the riverside path. They passed an empty house standing between a small boat-builder's shed and a beer shop. It was one that Sophie had noted as being in a quieter setting, and therefore possibly more suitable for Billy than the house they occupied. When the time was ripe she might suggest a move to him. Farther along the path they came to a point at which they faced an old-gold autumn sun sinking into a horizon of deep crimson, but Billy paid no heed to it. Sophie didn't despair. She knew that when he walked he sometimes started talking. And presently that was just what happened. Haltingly at first, he began to tell her what had been worrying him since his last trip to town.

Sophie had guessed that Sarah might be behind his present upset. She listened quietly and refrained from making any comment until they were back out of the chill and by the fire in the house. The burning coal crackled faintly in the grate and from the region of the jetty outside they could hear the boom of Josh's voice as he told some of the children to get inside out of the cold.

Sophie's immediate fear was that Gascoigne and Morley might allow their resentment to get the better of their professional ethics and drop a hint as to where Billy could be found. But even without that, there was no doubt that Sarah would redouble her efforts to create trouble, especially if no alternative arrangements were made to provide her with some sort of an allowance. If Sarah managed to destroy this hideaway, Sophie was afraid that even with her protection and help Billy's slender hold on sanity might break. Thinking this over, Sophie believed she had an answer to the problem.

'You know,' she said, 'I'm wondering whether it might not be worth trying to put Mrs Danby out of her misery.' And then she laughed at the look Billy gave her. 'Don't worry yourself—I'm no' suggesting any physical hurt to the lady. Nothing as drastic as that. What I mean is this: give her what she wants. Not only restore the cuts you have made to her allowance, but give her a little more. Then she'll have no cause to complain.'

Billy would have given an immediate blunt no to the suggestion if it had come from anyone else. But Sophie's opinion meant so much to him that he was able to ride out his first reaction without comment and then consider it calmly. He pondered for a minute before saying, 'I suppose I could get Harpur to handle it.'

'Why not Mr Gascoigne and Mr Morley?'

'I sacked 'em, didn't I?'

'You did,' Sophie said with an understanding smile. 'But why give them reason to feel badly done by? I'm sure they'd be delighted to be in a position to tell Mrs Danby that she's to benefit from an increased allowance.'

Billy grunted and said, 'I'll think about it.'

The matter wasn't discussed any more that night; but in the morning, as they lay side by side in bed, he said without any preamble, 'All right, Sophie. I'll load them boxes on to a horse-cab and deliver 'em to Clement's Inn. But I'm damned if Gascoigne's going to get that painting back!'

Later that morning in Gascoigne's office—where there was a conspicuous oblong patch of lighter brown on the wall—no reference was made to the disappearance of the watercolour. Gascoigne and Morley were too dazed to give it a thought, overwhelmed as they were with amazement and relief at the unexpected return of their client with the deed-boxes and instructions regarding an increase in Mrs Danby's allowance.

Gascoigne had already informed Sarah that Billy had taken his business out of their hands and that this meant someone else would be dealing with her allowance. Since receiving this notification, she had been staying in London with Georgiana and her husband and coming in daily to demand to know where her enemy could be found, insisting that the termination of his long association with the firm could only be the work of that scheming Scotswoman Mrs Booth.

Sarah's onslaughts against the lawyer and his clerk had been so savage and unremitting that they had been tempted to let slip some hint as to where the client in question might be found. Now they were vastly thankful that they hadn't: and although they did not know what had prompted Billy's change of heart, they were as certain as Sophie that all would be sweetness and light when they conveyed to Mrs Danby the glad tidings of the increased allowance.

But Sarah was to react in a way none of them had anticipated—not even Sophie.

Chapter 29

When she received Gascoigne's letter informing her that the firm would no longer be handling her allowance, Sarah had hurried to Queen Anne Street to get at Hannah again, warning her that she too would find herself left out in the cold thanks to the grasping Sophie Booth. So convincing was she that Hannah, like Gascoigne and Morley, had been tempted to reveal what she thought she knew about Billy's secret hideaway. But when Sarah, in her usual bullying fashion, accused Hannah of refusing to help her because of jealousy and spite, Hannah withdrew into her shell and kept what she had discovered to herself.

But Hannah had been left deeply disturbed by what Sarah had planted in her mind, and she began dipping into the sherry and gin even earlier in the day, becoming by nightfall a befuddled wraith, alone with her tribe of cats. Sometimes she fed them three times a day, sometimes she became so confused that she forgot to feed them at all.

The neglect of the gallery began on the doorstep. Rust and corrosion festered on the door handle and knocker. Paint peeled off the wood. The steps were almost concealed by a thick drift of dead leaves, some of which Hannah would gather up in her apron to tip on the fire inside.

Her cats roamed the house. In both the bottom and top gallery rooms, in corners and inside the dark tunnels made by the rolled-up canvases lying on the floor, they slept, procreated, sparred and urinated. Other rolled-up canvases were jammed upright into corners to keep out draughts. Dust and grime clung to everything, yet in the weak flickering light of a lantern or in the feeble flame from the grate, all around the rooms the paintings came to life. In them suns and moons glowed, gilded cities floated on gilded hills, dream ships rode at anchor in bays of light, and nymphs emerged from trees around shaded pools.

Ever since Billy had first left her at the gallery while he went away on sketching tours or to places unknown, Hannah had used his pictures as an escape—losing herself in them, drifting away. It had become her secret way of sharing something of his life—particularly after she had been inflicted with her private scourge. When her mind simmered and burned with drink, her reactions to the pictures were intensified to the point of vivid illusion, so that the clouds in the paintings seemed to drift by, ships sailed along, whales leapt out of the water, volcanoes erupted, nymphs joined hands and danced, and crowds and multitudes milled about and chattered. She heard it all too—winds, music, singing, eruptions, shouting; so much so that the sounds seemed to echo around the cold rooms. In this way, as she staggered about with a retinue of smouldering-eyed cats behind her, a lantern held up in one hand and a glass of sherry or gin slopping in the other, she journeyed to distant and mythical places.

One night, just over a week after Sarah had called to sow the seeds of her latest fear, Hannah was in the lower gallery room in front of a large alpine landscape when suddenly it seemed to her that someone or something trapped in a mountain was making a desperate attempt to break free. As a dreadful pounding came from the heart of the picture, she backed away from it—only to find that in another painting near it the attempt to escape was being made out of the sun itself. The orange ball in this picture grew and expanded until it was pulsating to the accompaniment of a sound so loud and terrifying that she left the lantern on the floor and clapped her hands over her ears to stumble screaming from it into the black hole of a doorway. But the sound pursued her and continued until the realisation began to penetrate her confusion that it was caused by someone knocking loudly on the street door.

Retrieving the lantern, she went to the door and found Sarah waiting impatiently.

'What was all that screaming about?' Sarah demanded, thrusting her way in through the opening. And then, when

Hannah slammed the door shut again without offering a word of explanation, she said, 'Is *he* here?' There was no need to mention Billy by name.

'No,' Hannah said sullenly.

'Has he been here?'

'If he has, I haven't seen him.'

Sarah could now see the state that Hannah was in. She had rarely found her as intoxicated as this, but it explained something to her. 'Oh, so that's it. Screaming drunk.' She grimaced. 'Kindly pull yourself together and try to understand what I'm going to tell you.' Shivering, she crossed to the meagre fire in the grate, saying, 'You know that I've been going every day to Gascoigne to see if he could tell me who was going to handle my money in the future. Well, he kept saying he had no idea what the new arrangement would be. But today he told me that our friend has reappeared. What's more, he's made it up and Gascoigne's to continue to pay me. But that's not all. Not only are the cuts restored, but I'm to get more!' She paused, and when Hannah failed to show any response she repeated impatiently, 'I'm going to get more. An increase. Do you understand? *More.*'

'More?' Hannah echoed blankly.

'That's what I'm trying to tell you. More money.'

Hannah shrugged indifferently. 'You're not complaining about that too, are you?'

'Yes, I am!'

Hannah was too bemused to show any interest. It meant nothing to her. She turned and started to scavenge around for something to put on the fire, leaving Sarah standing by the fireplace and still talking.

'It isn't like him to suddenly pay me so much out of the goodness of his heart. I'll wager that Scotswoman's behind it.' She waited for a comment from Hannah, but none came. 'Don't you see? If he can afford to restore the cuts and give me an increase, he must be worth an absolute fortune. And *she* probably put him up to this—thinking that if he paid me more I wouldn't bother him again and *she* could get her hands on everything. Well, it won't work.'

By now, Hannah was down at the other end of the gallery and obviously paying little or no attention. Sarah faced the fire, but it was dying fast and gave little warmth. Still shivering, she called to Hannah, 'Hurry up and do something about this fire. I'm freezing.'

As she held out her hands to the embers, she noticed that they had burned away to curious grey flakes. Then she heard a loud scraping sound and swung round sharply to see Hannah dragging an old blackened roll of canvas across the floor towards the fireplace. That explained the flakes in the grate: the remains of a roll of unused canvas. She stood to one side as Hannah grappled with the roll, eventually balancing it in her arms before dropping it lengthways in the grate. As it landed, there was a puff of grey ash and sparks; what little fire there had been vanished for the moment, leaving Sarah shivering. Then, as the heat began to burn into the underside of the canvas roll, vaporising years of the urination of cats, an acrid reek rose up out of the fireplace, becoming so pungent and suffocating that Sarah had to move away, saying to Hannah, 'Just look at you! In the state you're in, you wouldn't have the faintest idea if he *had* been here.'

Hannah floundered about, rummaging for more waste or debris to put on the fire. She pointed to the table in the centre of the room upon which letters were spread, all still sealed. What she intended to convey was that if Billy had been here the letters would have been either opened or taken away. Sarah understood her meaning.

As far as was possible whenever she came here, Sarah carried out a routine search—opening drawers and cupboards, probing into pockets of working jackets and greatcoats, reading opened mail and scrutinising anything else on which she could lay her hands. Deciding now to check on the unopened mail, she collected the lantern from where Hannah had left it on the floor and placed it on the table in order to conduct her inspection. There were many letters that intrigued her—one more than the rest. It was sealed with the name and arms of Henry Harpur, whom she knew to be the solicitor now handling Billy's will. As she examined it, holding it against the light from the lantern, it became impossible for her to put it down without knowing what was inside it; surrendering to her curiosity, she broke the seal and opened it.

What she read was a confirmation of her very worst fear.

'He's altering his will!' she called to Hannah.

Here it was, before her eyes, in black and white. Harpur was reminding Billy in this letter that a number of alterations were still awaited before his new will could be drawn up. But there were no specific details of what she wanted to know.

Hannah was distressed, but not for the reason Sarah expected. 'You shouldn't have done that!' she cried, coming to the table, half sobered by the sight of Sarah holding the letter and the envelope with the broken seal.

'It's just as well I did,' Sarah replied. 'Now, at least, we know the worst.'

'He'll blame me.'

'Tell him I did it. I don't care.'

'He'll still blame me.'

Ignoring this, Sarah went on, 'I can guess exactly what he's up to. He's going to alter everything in Sophia Booth's favour. I'll be fobbed off with ha'pennies. You see if I'm not right. We'll be left destitute, you and I ...'

Warmth reached out from the grate, where the flames now had a hold on the roll of canvas Hannah had dumped there. Sarah crossed from the table to the fireplace, taking the letter with her. She was thinking that she might well be able to get at Billy through Henry Harpur. If she called at his chambers and insisted on seeing him, she might pick up a clue to help her track Billy down. At the fireplace she began to read through the letter again, tilting the surface of the paper towards the glare from the flames.

'Give me that!' Hannah cried suddenly, lunging for the letter to put it back on the table. But Sarah was too quick for her, lifting the sheet of paper out of reach so that Hannah's blackened little hands clawed through the air. Hannah overbalanced and fell, lying on the floor, a crumpled bundle of rags, before slowly gathering enough strength to drag herself back to her feet.

Sarah watched coldly, making no move to help, suddenly aware that she was herself under observation. Hannah's cats prowled and watched intently; dozens of eyes swimming in the gloom—luminous greens, yellows, blues and reds—threatening in this incredible atmosphere where dirt and decay vied with the dusty splendour of poetic visions and gorgeous extravaganzas.

A little unnerved by all the eyes, but undeterred, Sarah taunted Hannah by holding the letter near to the fire, saying as she did so, 'That's where this should go.'

At that moment, a burst of light within the mass of flames caused Sarah to glance again at the fire—and then she realised what was burning there.

What she had assumed to be a roll of reject or rotting canvas was in fact a large oil painting, now slowly unravelling glimpses of colour as it writhed in its death throes. Patches of Turner skies, dazzling when the paint in them had only just been applied, shone with a brightness never before seen. Then, as tiny tongues of fire swept across the blue, the oils and pigments ran, sizzled and bubbled, and the skies swiftly darkened and died.

Stunned and incredulous, Sarah turned on Hannah. 'How long have you been doing this?'

'What?' Hannah stared at her through bleared and confused eyes.

'That!' Sarah cried, pointing at the canvas as it continued to contort and flash glimpses of its beauties in the flames. She let go of the Harpur letter, letting it flutter to the floor, and reached into the grate to rescue what was left of the painting. But as she grasped one end of it, her touch made it collapse in the middle. Hot air shot up the tunnel of the rolled canvas, scorching her hand, and she screamed 'How long, Hannah? How long?'

Unable to take in exactly what was happening, Hannah stood mystified until Sarah took her by the shoulders and swung her round to make her look into the hearth.

'Don't you see what's burning there?'

Hannah remained mute; she was beginning to comprehend.

'That painting's one of his big ones—the 500 guinea size at least,' Sarah said fiercely. 'It might even have been one of his favourites. Now—will you tell me how long you've been doing this?'

Without answering, Hannah began to breathe in sharp, terrified gasps.

Sarah flung another question at her. 'Does he know about this?'

'No,' Hannah whispered fearfully, 'no.'

'Of course he doesn't! If he did, would you be here now? You—or them?' Sarah swept her hand around to take in the restless cats. 'You'd be out on the street—all of you.' And pointing back at the fire she went on, 'Could you imagine him allowing you to stay here for one second more if he knew what you've been putting on that fire?'

Hannah began to sob, but Sarah was relentless. 'And what if he does happen to find out?'

'Please, no,' Hannah whimpered.

'What if someone were to tell him? I'm not saying it would be me, mind. But what if it got back to him?'

'No! Oh, please, no, no, no!' Hannah fell on her knees and grasped Sarah's legs, begging her not to tell Billy.

'What's to stop me, though?' Sarah asked. 'Why shouldn't I?'

'Sarah, please—please, no!'

For some moments Sarah allowed Hannah to plead, getting a perverse satisfaction from it, and then she broke the wretched woman's hold and stepped back out of reach.

'Very well, then. But in future you might put yourself out to give me a little more help with what I need to know. After all, it's as much for your benefit as mine.' And with another of those sweeping gestures that took in the cats, she added, 'And theirs.'

It was Hannah's desperation to protect the cats—her children—that caused her to act the way she did now. On her hands and knees she crawled over to a cupboard against the wall, pulled open the door and dragged a sheaf of watercolour paintings from a shelf.

'What are those?' Sarah demanded, coming over to her.

Still on her knees, Hannah handed them up.

Sarah snatched at them and started to go through them, but they meant nothing to her. She looked down impatiently at Hannah and said, 'Why are you showing me these? Is there something special about them?'

Hannah nodded slowly and miserably.

And then Sarah, looking at the watercolours again, caught

her breath in a rush of excited understanding.

'This place ... Is this where he's hidden himself?'

A cat mewed and rubbed itself against Hannah, and she reached out to stroke it as she nodded her head again. Tears blurred her eyes.

Chapter 30

Billy Turner sat in his rooftop eyrie, his face more deeply lined, his hair greyer. The sun came up through creeper beaded and jewelled with dew, and another placid autumn day began. Now that he believed he had settled matters down the river, he was at work again: filtering elements of the light into a mental version of the uncompleted picture on the easel in his painting-room below.

Sophie came up with some pancakes and coffee, and then went back to her housework. Down on the jetty, as the tide crept up the piles, the local urchins gathered to fish—every year or two saw a different lot of them. Within minutes, Josh Mottram took up a position near them, bellowing rebukes for their impertinence while they chattered back at him cheekily—although at that distance Billy couldn't hear their actual words.

He climbed down through the trapdoor and descended to his painting-room, where he had already set a palette with colours in preparation to get on with the canvas that currently engaged him. At this stage it was a mass of quenched colours—pinks, lemon-yellows, oranges, misty greens and blues—from which a number of shapes were slowly emerging. On what was already there he mentally overlaid what he had put together on the rooftop; but it didn't quite fit. He decided not to force matters but to seek a little diversion out on the jetty. Being close to the water—in particular the river that had been so much a part of his inspiration throughout his life—always helped him to sort things out when he was stuck at an embryonic stage with one of his creations.

In the hallway, as he picked up his umbrella with a fishing line wound around its end and took his old hat off a peg,

Sophie came from the kitchen to see him off. 'I hope you'll be catching something tasty.'

'I'll be competing against them boys, and they all seem to have the knack of mesmerising everything from a stickleback to a pike. If I'm to have any success, I'll need old Izaak Walton up there praying for me.'

'Oh, you're no' so bad when you put your mind to the task.'

'Trouble is,' he said with a grin, 'too often I don't.'

Sophie laughed, knowing how his mind was apt to wander when he was fishing.

When he left the house Billy also carried a small three-legged stool, which he raised in greeting to a passing neighbour.

The four boys near Josh bounced up at the sound of Billy's distinctively hard-heeled walk along the boards of the jetty and turned smiling faces to him. 'Good morning, gentlemen,' he said to them.

'Goin' arter the fish again, Admiral?' asked a boy Billy had nicknamed Shivers because of the way in which he showed his excitement when he had a fish on his line.

'I am. And don't any of you dare go warning 'em!'

The boys laughed and made popping noises that were supposed to be fish-talk as Billy set his stool between them and Josh.

'And how's the Lord's good friend this bright morning?' Billy inquired of the waterman as he sat himself carefully on the stool.

Josh, nettled by Billy's easy familiarity with the ragged boys, neglected to reply.

'Miserably sober, I see,' Billy went on, to the amusement of the urchins. 'Come on, now. Warm your soul with a little charity.'

Josh looked at him warily.

Billy pointed to the waterman's jar of worms. 'Spare a morsel of bait for a humble heathen,' he said.

Josh shoved the jar towards him and Billy chose a fat, purple worm and impaled it on his hook. He then gripped the umbrella just above the handle and swung the baited line out into the water. 'May the best of us win, gentlemen,' he said.

The boys and Josh settled down seriously to fish. But Billy

was only going through the motions. He was getting on with his own work.

For a start, he dismissed the uncompleted painting in the house from his mind. Instead, he thought about another idea he had been toying with since a recent boating expedition to Maidenhead with Sophie and Josh. After being caught in a windy shower, they had gone ashore, and Billy had seen the new railway-train rushing towards him across the bridge. It had excited him: he had wondered about having himself tied to the front of the engine in order to get an impression of its movement for a picture he had already entitled *Rain, Steam and Speed,* his concept of the new man-made dragon that was roaring and rattling across the face of the earth on a growing network of iron rails. After musing on what effects such a picture would allow him to present, he set it aside and half shut his eyes to weave into his visions the shimmer in the air and the sparkle off the rising tide. Alone, without shifting his position on the stool, he roamed among strange headlands and unknown bays, among phantom ships and mythical cities, across plains of light and into forests of the sun. Presently, these images gave way to that of the canvas on the easel back in the painting-room. What he was trying to pin down there —and in most of his pictures—was his ultimate quarry: light itself, as he had seen it breaking out and flooding over the lagoon of Venice.

As he mused, the upstream flow of river traffic became busier with the tide coming in. A private barge swept past, thrust by eight oarsmen; then a steam pinnace, its paddle-wheels thrashing the water, its smoke briefly smudging the sun. There was a sporadic stream of smaller boats, but as there was almost no wind those vessels under sail made poor time.

Billy remained undistracted by this pageant. And neither Josh nor the urchins paid much attention to it—except when a boat came in too close to the north bank and threatened to foul their fishing lines.

One of these boats caught Josh's eye because of the translucent red parasol that shaded the heads of its two women passengers in the stern seat. As it passed, he exchanged a nodded greeting with the waterman who was rowing and then returned to his fishing. He failed to notice the slight lifting of the edge of the parasol as the woman holding it peered across to the end of the jetty. Even if he had been watching, the woman's face was visible for only a moment before the edge of the parasol hid it again; and from so brief a glimpse he would have been unlikely to have recognised Sarah Danby.

Sarah had used her knowledge of the burned canvases to blackmail Hannah to accompany her up the river, claiming that she needed help in trying to identify the stretch shown in the watercolours. But there was more to it than that. She wanted to involve Hannah as deeply as possible in her intrigue in order to secure an even greater hold over her. It still rankled that Hannah had withheld such vital information from her.

From the moment Hannah had been helped on board the boat at the Westminster wharf, every muscle and bone in her frail body had been locked stiff with fear. Although sharing the shade of Sarah's parasol, she felt that the sunlight was boring through the cloth of her bonnet and exposing the disfigured side of her face to the slint-eyed scrutiny of the waterman. It was so long since she had been farther from the gallery than to the markets or to an engraver or framer that all previous outings might have occurred in another life. Her terror of the open air and direct sunlight, quite apart from her qualms at being out on the river in a thin wooden shell, left her too confused to be of any help in identifying anything at all, the banks either side of the river becoming in her eyes featureless blurs.

It was from a point a hundred yards downstream from the jetty that Sarah had first sighted the hunched, thickset figure seated on the stool. What made her almost certain at first glance that she had found what she was looking for was the umbrella-fishing rod. Looking now from side to side of the river, she thought that what she saw bore a strong resemblance to the scenes depicted in the watercolours: and from this point on, until the waterman brought the boat opposite the end of the jetty, she took good care to keep herself and Hannah well concealed under the parasol. When she raised its edge and peered across, her hopes were confirmed. There he was.

She resisted an urge to shock him by revealing her presence.

It would be interesting to see his reaction, but that was not what she had planned. She had no intention of confronting him this time and having him dodge away to some fresh retreat.

As the boat continued upstream, Sarah said nothing to Hannah about what she had seen—she did not speak at all until they had gone another four hundred yards or so, when she told the waterman to make for the northern bank. A few discreet inquiries not too far from the jetty might reveal the exact location of the latest hideaway. The waterman looked over his shoulder for a suitable place to land and then, trailing one oar in the water, he ploughed hard with the other oar and swung the boat in to a spit of dry sand jutting out from the bank. When the boat had come to a firm, gritty stop under overhanging branches, Sarah stood up and stepped ashore.

In an exhausted voice, Hannah asked, 'Where are you going?'

'Just for a short stroll,' Sarah told her. 'To stretch my legs. You stay here. I shan't be long.'

Before she started along the river-path the waterman said to her, 'Should ye be wantin' to go farther up river, ma'am, it's but an hour to the turn. The price goes up if I has to row against the water.'

'I'm hoping this will be far enough,' Sarah replied. Then, carrying the parasol above her head, she set off down the path.

Not happy at being left alone with the waterman, Hannah looked around nervously, jumping with fright when a leaf landed in her lap from a branch overhead. Other leaves, yellow and russet, came away from the trees and tumbled down through shafts of muted sunlight.

Slowly, as she watched Sarah heading along the path, something began to seep into Hannah's mind. She took a closer look at her surroundings. And she began to realise that this stretch of the river was remarkably like what she had seen in those tell-tale paintings at the gallery.

The waterman eyed her quietly. He found her and the other woman a strangely ill-matched pair. From the few remarks he had overheard, it seemed that they were searching for a particular place—without much enthusiasm on the part of this one. He sensed the animosity between them, and it was obvious to him that the decrepit hag was petrified of the smartly-dressed one. It was also clear that she was terrified of being left alone with him, and he was not at all surprised when she suddenly scrambled out of the boat and stumbled along the river-path in pursuit of the other woman.

At the end of the jetty, Billy nearly lost his umbrella when a fish accommodatingly hooked itself. The umbrella would have been dragged out of his hands but for Josh, who grabbed it and landed the catch—a plump roach—unhooked it, rebaited the line with another worm and then handed the makeshift rod back to its dazed owner.

'Very careless of me,' Billy said by way of thanks and apology.

The boys were jubilant. It wasn't the first time the Admiral had almost fallen asleep and caught a fish without trying.

Josh had seen this happen before, too, but he was well aware of the reason for it: the Admiral had been in another world. Since his glimpse into that world, Josh had always been conscious of the great powers this man secretly possessed, and it was often as much as he could do to suppress his wonder.

Billy returned to his visions. Only his outward self was involved in the act of fishing, and when another fish nibbled at his bait he had to be told about it. He apologised again, only to drift away once more.

Josh and the boys ran up a good tally of roach, bream and chub between them as the upstream river traffic became even busier, reaching a peak in the last hour before the turn of the tide. By this time the boys were ready to abandon fishing in favour of another pleasure, and presently one of them looked towards Billy and piped up, 'It'd be a good day for that piece o' magic glass today, don'tcha think, Admiral?'

It took a moment or two for Billy to react to this as his gaze followed the youngster's pointing finger towards the sun. Then, shutting one eye and squinting with the other, he said, 'Yes, I do believe it would be.' And with the eyes of all four boys on him he held his umbrella rod with one hand and dug into his pocket with the other, prolonging the suspense before bringing out the compact leather box in which he carried the prism these days, then snapping it open to reveal the glass jewel cushioned in a bed of yellow-orange velvet. 'Would this be what you're wanting?'

They nodded in unison and he handed it over, together with a small sheet of white paper from the same pocket—and, of course, his hat with the hole bored in the crown. Having obtained three of the four essential items, the urchins looked to one of their own number for the last one. A boy called Ned wore an ancient man-sized frock-coat into which he had been growing very slowly, having as yet a good twelve inches of shoulder and sleeve either side to fill, and he was called upon to hand over the garment for the benefit of all.

Josh had seen his young fellow-anglers go through the procedure many times before and he knew what happened inside the hat, but he didn't approve. By breaking up that ray of light into bands of colour, the boys were taking apart something that the Lord had put together. This, to Josh, smacked of sacrilege—and he couldn't quite forgive the Admiral for instigating it.

Letting the boys get on with it, the hatless Admiral returned to his reveries, And when a woman's cry rang out somewhere not far up the river, he failed to hear it. But Josh turned, and the heads of the four boys came out from under the coat.

They saw the tiny figure of a woman stumbling along the river-path towards another woman, who stood waiting under a red parasol. As they met, the two women appeared to engage in a short argument—nothing of which carried as far as the jetty. Both then walked with the parasol held well down over their heads towards the blacksmith's forge. They paused to peer inside and then the larger woman lowered the parasol and they entered, disappearing from sight.

By this time the boys had lost interest and were back under the coat with the hat and prism, but Josh continued to watch and ponder. He recalled having seen that same red parasol travelling upstream only a short time ago, and some instinct told him that the presence of the two women ought to be investigated: so he hauled in his line and left it lying on the jetty as he stood up. Thumping one of the boys on the back through the coat, he said, 'When you've finished meddlin' with God's sunlight underneath there, keep a watch on the Admiral's line for 'im.'

He received a muffled assurance that this would be done, followed by an equally muffled threat of a punch on the nose if he continued to upset the delicate balance between hat, prism and sunlight with this thumps. Overcoming the temptation to lift the coat and clout the culprit, he started out with long strides, swiftly covering the length of the jetty and the ground to the blacksmith's forge, where he took up a position at the side opposite the Admiral's house. All he could hear was the low roar of the furnace; and then the clanging started up and the two women emerged.

Sophie's description of Sarah Danby had been remarkably accurate. Josh recognised her immediately. He was torn between trying to hear what she was saying to her companion and rushing off to warn Sophie. The clanging from the forge defeated his first object, but he waited to see what the women's next move would be.

Obviously the blacksmith had innocently provided the information they had been seeking. The woman Josh knew to be Sarah Danby pointed to the Admiral's house and, putting up the parasol again, took the arm of her reluctant companion and urged her to start walking, keeping the parasol well down over their heads.

Josh had seen enough. Although these two women went on past the house, Sophie had to be told about them.

In Billy's painting-room, Sophie was taking the opportunity of his absence from the house to do a little tidying and dusting. She picked up a bunch of his brushes, handling them fondly. They were worn and wispy, and she was amazed again at his ability to create such wonders with such tattered tools—although she knew that he had a sentimental attachment to them and disliked having to discard them.

Looking over the canvas on the easel through half-closed eyes, she waited for something to emerge out of it. In others, the shapes and patches of colour sometimes became cities on hills, bays, inlets; and bridges, towers and castles might be vaguely discerned. The picture she was examining was already drenched with light. In it she saw a headland, and then she didn't; she saw the mouth of a river, and then she didn't see that either; but the faint suggestion of a tree seemed to float out towards her. It was plain to her that something new had been happening in Billy's work. Whenever she entered the painting-room now, it was as if even more light had been captured and brought inside these four walls—sometimes such unearthly light that it made her gasp aloud. In contrast, standing against the wall nearby was a stark reminder of another turning his work was always liable to take—the painting left dark and half finished after his fight with Sarah at the lawyers' chambers.

The back-door bell rang in the hall. There was an urgency about it that made her hurry down the stairs and out across the garden to unbolt the gate. Josh slipped through the moment it opened; and as soon as he had told Sophie what he had seen she led the way back into the house, along the hall-way and into the ground-floor sitting-room.

Through the gauze curtains, they could see Sarah and Hannah walking back towards the house, having inspected the immediate surroundings. As she watched them getting nearer, Sophie spoke in a flat, measured voice—so devoid of emotion that in a curious way it was full of it. 'One short glimpse of Mrs Danby and the peace of this place will be wrecked for the Admiral for all time.'

Sarah and her unwilling companion were almost opposite the front of the house now. At any moment they might switch direction and head out along the jetty to where Billy sat in blissful ignorance. To Sophie there seemed to be only one course of action—and it had to be taken immediately. 'Quickly,' she said to Josh. 'Let's get them inside.'

Events moved with such speed then that the two unsuspecting women hardly knew what was happening to them. Within seconds, Josh and Sophie had rushed out to them; Josh clamped a huge hand on the upper arm of each of them and steered them firmly and hastily through the door and into the house. On the way, Sophie took the parasol out of Sarah's hand and collapsed it to make their entry simpler. Before Sarah or Hannah had time to utter a word of protest, they found themselves inside the hallway with the door firmly shut behind them.

'Well, Mrs Danby,' Sophie began, a little breathless herself. 'It's good of you to call.' She returned the folded parasol to its indignant owner, and turned to Hannah. This was the first time she had seen her and Sophie was appalled at the appearance and terrified state of the unfortunate little woman who had once been so fresh and radiant. She wanted to be gentle with her, but so much was at stake that she had to remain cool and reserved—outwardly, at least. 'I imagine you to be Miss Hannah,' she said. 'How do you do? Please come through into the sitting-room—both of you.'

As Sophie led the way, Sarah stood still in obstinate refusal, until she became aware that the hulking waterman was looming behind her and so she followed. Hannah crept along behind her, trembling uncontrollably. Josh came last, his big heart filled with pity for the shrunken wraith of a woman. He had actually felt the fear palpitating in her stick of an arm when hurrying her into the house.

From the sitting-room they could see out through the misty haze of the curtains to where the man responsible for bringing together Sarah, Hannah and Sophie now crouched hatless on his stool at the far end of the jetty. Between them, these three women were now in a position to decide his fate. His imagination was working at such a pitch of sustained intensity that the shock of seeing Sarah here in his haven could strike like an anchor crashing out of the sun into his reason, sending him the way of his mother. Of the three, only Sophie was conscious of this.

Sarah had regained her breath by now, and some of her composure. This was not at all as she had planned, but she was determined to brazen it out. 'Are you in the habit,' she asked Sophie coldly, 'of dragging innocent passers-by into your house against their will?'

'No,' said Sophie, 'not innocent ones. Only those who come prying with the deliberate intention of causing trouble.'

'Hannah and I were merely taking a walk,' said Sarah, drawing herself up. 'What do you mean?'

'I mean that you think you've winkled him out again.'

'Think?' Sarah mocked. 'I *know* it!' It was galling to have been pounced upon and rushed in here, but she had absolutely no doubt that she could dictate her own terms. She gave a theatrically disdainful laugh and went on to boast of how, through the watercolour paintings, she had discovered where to search for Billy's hideaway and what she proposed to do with the information now that she had it. 'I'll be giving that snivelling Gascoigne an ultimatum. Our friend out there must keep me in his will and at the same time put an end to his association with you, Mrs Booth. You are obviously an evil influence on him.'

Sophie let her have her say, keeping an eye towards the jetty just in case Billy decided to pack up his things and come back to the house. Then she turned to Hannah. 'I am most surprised to find you a party to this, Miss Hannah. Most surprised indeed.'

Hannah was near collapse. She began to tremble even more, totally incapable of making any reply. Sarah spoke for her, saying scornfully, 'Can you imagine her coming all this way of her own accord? I had to drag her along.'

'I had assumed as much,' Sophie said, turning back to Sarah. 'I wonder, though—have you stopped to consider the outcome should Mr Turner discover what you have done to this poor lady?'

A flicker of alarm showed in Sarah's eyes.

'He would never forgive you, Mrs Danby,' Sophie continued. '*Never*. Knowing him as I do, that I can confidently assure you.' And when Sarah remained silent, she pressed on. 'Haven't you any idea of the storm and nightmare you have caused that man with all your hounding and persecution? I've had to see him through weeks of darkness and despair. You destroyed one haven for him at Wapping, and another at Margate—and now he's found one here. He's working as he's never done in his life before. The proof's upstairs on the easel in his painting-room. A vision. Yet the further he goes, the more defenceless he becomes. It is my belief—my fear—that if he were to see you here now in this place he so loves, it might well destroy him. It could plunge him into a state of mind from which it would be impossible to rescue him.'

Sarah remembered the stricken look on Billy's face in the lawyers' chambers at their last encounter; although she said nothing she looked perturbed.

'Yes,' Sophie said. 'You know what I mean well enough.' She had been groping for some line to take against Sarah, and even though she had undefined reservations about this one, she had to try it; she had no other. 'If you know what is good for you, Mrs Danby, you'll listen to me.' She pointed across to the desk in the corner of the room. 'He takes a lamp over there of an evening to work on something that concerns you—both you and Miss Hannah, in fact. His will.'

As Sarah made a quick impulsive move to thrust past Sophie and get to the desk, Josh's hand shot out and fastened an iron grip on her shoulder, drawing her back.

'You brute!' she shouted, trying to wrench free. 'How dare you!'

This brought a sudden gasping cry from Hannah. 'He'll hear you! He'll hear you!' It wasn't for herself she feared but for her teeming family of cats back at Queen Anne Street.

A quick check through the curtained window failed to show any reaction from either Billy or the urchins. They hadn't heard anything.

Hannah subsided into an armchair; she made no sound but tears ran down her cheeks. Sophie's instinct was to go to her and comfort her, but she had to steel herself against it. Time was short and there were still things to be said and decided.

'I have no doubt whatsoever,' Sophie said, 'that Mr Turner will always see to it that Miss Hannah is cared for. He has assured me of that. But as for yourself, Mrs Danby, I would not be so sure. The trouble is that you have it fixed in your head that he will always provide for you—no matter how far or how ruthlessly you push him.'

'Oh, but he will,' Sarah said confidently. 'He made a promise to his father.'

'He has honoured it quite long enough,' Sophie said. 'His father exacted that promise on behalf of the children—and they've long since grown up, married and ceased to be your responsibility—or his. He has more than repaid you for any pleasure he might once have found in your company. It is my opinion that he owes you nothing.'

Sarah opened her mouth to dispute this, but Sophie talked her down. 'I want you to leave now, Mrs Danby, and take Miss Hannah with you. But first I want you to undertake to do as I say. If you do not, then I shall see to it that your allowance is stopped. And not only that: I shall see to it that you are cut out of his will and never put back into it again.'

Although shaken, Sarah remained defiant. 'You couldn't do it!'

'Oh, I don't know,' Sophie said with a calmness that carried conviction. 'I pride myself that, if I really care to try, I can persuade that man out there to my way of thinking. For instance, I have my eye on another house near here—one that I believe to be more suited to his needs. He might be reluctant to make the move if the proposal were to be put to him today; but when the time comes, I'm sure he'll quietly go along with what I suggest.'

'You're terribly sure of yourself!'

'Perhaps I have reason to be. After all, I was the one who persuaded him to restore and increase your allowance when all your efforts had failed. And I honestly believe that I could persuade him to change his mind again—though not to your advantage this time. So will you go now? And please leave by the back door. Josh will show you the way;' then, very distinctly, 'Don't ever come back. And never breathe a word to anyone about this place. Above all, never pester that man again in any way. Those are my stipulations. Should you break one of them, then I promise you solemnly that you will be cut out of the will—and, moreover, that Mr Turner will cease to support you.'

Sarah tightened her grip on her parasol. 'For a *lady* with such influence, isn't it rather surprising that you haven't got him to marry you?'

'And land him in bigamy?' Sophie said.

'But how could you?' Sarah demanded. 'I understand you to be a widow.'

'That is true. Twice over, in fact. But that doesn't make *him* free to marry me.'

'But *he's* never married.'

'Don't you believe it!'

In what was for her a rare show of panic, Sarah gasped, 'Married? I know nothing about this—nothing at all.' She turned on Hannah. 'What do you know about it? What have you been holding back this time?'

All Hannah knew was that she wanted to get away from here and back to her cats as quickly as possible. She had lost track of the conversation and had no idea of what Sarah was arguing about now.

Turning back to Sophie, Sarah said, 'If he's not married to you, who is it?'

'His work,' Sophie told her simply. 'And from all accounts he was betrothed at a very tender age. It is a marriage I would no' want to break up.'

Staring at Sophie, Sarah said, 'I believe you're as unbalanced as he is.'

Sophie smiled, and glanced out through the curtains. 'I rather think he's preparing to come back in, so will you kindly hurry along?'

It was a bluff, but it seemed to work.

Hannah jumped up and seized Sarah's arm and started to pull her out to the hallway, pleading, 'My cats! Let me get home to my cats!'

Sarah broke away so violently that she knocked Hannah's bonnet to the back of her head. She quickly pulled it into place, but in that moment Sophie glimpsed the side of her face. Shocked and repelled by what she had seen, Sophie now fully realised why Hannah had become a recluse. More than that, it gave her a new understanding of Billy's attitude towards Hannah. Until now, she had harboured the uneasy feeling that, in his deliberate avoidance of Hannah whenever possible, Billy had been less than considerate; but the sight of the hideous disfigurement made it clear why Billy, the seeker of beauty, had become loth to face her. It was a tragedy, and Sophie was filled with a great sympathy for both of them.

In this brief lull, Sophie lost her hold on the situation. Sarah had only to look through the curtains to see that it had been a bluff. Billy still sat stooped on his stool.

'You very nearly tricked me into going,' she said to Sophie. And with growing confidence she went on, 'That isn't the only trick you've tried on me, either, with all your glib talk. What if William should see me here? What if he should go the way of his mother and end up in the madhouse? Why should I worry? Gascoigne once assured me that my allowance would continue to be paid in full.'

Sophie was momentarily lost; but then her mind cleared. It was useless to plead with Sarah. There seemed to be only one way of dealing with her now: to call her bluff. Beckoning Sarah to follow, she went from the sitting-room to the hallway, and then along to the front door.

Before opening the door, Sophie turned to Sarah who stood back in the hallway, with Hannah and Josh beside her. 'If the shock of seeing you here proves too much for Mr Turner, then you'll be all right—your allowance will continue. But if he rides out the shock, then he'll no' be needing me to influence him in deciding what's to be done about your allowance and your place in his will.'

She opened the door, so that there was an unobstructed view out and across to the end of the jetty.

'It's for you to decide,' Sophie said, standing back, so that Sarah was free to walk past her—if she so dared.

It was at this point that Billy roused himself from his day-dreams and rose from his stool.

Billy remained unaware of Josh's absence as he slowly wound in his fishing line, making a wet bulge of it on the end of his umbrella. He had caught what he had really come here for—exactly what he needed to finish the picture on the painting-room easel. And this was not all he had settled. He looked down to where two of the boys, Ned and Shivers, still played with his hat and prism under the coat.

'Well now,' he said loudly to attract their attention. 'Do you young gentlemen under that coat realise that you're getting a very special look at God in that hat of mine?'

Ned and Shivers peered out curiously from under the coat.

'God?' said Shivers.

'Yes, gentlemen—God.' Billy looked around for Josh, then shrugged when he found him missing. 'In Mr Mottram's Bible it says, as I know he's often told you here, that there's God the Father, God the Son, and God the Holy Ghost. Three of 'em. But mark what that prism says. Get under that coat again and take a good steady look at it.'

The heads of Ned and Shivers vanished, and the other two boys—who had been listening wide-eyed—raced in their fish-ing lines and fought their way under the coat too.

Billy gave the four of them time to adjust the rod of light in relation to the prism, waiting until all was absolutely still under the coat before saying, 'There are some who say—and I admit I agree with 'em—that there are three main Gods where colour is concerned—red, yellow and blue.' He broke off for a moment, and then continued as though no longer addressing a bunch of tattered mudlarks. 'Where light is concerned, however, the prism gives us another hierarchy.' His voice slowed, and he named its members. 'God the Red ... God the Orange ... God the Yellow ... God the Green ... God the Blue ... God the Indigo ... God the Violet ...'

In the silence that followed, he allowed the boys to watch for a little longer before peeling the coat off them and saying, 'I'll have my piece of glass back now, gentlemen, if I may.'

The boys leaned away from the mouth of the hat to make way for his hand, and he reached in and grasped the prism, lifting it in his clenched fist above his shoulder. He opened out his fingers, balancing the prism on his palm—and it was as if he had converted it from a thing of banded colour to a piece of solid light chipped off the edge of a ray of the sun. He twisted his wrist a fraction, this way and that, making the prism's polished surface beam and flash. 'Put all seven together and look what you have now ... one. The one great God who is life to us all ... light.'

He displayed the jewel for another few moments to their wondering eyes, Then he sat it back in its plush-lined leather box, which he clicked shut and slipped into his pocket. His hat was handed back to him with the sheet of white paper inside it, and he put it on his head without removing the paper. And then, hooking his fingers into the gills of the two fish he had inadvertently caught, holding them in one hand and the stool and the umbrella in the other, he set off along the jetty, his heels jabbing cheerfully at the boards.

The sound carried ahead of him and entered the house through the open door. Sophie remained just inside, with Sarah still standing back in the hallway. She hadn't moved since Sophie had opened the door. Nor had Hannah or Josh; Josh was ready to reach and grab Sarah, while Hannah simply didn't understand what was happening. All of them had seen Billy lifting the prism and talking to the boys, but they had not heard what he said. In a few moments now he would reach the bank.

Sophie looked back along the hallway to Sarah. If she was to make a decision, now was the time. Sarah's bosom rose and fell rapidly in fury and frustration; she knew now that she didn't have the courage to accept Sophie's challenge.

'All right—close it!'

And Sophie quickly shut the door. From that moment the departure of Sarah and Hannah matched the speed with which they had been brought into the house. Josh grabbed Sarah's arm and forced her swiftly ahead of him down the passage, while Sophie led Hannah behind them.

By the time Billy let himself into the house from the front, dropping the stool, the umbrella and the two fish in the hallway, Josh and Sophie had escorted Sarah and Hannah out of the back gate and started them on their way behind the blacksmith's forge and on to the river-path, along to where their boat and waterman waited. They were to get into the boat and tell the waterman to cross the river at right-angles and then row down close to the south bank.

The waterman complied, even though it meant a hard haul against the last of the incoming tide, his two passengers now dead weight as they sat hunched close together in the stern under the parasol. Josh watched the boat until it reached other craft down the river and became lost to sight.

Sophie returned to the house by the back gate and saw the last of the boat through the parted sitting-room curtains. She went into the hallway to pick up the two fish Billy had left there before he had climbed the stairs to his painting-room, where he had picked up his palette and set to work without a second's delay.

By the time Sophie went up to the painting-room, carrying the two fish on a plate, Billy had nearly completed his picture. She saw that she had been right in what she had discerned. It was still the same paradisaical place of colour and light that she had seen before the arrival of Sarah and Hannah, but the mouth of the river was just that much plainer, the headland stood out a little more, and the tree was now almost linked with the earth even though it remained little more than a plume of golden-green and pink—so ethereal that its slight inclination to one side could have been caused by nothing stronger in the way of a breeze than the mere passage of light through its foliage. Yet the picture could so easily have ended up a stark and frightening thing if Billy had so much as suspected the presence of the two women who had come and gone.

Fighting her emotions and struggling to keep her voice normal, Sophie said, 'I see you did yourself proud on the jetty. How would you like the fish done?'

Billy stepped back from the painting, glanced down at the roach on the plate and grinned as he said, 'Them two fish were very obliging the way they allowed themselves to get hooked, so we'd better treat 'em well. Let's have 'em baked in wine, with herbs.'

He turned his attention to the painting again and cocked his head to one side for a new angle on it. The movement reminded him that he still wore his hat; he took it off, dislodging the sheet of paper, which fluttered to the floor. 'You know something, Sophie,' he said, glancing at the paper and then looking back at the painting, 'I believe I've got the answer to the mystery of it all. Came to me clearer than ever out there on the jetty. It's the only answer ... must be ... otherwise we're all sunk. The sun is God.'

Sophie released her pent-up feelings in laughter—a laughter which threatened to engulf her, balanced as it was on the knife-edge of tears. At long last she felt that she had secured a really safe haven for him. But in truth, she was that haven.

Note

J. M. W. Turner was born on 23 April 1775, and died at Chelsea on 19 December 1851. His last words were, 'The sun is God.'

Some twenty-five years after his death, Boudin, Degas, Monet, Pissarro, Renoir and Sisley were among the Impressionists who jointly stated:

'A group of French painters, united by the same aesthetic tendencies ... cannot forget that they have been preceded ... by the Great Master of the English School, the illustrious Turner.'